## Praise for the Elliot

"The irrepressible heroine is delightful and her ongoing banter is nonstop fun."

*— Ellery Queen Mystery Magazine*

"Lynn captures the flavor of the South, right down to the delightfully quirky characters in this clever new mystery series. Elli Lisbon is the Stephanie Plum of the South!"

*— Krista Davis,*
*New York Times* Bestselling Author of the Domestic Diva Mysteries

"Elli Lisbon is proving herself to be the most lovable OCD PI since Adrian Monk."

*— Maddy Hunter,*
Agatha-Nominated Author of the Passport to Peril Series

"A must-read mystery with a sassy sleuth, a Wonderland of quirky characters, and a fabulous island setting that will keep you turning pages."

*— Riley Adams,*
Author of the Memphis Barbecue Mysteries

"Back for another episode of juggling sleuthing, professional responsibilities, and complicated personal relationships...Lynn whips all these ingredients into a tasty southern mash of star-crossed romance, catty but genteel one-upsmanship, and loveable oddballs that should please fans of humorous cozies."

*— Alfred Hitchcock Mystery Magazine*

"A solid and satisfying mystery, yes indeed, and the fabulous and funny Elliott Lisbon is a true gem! Engaging, clever and genuinely delightful."

*— Hank Phillippi Ryan,*
Agatha, Anthony and Macavity Award-Winning Author

"Elli is one of my favorite characters and I love her strong sense of being, her spunkiness, and her determination to do what needs to be done. Boasting an eclectic cast of characters, clever and enticing dialogue and the perfect backdrop of the Ballantyne estate and Sea Pine Island, this is one of the best books in this delightfully captivating series."

– *Dru's Book Musings*

"With an intelligent woman sleuth, a unique blend of quirky supporting characters and a well-devised mystery plot, *Board Stiff* is delightfully entertaining."

– *Fresh Fiction*

"Elli is an admirable and engaging heroine. Deft writing and clever dialogue further ensure that readers will be looking forward to the next installment in Elli's adventures."

– *Kings River Life Magazine*

"An engaging read that grabbed my attention from the start...With witty banter, a likable cast of characters and a visually appealing setting, this is a great start to what I hope is a long running series."

– *The Cozy Chicks*

"'I used to be able to juggle six wet cats while balancing a bowl of Jell-O on my head. Now I couldn't locate a cat if I stood in a barn with a can of tuna in one hand and a mouse in the other.' Elliott's self-effacement makes her an unusually lovable protagonist, especially when she lets fly with comments like that."

– *Mystery Scene Magazine*

"Packed with humor, romance, danger and adventure, this is a good mystery full of plot twists and turns, with red herrings a plenty and an ending that I found both surprising and satisfying."

# SHAKE DOWN

**The Elliott Lisbon Mystery Series**
**by Kendel Lynn**

<u>Novels</u>

BOARD STIFF (#1)
WHACK JOB (#2)
SWAN DIVE (#3)
POT LUCK (#4)
SHAKE DOWN (#5)


<u>Novellas</u>

SWITCH BACK

AN ELLIOTT LISBON MYSTERY

# SHAKE DOWN

*Kendel Lynn*

HENERY PRESS

Copyright

SHAKE DOWN
An Elliott Lisbon Mystery
Part of the Henery Press Mystery Collection

First Edition | March 2020

Henery Press
www.henerypress.com

Trade Paperback ISBN-13: 978-1-63511-587-1
Digital epub ISBN-13: 978-1-63511-588-8
Kindle ISBN-13: 978-1-63511-589-5
Hardcover ISBN-13: 978-1-63511-590-1

Printed in the United States of America

*For Ruth*

## ACKNOWLEDGMENTS

I'm deeply thankful for the life of love and encouragement that surrounds me.

Thank you to Pat Allen Werths, Molly Weston, Cathy Pickens, Hank Phillippi Ryan, Dru Ann Love, and much love to my mom, Suzanne Atkins.

I can't possibly express how grateful I am for the authors and staff of Henery Press. I shall forever be thankful. Special gratitude to Maria Edwards and Christina Rogers for making the Hen House stronger and more vibrant, and to Art Molinares for making the dream possible.

# ONE

(Day #1: Saturday Evening)

Even two miles from the shoreline, the warm night air smelled of tangy sea salt and brine. It drifted through palm trees and sweet magnolias, swaying the paper lanterns on the patio of the Ballantyne Foundation's Big House on Sea Pine Island, South Carolina.

I was enjoying the remnants of an early evening dinner with twenty board members and committee members. We sat poolside in thick-cushioned chairs beneath wide umbrellas. Carla Otto, the Ballantyne's renowned resident chef, had made a spread worthy of a *Southern Living* photo shoot (and a spot on any Michelin-starred restaurant's menu). She was testing new recipes for the upcoming end-of-summer Ballantyne Beach BBQ the following weekend. We dined on juicy thick-sliced brisket, maple bacon beans, grilled cob corn, and pickled cole slaw. All served with frosty glasses of watermelon hibiscus sangria.

"This corn on the cob is amazing," I said.

"It's the butter," Carla said. Her bright eyes framed with orange specs, her smile as big as her curly black hair. "The soul of the dish. Herbed goat cheese compound melts into cream on contact."

As Director of the billion-dollar Ballantyne Foundation, I participated on all fundraising committees, and happily, all menu tastings. For this year's late summer event, I was on the fringe of the committee. Barely a bystander, and I was loving it. My only responsibilities: Setup and centerpieces. A snap.

Jane Walcott-Hatting, chairwoman of the Ballantyne Board of Directors, served as co-chair of this particular shindig alongside Carla. Jane was basically Carla's opposite. Stern, rigid, and always preferred the vinegar approach over honey. However, they did make a dream team. Like having Martha Stewart and Leah Chase plan the party. Which was perfect, as our board was down three members for this event. Matty had taken his Sea Pine Prep senior class on a research trip (code for kayaking), Chas was at a banking conference (code for golfing), and Deidre's husband surprised her with their third cruise of the year (code for doing whatever you please when you're retired).

"Before we break," Jane said. "Let me remind core committee members, we have meetings in the board room at eight sharp each day this week starting Monday. Do not be late. Elliott, you are not core."

"I'm aware." I raised my glass, taking another generous gulp of sangria, and relaxed into my cushioned chair. The umbrellas were up, but the sun had already gone down.

"The host families each receive their own table," Jane said. "Carla, at last count, we had twenty-two, correct?"

"Twenty-five," she replied. "This morning, the Spiritual Guidance Center in Summerton added three newly-trained families."

Summerton County, where Sea Pine Island resided, lacked formal housing and meal facilities for the homeless community. In its absence, residents volunteered to open their own homes, providing food and shelter, many times clothes and necessities, to those in need. We dedicated this year's annual Ballantyne Beach BBQ to those host families. We wanted to celebrate the selfless acts of kindness they generously offered to their neighbors. It also encouraged the Ballantyne's wealthy donors, those who bought tickets to the BBQ, to open their wallets to a new homeless shelter initiative.

"Elliott," Jane said. "Make that happen."

"Already did," I said. "We'll have thirty tables with twenty-five cake centerpieces. The other five tables will have either gluten-free macaron towers or tiered vegan fruit tart displays."

As Jane continued her list of last-minute directives, I spotted Juliette Pete walking through the Big House. I jumped up and jogged across the deck and through the patio doors to catch her. She was packing cake boxes onto a large folding cart.

"Juliette, wait," I said. "Let me help."

"Good Lord, Elliott," she said. "You've already done so much to help me." Her long blonde ponytail swung round as she packed. She placed the last stack, then grabbed the wagon handle.

I helped her keep it stable as we rolled it through the foyer, silently crossing the polished plank floors to the side door leading to the porte-cochere.

Sid Bassi, my closest friend, entered and held the door for us. It took less than five minutes for the three of us to transfer the wagon and its cargo to Juliette's SUV. She snapped the trunk shut with one hand. The words "Cake & Shake" were written in elegant script across the rear panel.

"I cannot wait for next week," Juliette said. "I'll have twenty-two perfectly—"

"About that," I interrupted. "May I request three more? Making it twenty-five?"

She laughed. "Of course, I have an extra six planned. So that'll be twenty-five perfectly decorated superhero-themed cakes ready Saturday morning. And, of course, eighty gallons of ice cream for the shake maker."

"Eighty?" Sid asked. "This for the Beach BBQ, right? Not the Met Gala."

"Have you tasted her shakes?" I said. "The Met Gala should be so lucky."

"I'm so lucky," Juliette said. "Thank you, really. Letting me bake cakes and make shakes in exchange for a dream wedding? You're an angel."

"You're a lifesaver," I said. "Those cake centerpieces will be the talk of the island. And us leaving the party décor overnight on the beach is hardly a fair trade."

"Ha! You haven't seen the prices for twinkle lights, tents, and a tiki bar installed on sand."

I smiled and hugged her. As the person who secured that particular aspect of the upcoming party, I had indeed seen those prices.

"If you need me, ladies," she said as she climbed into the driver's seat, "I'll be baking and shaking. Except tomorrow. I'll be showering my adoring bridesmaids with gifts and mimosas at the Wharf." She snapped her seatbelt. "How did my life get so perfect?" She waved and pulled out, driving down the palm tree-lined drive and into the night.

"I'm calling it," Sid said to me with her own hug. "One more glass of sangria and I'm crashing at your house. I'll see you tomorrow at the Showcase."

"What time you arriving?"

"Nine a.m. sharp," she said. "Maybe eight, as it's opening day. You know there's always a line on the first day. I have two separate listings on that block. I'm hoping to tempt Millie Poppy Pete."

"Good luck with that. She'll never sell her house."

"Says you. She hasn't witnessed my Annette-Bening-*American-Beauty*-I-will-sell-this-house-today mode."

"Okey doke. See you at noon. Or noon thirty. Maybe by then you'll have it listed."

"Maybe by then I'll have it sold."

*       *       *

Millie Poppy Pete's house was in the middle of a short lane on the dunes of South Pebble Beach. While it was off-plantation, meaning no gates or uniformed sentries to guard them, the far end of South Pebble Beach bordered Harbortown. One could walk mere minutes down the sandy beach, take advantage of Harbortown's miles of Magnolia-shaded pathways and seaside restaurants, and then return home to their own equally lovely neighborhood, all without having to pay the high maintenance fees or follow any strict regulations.

A printed yard sign adorned with colorful balloons indicated Millie Poppy's house was the first stop on the Sea Pine Island Home Showcase, an annual tour of our beachiest residences. The early birds had long since moved onto the other homes, and the post-church, post-brunch, post-why-get-out-of-bed-early-on-a-Sunday crowd was just wandering in.

Guests mingled through the rooms, admiring the knotted pine floors, reclaimed wood ceiling beams, and hand-plastered walls. Hues of blue from Wedgwood to navy popped against the bright whites of the rugs and sofas. Halfway to the sunroom, a quartet of three-tiered cakes were displayed on a dessert table set amongst delicate macarons and petit fours and a spray of business cards with Cake & Shake letterpressed into the parchment.

Millie Poppy greeted me with a wave as I entered her dream home. It had not yet been listed, or sold, by Sid. Probably because you didn't sell a dream home, you bought one. Millie Poppy was standing at the slider to the sunroom. Her husband, Sam Turnbull, was tending their award-winning rose garden. He wore a wide-brimmed straw hat, thick gloves, and carried a hand-held trowel. Rows of blooming flowers in yellows and pinks ringed a fire pit, itself ringed with Adirondack chairs. Sam rearranged mulch along the far fence, patting the soft mounds, and by Millie Poppy's tone, I'm guessing he'd been at it all morning.

"Sam, honey, it's perfect," Millie Poppy said. "It's been perfect. You come on in and say hello. Elliott Lisbon just arrived." She hugged me quick when I approached. "That man acts like this is the Annual Garden Club Tour, not the Home Showcase."

"The roses are gorgeous," I said. "Looks like every single blossom is in perfect bloom."

"Don't listen to me complain, those beauties are the reason we get the first spot on the tour," she said. "Now let's talk about you. You're sweet as a peach for helping my granddaughter with her wedding. How can we ever thank you?"

"Please, you and Sam and Juliette have all thanked me enough. It's my pleasure, I promise. And really, it's my job."

"The way I hear tell," Sam said, brushing soil from his gloves, "your job is investigating petty theft."

"Petty, honey, isn't the half of it," Millie Poppy said.

"Oh, you're a half short indeed. Our Elli can get anyone out of a pumpernickel." Zibby Archibald wobbled over, a ring of dahlias in her hair. On the spry side of eighty-eight, she was our oldest and most beloved Ballantyne board member.

"Peccadillo," I said. "But yes, I'm working toward my South Carolina PI license."

"She's very close to meeting the hourly requirement," Sid said. She had walked up behind Zibby, towering over her. Sid resembled a professional beach volleyball player while Zibby resembled Aunt Clara from *Bewitched*.

"Yep," I agreed without hesitation. "Only about four thousand hours to go."

"That's the spirit," Zibby said. "Every armadillo counts."

Millie Poppy's phone rang. She glanced at the screen.

"Excuse me a sec," she said, walking into the bright sunroom. Its glass walls were dressed in floor-to-ceiling plantation shutters, the slats open to let the sunshine in. Millie Poppy had barely reached the window before she turned. Her face was pale, her brow was crinkled in confusion. "That was Tess, one of Juliette's bridesmaids. She asked if Juliette was here."

"Here?" I asked. "Her brunch was at the Wharf, right?"

Millie called out to Sam, asked him to find Tucker. I hadn't seen Tucker when I walked in, but as he was both Sam's grandson and Juliette's fiancé, I figured he had to be close.

We all joined Millie Poppy in the sunroom and she repeated her short phone conversation. "Tess asked if I'd seen Juliette. Or Daphne. That's her maid of honor, Daphne Fischer. Why would I have seen Daphne? They're supposed to be at Juliette's brunch." She checked her watch. "Close to three hours ago."

Tucker pulled out his phone and started dialing. So did Sam.

"Tucker, when did you last talk to Juliette?" I asked.

He answered me as ringing sounded from the phone pressed to his ear. "I didn't, not today. Not actually talk to her. She texted this morning saying she was running late for the brunch. Then just 'love ya' like normal, and that's it. She spent the night in Summerton with Daphne and Tess. I thought."

Millie kept hitting redial on her phone, her face becoming more drawn with each button push. Sam began making his own calls, starting with the Wharf.

As we crowded together in the sunroom, more Home Showcase visitors arrived, filling the house almost to capacity.

Sid grabbed Zibby's hand. "I'll shepherd the tour visitors, encourage them to move on to the next house. Zibby, you handle the cake table. Box up slices as quick as you can."

"Nothing persuades an exit like a parting gift," Zibby said.

Ten minutes into phone dialing, which was escalating from

urgent to frantic, Juliette fast-walked into the house. She squeezed past the remaining Showcase stragglers and stopped at the sunroom doorway.

Millie Poppy nearly cried and hugged her tight. "Honey, where have you been?"

"Where've I been?" Juliette said. "What's happening here? I received fifteen messages from the three of you. My phone keeps rolling straight to voicemail."

"Daphne didn't show up at your brunch," Tucker said. "Tess called in a panic. Did you show up at your brunch?"

"I've been looking for Daphne all morning. Like since nine. I saw all the voicemails from you guys and thought the worst. Came right home." She turned to me, distress coloring her features with a wash of pink. "I can't drive and think and talk and text at the same time. I don't have Bluetooth."

"Tell us what you know," I said.

"Daphne didn't show up at the Wharf," Juliette said. "She never answered my texts or answered anyone's texts." She ran her fingers through her hair and plopped into the sofa. "I checked our apartment. Her car's gone. So is her purse and her phone."

"Did you two have a fight, honey?" Millie Poppy asked. "Is she upset?"

"Any reason she wouldn't go to the brunch?" I said.

Juliette shook her head slowly, confusion distorting the wash of pink. "It's all been good. Hectic, but good."

"What about this morning?" Tucker said. "Didn't you guys go to the Wharf together?"

"I texted Daphne after the Ballantyne party last night to see if she wanted to meet up with me and Tess," Juliette said. "But she said no. She was beat. Wanted to rest and be fresh for today." She looked up at the four of us watching her. "I thought she was planning a surprise for the brunch, so I didn't push it."

Tucker sat down next to her and wrapped her in a hug. "It'll be fine. She'll turn up. Hell, she's probably just late." Juliette looked up at him and he held her hand. "Really, really late."

"Thanks," Juliette said and kissed him on the cheek.

"Honey, wasn't Daphne home when you woke up this morning?" Millie Poppy Pete said.

"I wasn't home last night," Juliette said, then turned to me. "We're roommates, me and Daphne. But last night I stayed with Tess. I started texting Daphne as soon as I got to the apartment and saw she wasn't there." She took a deep breath and sat up straighter. "We can't just sit here. I can't just sit here."

"What do we do?" Millie Poppy asked me. "You're the investigator. What's our next step?"

"It's only been a few hours," Tucker said.

"Well, we have to call the police, that's obviously the first step," Juliette said. "But we have to wait forty-eight hours. Isn't that what the rule is? But that seems like too long to have to wait."

"It's only twenty-four hours, honey," Millie Poppy said.

"It's actually neither of those things," I said. "The rule is more fluid. It's common sense and reasonable judgement. You answer two simple questions: Is this out of character? Is there a reason to think she's missing?"

"Yes, absolutely," Juliette said. "Something's not right."

"Or maybe not, Jules," Tucker said. "We shouldn't overreact. You know how she is. She'll be back in a day or two. You'll see."

Sid leaned in from the doorway. "Almost cleared out, and I moved the Start Tour sign next door. I heard you talk about Daphne. Any news?"

I shook my head as Millie Poppy spoke up. "Elli, will you file a missing persons report? Can you do that today? It's Sunday. Does that matter?"

"We should definitely file a report right away, right now, but, Juliette, you should be the one to call," I said. "You'll be able to answer all their questions accurately and quickly."

Millie Poppy started swiping and tapping on her phone. "I think I have the non-emergency number on here somewhere. Part of the community beach watch."

"Just call 911, Juliette," I said. "Tell them everything. Starting with the last time you talked to Daphne, and don't leave anything out."

Juliette began dialing as Millie Poppy, Sam, Tucker, and I joined Sid in the living room. It was half-past two in the afternoon, so this part of the Showcase only shut down about two hours early. Zibby stacked the last four cake boxes and declared them tucked in for transport.

"Thank you, Zibby," Millie Poppy said. "And you, Sid, and you, Elli."

"We'll clean up the rest," Sam said.

"Please help us find Daphne," Millie Poppy said.

"Of course," I said. "I'll head to the police station after I leave here."

Sid grabbed her oversized leather handbag, which resembled more of a satchel than a purse, and we walked out the front. Tucker ran up to meet us in the driveway.

"Do you really think you can find her?" he asked.

"Well, you said something about Daphne, like, 'you know how she is,'" I said. "It implied she's done this before. Taken off without telling anyone."

"Yeah, she's done it a couple times," he said. "She goes off the grid. She's a wanderer at heart. Puts her pack in the car and hits the road on a whim."

"You told Juliette you thought it'd be okay," I said. "Did you mean it, that Daphne simply left town for a few days, even though the wedding is approaching?"

Tucker looked back at the front door and lowered his voice. "No way. Daphne would never do that to Juliette. Not now. Not this week. Something's definitely wrong."

I thanked him and he walked into the house. I climbed into my blue Mini convertible while Sid walked to her Mercedes SUV.

"Why didn't you call dispatch for them?" Sid asked. "Seems like you're the one with all the connections."

"Because 911 calls are recorded. If something's really wrong, then the investigation has already started."

# TWO

I drove north on Cabana Boulevard toward the top of the island. Sea Pine Island was shaped like a shoe, and Cabana ran from heel to toe and over the Palmetto Bridge to mainland South Carolina. South Pebble Beach, where Millie Poppy lived, was near the heel side of the arch, and I was headed to the police station, near the toe, not too far from the bridge. Though the entire island was only about seven miles long, so really, almost everything was not too far from the bridge.

The Island Civic Complex housed the police station on the east side and the library on the west. It resembled a park shaded by tall pines, blooming crape myrtles, and a smattering of magnolias. After parking and putting the Mini Coop's top up to avoid tree-sapped seats upon my return, I crossed the quiet lot and entered the worn lobby. A pair of senior volunteers greeted me, then buzzed me straight through the unmarked door directly behind them. Being a PI-in-training under the tutelage of Captain Sullivan had its privileges.

A long hall papered with announcements and flyers (always a motorcycle or RV for sale or wanted) led into the main station room. Sets of cubicles filled the inner space while offices, interrogation rooms, and holding cells filled the outer. Phones intermittently rang low, fingers lightly tapped on keyboards, voices echoed from the break room at the far end. The entire building was bathed in a yellow hue courtesy of fluorescent lighting. I wound around the perimeter of cubes to a trio of offices, stopping at the one in the center.

Lieutenant Nick Ransom sat at a large desk, the metal kind found in every government office nationwide. Beat up, but sturdy, dark gray with plenty of scratches and dents. It contrasted with his tailored Italian dress shirt, stainless Patek watch, and Jamie Fraser good looks, minus the red hair and Scottish accent. He was lieutenant of the Sea Pine Police, my next-door neighbor, and the newly rekindled love of my life. Though we were still working that last part out.

I hadn't even said hello, had barely leaned a shoulder in the doorway, when he started talking.

"She hasn't been missing very long," he said. "We're talking, what? Four hours? Also, not our jurisdiction. One Daphne Fischer, aged twenty-three, lives Summerton. Which, as you know, is unincorporated and belongs to the Summerton County Sheriff's Office."

"This has been an episode of facts with Lieutenant Ransom," Parker said from behind me. Corporal Lillie Parker was cat burglar lithe and ballet dancer fluid. She was Ransom's right hand on the force, and a force in her own right.

I took a seat across from Ransom and left the door-leaning to Parker.

"Our dispatch received the initial 911 call and then immediately re-routed it to the Sheriff's Office," Parker said. "She a friend?"

"Friend of a friend," I said. "Her best friend's grandmother is a longtime acquaintance of the Ballantynes. I've met Daphne maybe four times in the last couple months. She works at the Cake & Shake."

"Brown Butter Peach," Parker said.

"Strawberry Shortcake Custard," I said.

"Mexican Chocolate," Ransom said. "With Don Julio Real."

"You win," I said.

He took out a silver pen and his notebook and jotted a few lines. "I'm on a joint task force right now, but I'll call Sheriff Hill, see if he can make this a priority."

Parker handed me a thick manila envelope. "This is a missing persons starter kit. I know, bad name, but that's what it is. It outlines the steps to take before starting a physical search. Who to call, where to look, hospital numbers, stuff like that."

"I've never worked a missing persons case," I said. "At least, not like this. Do we start hanging flyers?"

Parker nodded to the envelope. "Yes, definitely. That lists tips on how to make posters and where to place them. Sorry about your friend of a friend. Hope they find her soon." With another nod, she pushed off from the doorway and returned to the clattering main room.

"Joint task force, huh?" I said. "Sounds fancy."

"We have official credentials and everything." He walked around his desk and leaned on the corner. "I'm sorry about your friend, too. But like I said, it hasn't been very long. Just a few hours."

"That we know of. But agreed, it's still really early."

I touched his hand. It was tan and strong. Fine scars stood out, marking time from his former life as an FBI agent. His secret crime fighting days, the ones that precipitated his sudden departure from our college romance, causing a twenty-year pause I was still adjusting to.

"I'm here if you need anything," he said.

"Thank you." I stood and smiled. "And I'm here if you need anything. Those joint task forces can be tricky."

I left the hum of the station's inner workings and thanked the volunteers at the welcome desk. Once outside in the sunshine of the late September day, I slipped into my Mini Coop and dialed Sid. "Have you heard anything?"

"Not a word," she said. "The Home Showcase officially moved on from Millie Poppy's, but her driveway is still packed. Friends and family have been trickling in all day."

"I'll reach out to Millie Poppy. She can talk to Juliette, see what they want to do. Parker gave me instructions on how to start a search."

"What do you think?" Sid asked.

"I think it's much too early to worry. Concern, yes. But worry? We're talking about half a day. Tucker said she takes off every now and then. I mean, who hasn't gotten caught up in something and run late for half a day?"

"Yeah," Sid said, then waited a bit. "But if it was my bridesmaids' brunch, you wouldn't get caught up in something that day, right?"

I glanced at the missing person packet. "Right."


Living on a small island meant everything was conveniently located. The Civic Complex was less than a mile's drive to the front gates of Oyster Cove Plantation, the beachfront community that housed both my seaside cottage and the Ballantyne Big House. The large manse rose like a stately Southern estate on a hill at the crown of a residential drive. It topped out at close to seventeen thousand square feet, including Mr. and Mrs. Ballantyne's private residence which spanned the entire third floor. Edward and Vivienne Ballantyne had converted the family fortune into the family foundation some fifty years earlier. They kept the seventy-five-acre grounds and massive estate, and hired management staff and formed a board to manage the operations. This left them free to travel the globe in search of additional charitable organizations—educational, environmental, social—to setup programs and donate money.

I joined the foundation fresh out of college. About ten years after that, Mr. Ballantyne renovated the music room to create my office when I officially became director. Not a huge surprise, as I'd been close to both Edward and Vivi since toddlerhood, but a huge responsibility, as I'd been close to them since toddlerhood.

I popped into the Big House on my way home from the station and no sooner reached my desk when Tod Hayes, Ballantyne Administrator, stuck his head through the open doorway. "Edward is on the line," he said. "Also, Jane needs you to arrange additional musical entertainment for the BBQ, Carla needs you to order twelve dozen peonies, and Zibby needs a new hat. Preferably one with a flamingo feather. She specifically asked me to tell you that."

"I'm not on the committee, Tod."

"And that matters how?"

"Remind Jane, that's how." I waved him away and picked up the phone. "Mr. Ballantyne, what a wonderful surprise. How are you?"

"Elliott! My dear!" He shouted into the phone, his voice robust and welcoming. "The Rocky Mountains are magnificent. Next time, you must come with us!"

"I would love to, sir," I said. "And the summit? It sounded like council was presenting real solutions. I hope it's everything you wanted to hear."

"Indeed, my dear. The Homeless Alliance is chock full of invigorating ideas. It's been educational, and yet, quite heartbreaking." He cleared his throat, and I heard Vivi's voice in the background. "We're all over it, my dear. Our Housing First Initiative will get off the ground this winter. This winter, indeed!"

"That's exciting, sir. Please let me know what you need from me, and I'll get it done. The board is looking forward to the presentation after the BBQ."

"Of course, we know you will," he said. "You're our secret weapon in the fight against homelessness. Now tell me, what's this I hear about Millie Poppy Pete's granddaughter? She's nearing a panic."

"It's her granddaughter's maid of honor, Daphne Fischer. She didn't show up for an important brunch today, and no one can seem to locate her. No calls or texts or any word of any kind. I'd like to spend some time on it tonight and tomorrow, if need be. The first twenty-four hours are vital."

"Vivi already spoke with Millie Poppy and assured her she has our full support. As do you, my dear."

"So no problem for me to use Ballantyne resources?"

"We wouldn't have it any other way," he said. "We'll be home early Saturday, in time for the Beach BBQ. We're bringing three members of the Alliance. You'll make sure we have plenty of VIP seating on the sand, then? They've never visited this side of the Atlantic."

"Absolutely. I'm looking forward to seeing you both."

"It's been too long on this outing," he said. "It'll be nice to spend some time at home with you. You telephone when you have news. See you Saturday!"

The Ballantynes had been close friends of my parents, who passed when I was in college. So now, Edward and Vivi were my only family. Though even as a small child, it sometimes felt as if they were my only family. My parents loved me, but the Ballantynes felt like home.

Sufficiently grounded, I started my investigation by calling the Summerton County Sheriff's Office. I was routed to the desk sergeant who routed me to an investigator's voicemail. I let him know who I was, why I was calling, and requested a return call as soon as possible. Sooner than that, if possible.

It was now after five. No messages, no texts. No word from

or about Daphne.

I riffled through the missing person packet and hollered for Tod. Professionally, of course.

"We need flyers," I said when he leaned into my office. "I'll ask Juliette to drop off a picture of Daphne. Or maybe she can email it?"

"I'll get it from the web."

"Which web?" I asked.

"Juliette's wedding website, the Cake & Shake website, Facebook, Instagram, any singular social media site—"

"Fine. You're on it. I get it."

"Offering a reward for information?"

"Definitely," I said. "Let's start with...I don't even know. What price do you put on information?"

"Ten thousand dollars?"

"Sounds hefty enough to grab attention. I'll talk to Mr. Ballantyne. You add it to the flyer."

"We'll have them printed and delivered within the hour," he said and disappeared.

It was actually thirty-seven and a half minutes, according to the receipt. The delivery kid dropped off a banker's box full of flyers. They landed with a thud on the antique sofa table near the staircase. He'd no sooner exited through the Big House's massive double-doored front entrance when Sid arrived. She led a short line of people all hurrying inside behind her: Juliette, Tucker, Millie Poppy, Sam, and a guy about thirty years old. He wore his hair long and sandy, fresh from the beach. Another five cars rounded the circular drive as they entered, so we left the doors open.

The impromptu group met right in the foyer. Tod handed each person a stack of flyers while I explained the instructions Parker had provided. "We hang these within a five-mile radius of Daphne's apartment and everywhere on the island. We used

the Summerton Sheriff's Office phone number for the contact."
Which reminded me I needed to call the Sheriff's Office and tell
them that. "And there's a $10,000 reward for information
leading to her location." Which reminded me I needed to call
Mr. Ballantyne and tell him that.

Zibby emerged at the top of the wide center staircase with a
cardboard box that rattled with each uncertain step she took.
Tucker ran up and grabbed it from her, then she placed a hand
on his elbow for the rest of their descent. Once down, Tucker
distributed the contents: Tape guns loaded with thick rolls of
clear packing tape.

"Fast food chains, restaurants, groceries, banks and ATMs,"
I continued. "We have dozens of condo complexes and gated
communities. Give one to every gate guard."

Twenty-somethings assembled in the foyer, at least fifteen
to twenty, all wearing a variety of sunwear: Shorts, tees, flip-
flops, hats.

"Juliette, Millie Poppy, Sam, Tucker," I said. "You each grab
three or four friends. Create teams and split up the flyers and
destinations. Might have more room out in the drive."

"And Alex, too," Juliette said, pointing to the beachy guy
they walked in with. "That's Daphne's boyfriend, Alex Sanders.
He should be a team leader, too."

He gave me a what's up chin tilt and followed the crowd
outside to the front steps.

"Is that it?" Juliette asked. "Anything else?"

"Recruit your most charming, forward, extroverted friends
to approach the nearest pizza places. Ask the drivers to put
flyers on every delivery box. John's Pizza on the island is my
number one speed dial, so I'll call John." She nodded and
divided the remaining tape guns and flyers into smaller boxes.

The hardest part wouldn't be finding spots to hang the
flyers, it would be finding spots where they would be seen. The

entire island benefitted from the foresight of city planners and island ordinances going back multiple generations. Their collective vision kept the island fairly close to how nature intended. It was covered in flora and fauna with even the roughest of dirt roads bordered by flowering bushes, swaying marsh grass, and towering trees. It was gorgeous and peaceful and almost impossible to locate modern buildings by sight. Every shopping center, municipal building, and condo complex was bermed by landscaping twenty feet deep.

We could post flyers on poles and in windows, but people would need to be directly in front of them to see them. We'd be largely unable to attract the attention of passersby along the main roads. At least on the island. Though while Summerton itself had less restrictive building regulations, it still clung to plenty of its neighboring island's landscaping ideals.

Sid and I divvied up the rest of the initial duties as outlined in the packet. We needed to reach out to the hospitals (again), and I needed to call the Sheriff's Office (again).

Juliette stopped me on her way out to the caravan of cars lined up in the drive. "Can this really help? The flyers all over town?"

"It certainly can't hurt." I hugged her. "Someone will call. Daphne will call. It'll be okay."

I did not tell her what I was really thinking. It had now been nearly a full day with no word. Thoughts of the importance of the first twenty-four hours had played on a loop in my head since I'd spoken with Mr. Ballantyne.

I texted Ransom: *I know it's not your case, but anything you can do?*

He texted back: *Keep posting flyers. Sheriff said no one's heard from her since last night.*

Me: *That cannot be good.*

# THREE

I spent the rest of that evening making calls until the list had ended and hanging flyers until the box was empty. I felt mixed relief when my phone calls netted no results. At least when inquiring at places like the morgue and the hospital. My stomach tensed with each ring, each request for information on any young female patients. Thankfully, there were no Jane Does, dead or injured, within one hundred fifty miles of Summerton, even when I inquired far north along the South Carolina coast and into Georgia and Florida.

The pure blue sky lightened my bedroom through the skylight in the ceiling. I loved how the natural light slowly roused me from my sleep. The gentle swishing of ocean waves dancing on the sand drifted through the open windows. My second-floor master faced the sea. Though calling it a master made it sound grand. My cottage was exactly that: A cottage. Two bedrooms and a bath up, a compact kitchen, living room, and half-bath down. The décor included a mix of retro beach and vintage games with handmade rag rugs on the wood floors. An aged-plank patio overlooked the wide hard-packed sand beach and miles of sparkling sea clear to the horizon.

I grabbed a bowl of cereal and a fresh notebook and continued the investigation into the disappearance of Daphne Fischer. I'd originally started my investigative career in college with a major in Criminal Justice and a minor in Nick Ransom. He swept me off my feet during a slideshow in our shared evidence class. Literally. He caught my crumpled faint after a particularly graphic crime scene photo slid onto the screen and I slid onto the floor.

We were inseparable until he left me an answering machine message saying we'd meet again someday. He had been recruited by the FBI, and it turned out someday meant twenty years in the future.

Determined to become a skilled investigator, I vigorously pursued my degree for another two years before realizing my queasiness wasn't abating, and class situations were only getting queasier. I never saw it as a sign of weakness, just that I had other strengths. Like running a billion-dollar charitable foundation and performing discreet inquiries for eccentric patrons and their minor transgressions. It's only slightly shocking how many there were.

Though a missing woman was most definitely not a minor inquiry. Nor was it anything to keep discreet. Finding Daphne would require us to go wide and go loud. Getting the word out would be essential. The discreet part would enter in as I delicately nosed into her private life. Everyone held secrets, and I didn't relish prying them from their hidey holes.

At this point, I didn't have much to add to my notebook. I listed the names of everyone I'd met so far, including Alex Sanders, her boyfriend, and Juliette Pete, her best friend. I needed to get the names of her other friends, acquaintances, co-workers, and neighbors. Though the Summerton County Sheriff's investigators would handle the bulk of the questioning of those close, and not so close, to her. The conventional way to investigate. Logging interviews and canvassing her neighbors, all by the book.

Not being sworn to uphold anything, I had the freedom to

be more unconventional.

After a quick, but thoroughly-routined shower, hair, and dressing process, I popped into my Mini. With the top down and a hat on my head, I zipped down Spy Hop Lane toward the Oyster Cove Plantation's guarded gates and onto Cabana Boulevard.

I wanted to start today's investigation at the end and work backward from there. Not where she was last seen, but where she was last supposed to be. Juliette said Daphne never arrived at the brunch, but maybe she had, and no one knew it.

The Wharf was an award-winning fine dining restaurant offering sumptuous cuisine and spectacular views. It bordered the Intracoastal Waterway three miles down Old Pickett Road on the north side of the island. I parked amongst the cars dotting the asphalt near the front entrance. It was Monday, and though the Wharf only served dinner during the week, the staff usually began their daily preparations in the morning hours.

I entered through the heavy wood door into a rustically elegant foyer. The hostess stand stood empty, as did the high-backed chairs that lined the porch window. The sound of flatware clanking against porcelain drifted from the main dining room. I passed the dark coat check closet and leaned into the special events room.

Clearly, this was to hold the bridesmaids' brunch. Petite sprays of peonies and hydrangeas in vintage jars ran down the center of a long table covered in a starched white cloth. Ribbons adorned gold boxes of chocolates at each place setting. A plastic bin, neatly packed, included Tiffany blue gift boxes and fragrant sweet lilies. The room looked beautiful, decorated for hope and romance. But now, a day later, the gifts unopened and the lights switched off, it was abandoned and silent.

I quietly closed the door and entered the main dining room. Four-tops were placed along a wall of windows. Beyond the glass, ropes of Spanish moss hung from thick oak trees, their tangled roots buried in the waters of the Intracoastal. Several sailboats drifted lazily in the morning sun, its rays shimmering off the calm waves.

Chef Tom Carmichael, the Wharf's proprietor and head chef, was eating brunch near the window with Jane, our Ballantyne board chair. I'd recently discovered they were dating. It was a combustible connection to match up these two strong personalities. One egotistical, the other unpleasant.

"Elliott, I didn't know you were joining us," Chef said. "Here, grab a plate." He half-stood to reach for a china plate on the table next to his.

"Oh, I can't stay long," I said. Possibly too soon. I'd just noticed the array of gooey glazed cinnamon rolls, fluffy frittatas, and sweet peach Bellinis. My favorite cocktail. I stifled a sigh and continued. "I'm sure you heard about Daphne Fischer."

"Obviously," Jane said. "I know everything happening at the Ballantyne."

"Anything interesting with the brunch yesterday?" I asked Chef. "Perhaps Daphne arrived before everyone else? Maybe she snuck in or popped by after everyone left?"

"Not that I know of," Chef said. "And I know everything here."

A couple of know-it-alls.

"Nothing suspicious, if that's what you're asking," Chef continued. "Nothing strange, other than a no-show bride. But that's not as unusual as you think."

"Oh?"

"We host about two of those brunches a month. A bridal shower makes it real. The point of no return."

"True, but in this case, it was the maid of honor who was a no-show," I said.

"That brunch made it very real for her, too," Jane said.

"Always a bridesmaid."

"You can look around the restaurant if you want," Chef said. "As long as you stay out of the way. We don't open for dinner until four, but we're prepping for a special prime rib this evening."

I left them to enjoy their decadent brunch, weaving my way past uniformed servers. They placed heavy silver forks and spoons at dining tables around the room. Assorted kitchen staff in white coats clanged pans and sliced and diced through the swinging kitchen door.

A screen door with a mighty strong hinge led to an outdoor dining deck. Tables and chairs, more casual than their indoor counterparts, were shaded by tall square umbrellas. From this vantage, I could see the Palmetto Bridge spanning the land between Sea Pine Island and Summerton. A breeze flapped the sails of the boats, and pelicans and gulls intermittently dove and soared overhead.

I thought about this lovely setting. The room decorated with care. Elegant gifts and flowers. I wondered if Daphne ever arrived. Or even made it onto the island. Not a single trace of her stood out. There were no security cameras, no debris, no human footprints. Just an extension of the quiet from the special events room.

I followed the weathered path through the towering oaks and billowy Spanish moss to the parking lot. Additional staff members trickled across the pavement from their cars to the entrance. Missing persons posters were taped to light poles throughout the lot. I'd missed seeing them when I parked.

Apparently, so did the arriving staff. No one even looked at the flyers. Just heads down, holding aprons, putting on chef coats, hurrying into the restaurant. Not a glance at Daphne's smiling face. Her hair curly and long, the top half casually knotted atop her head. The words MISSING in tall black type framing the top of the photo.

It almost seemed futile. We'd need to post thousands of flyers, and yet, how many people would actually see them? We'd need the exact right person to look up at the exact right time and remember something about a stranger, something insignificant to them. More than futile. Impossible.

I sat in my car and looked up at the sky. "I'm going to find you, Daphne. I promise you that."


Sid had left me a voicemail while I was inside the Wharf. No news. Simply an update that the search would start from the Cake & Shake that morning. But before I joined them, I needed to meet with the investigator from the Sheriff's Office. I was over the bridge and halfway to the Summerton County Courthouse when the desk sergeant phoned, rerouting me from the main Sheriff's Office on the other side of the sound to the Summerton substation.

I'd already passed the turnoff to Poplar Grove, an elegant gated community situated on the May River, so I flipped around on Cabana, then made my way down the exquisite winding drive. It was bordered by climbing wisteria and vintage-looking gaslight lanterns. The police substation blended into the elegant surroundings. It was an iron and stone building about a mile before the main gates. While one might imagine the outpost quaint, once inside, one saw the bustle of a modern station.

A uniformed officer handed me a pass on a lanyard and showed me to a second-floor office with a view of the river—if you stood tiptoe, leaned to the left, and gave a good squint.

Sheriff Willem Hill, the youngest sheriff to be elected in the history of the county, was finishing up a phone call. He waved in greeting, then indicated a seat across from his desk. Though young for the county when he was elected ten years earlier, now he was mid-forties with hair cropped short and a trim goatee showing initial hints of gray. His smile reached his eyes and he lifted a finger to signal one minute.

It gave me time to adjust my expectations. I'd been expecting to meet with the lead investigator, possibly even a uniform. Definitely not the Sheriff himself.

I said as much when he turned his attention to me.

"I like to stay involved," he replied.

"Uh-huh," I said.

He laughed. "Also, Captain Finnegan called and name dropped."

"Me?"

"Ed Ballantyne."

"Gotcha," I said.

"It's nice to finally meet you in person," he said. "Now what can I help you with?"

"This is my first missing persons case," I said. "What happens next? Daphne's been missing nearly thirty-six hours. No one's heard from her since Saturday night, correct?"

"As far as we can tell," he said. "We've opened a file, and we have two investigators working on it. Are you the local contact, with her family being out of town?"

"I am. We've called the hospitals and morgues from Charleston down to Jacksonville and began hanging flyers last night."

"Sounds right," he said. "That's exactly what you should be doing when it comes to a missing person. We've also been making calls. Talked to her mother yesterday. She's of the impression Daphne left because of the wedding."

"Really? I'm of the impression she was the maid of honor in that wedding. Her duties pretty much put her in town all week."

"True enough," he said. "But she has a right to be wherever she wants. And a reason to not want to be at that wedding. It's not odd a woman might not want to help her competitor marry the man of her own dreams."

"Competitor? What competition?"

"You've lived here for what, twenty years, and you haven't heard of *Down the Isle*?"

"The bachelor dating show?"

"That's the one," he said. "Filmed right here in Summerton County, over on Thatch Island."

"Seriously?" I had always assumed the tv crews filmed the exterior shots around Summerton and the beach, but the whole house and all the episodes were actually recorded on some studio in Los Angeles. "You're saying Juliette and Daphne were contestants on *Down the Isle*, and while they look like best friends, they're not?"

"Ask Juliette about it. I'm going to. You might find out that Daphne skipping that bridal party luncheon isn't such a big surprise."

"Even though she was maid of honor, you think Daphne willingly left town? Over a tv show?"

"Like I said, her mother seems to think so. Says she probably went home to Nashville or at least took to the road."

"I'm assuming you've checked the cell tower pings?"

He studied me. In the pause I realized he had cited how long I'd lived on the island, down to the year, give or take. I knew when he was elected Summerton County Sheriff, but his was a widely publicized public position. Mine was not.

"This PI license you're pursuing, you seem to be committed," he said. "For someone not in the business. A couple of nasty cases over at your Ballantyne Foundation recently. You handle yourself pretty well. You see a future in investigations?"

"Thank you," I said. "I'm not sure about all that. Nasty is a strong word. Life is actually pretty slow on our island."

"The May Bash, the Nutcracker ballerina, something with a

burned boat, the tragedy at the Irish Spring, missing Pomeranians—"

"You seem well informed," I said, shifting in my seat.

"I'm in the next city over, not the next state," he said with either a smirk or a smile. I didn't know him well enough to differentiate.

"Back to the cell phone pings. You check them?"

He leaned back in his chair, a large black leather office chair with hearty springs.

"I have the full support of Captain Finnegan and his entire Sea Pine Island police department," I added with a touch of my own smirky smile.

"Which we're not, but I appreciate the name drop."

"Back atcha. I'm just saying, it's a cooperation. And I'm the official liaison for the family, as we've also already established. Seems inside the realm to share what you know at this early stage."

"Fair enough," he said. His chair sprung forward and he rustled a paper on his desk, as if checking his notes. "I was able to get a court order to look at her phone records for Saturday and Sunday. Her phone pinged a few times on the island between 9:13 p.m. and 10:47 p.m. on Saturday, then it stopped about an hour later. Looks like the phone itself turned off then, and it hasn't turned back on. We'll keep checking."

We exchanged a quiet stare. "Basically, if she left town, she turned her phone off when she hit the road?" I asked.

"Squares with her mother's opinion. Seemed sure she knew her daughter well enough to not be worried."

I sighed. It didn't square with Juliette, her closest friend. And I tended to think close friends knew more about us than our parents, even our mothers, and certainly a boyfriend probably knew us best. And hers had shown up at the search. "Alex Sanders, her boyfriend, have you talked to him?"

"Yep, again this morning" He hesitated, then shrugged. "Works over at Island Rentals near Sugar Hill, been dating Daphne for about six months. You probably know all that."

"You said 'again,' as in you talked to him once already?"

"He's coming back to talk tomorrow," he said. "He's out hanging flyers. I know where he is. I'll keep an eye on him."

"Me, too."

He stood, extended his hand to shake. International code for "interview over." He escorted me to the stairway. "Anything else, detective?"

"You have my number?" I asked.

"And I'm not afraid to use it."

# FOUR

As I drove through Summerton, I arranged to meet Juliette at the apartment she shared with Daphne. It was a more-shabby-than-chic rental community on the Summerton side of Palmetto Bridge. Eight or ten brick-and-wood-sided buildings, each two stories with exterior staircases, were set at angles. Asphalt lots were bordered by spaces covered with metal carport roofing. I circled around to the back of the complex and found their unit on the second floor without trouble.

Juliette held the door as I entered the compact entry. "What did the Sheriff say?"

"Pretty much everything I mentioned on our call," I said. "Daphne's phone last pinged on Saturday night, and her mother thinks she willingly left Summerton so she wouldn't have to attend your wedding festivities this week."

I'm not sure which news made Juliette's features deflate so fully: That Juliette hadn't been heard from in two days or that she hadn't wanted to be here in the first place.

"Tell me about *Down the Isle*," I said. "I've never watched a single episode."

"Really?" She half-smiled at that and wandered into the kitchen part of the living room-kitchen combo. "Two years ago, almost, I guess. I was on the show. So was Daphne. We were two of eighteen Single Ladies."

"Really?" My turn to be surprised.

"That's where we met," she said. "That's where I met Tucker, too."

"But your grandparents are married to each other."

She laughed. "I know, right? We'd never actually met." She took a deep, cleansing, yoga breath and seemed to gather her thoughts. Or gird herself to tell the story. "Daphne's from Nashville, not sure if you knew that."

"Let's assume I know nothing about any of this."

"Okay, right. Good point. Daphne's momma encouraged her to audition for the show. So did Millie Poppy. Encouraged me. Can you imagine, these two women urging their daughters, granddaughter in my case, two states apart to go on tv to find a husband? And we agreed.

"Anyway, Millie Poppy adored Tucker. He lived out in San Francisco back then. Had only visited Sea Pine a handful of times over the years. Serious bad blood between his grandfather and his dad. Never once called Sam Grandpa."

"Like you don't call Millie Poppy Grandma?"

"I know, right!" she said with a light laugh. "I'm telling you, he and I are the same. My family tried to get 'Nanna' to stick, but everyone called her Millie Poppy. She loved her name. For a while, when I was really little, I called her by her full name: Millie Poppy Pete. I'd say, 'Millie Poppy Pete, can we go to the beach? Millie Poppy Pete, what's for dessert?' It tickled her to giggles, then I'd giggle. How could I ever call her Nanna? Anyway, Millie Poppy Pete always wanted to fix me up with Tucker, and when she heard from Sam that he was the Eligible, why she—"

"Eligible?"

"That's what they called him. Didn't want to get us confused with the other bachelor show."

"Makes sense," I said.

"Millie Poppy thought time was running out to get us together. Though she never told me all these matchmaking plans until it was over and we ended up engaged. Pretty pleased with herself." Juliette smiled and poured us water from a pitcher, then handed me a cupcake from a domed plate. "Lemon raspberry with cream cheese frosting," she said, almost absentmindedly.

"*Down the Isle* started with eighteen Single Ladies. We all met Eligible, Tucker, on day one, in the evening really, after we moved into Isle House. It's over on Thatch Island. It's gorgeous. Plantation house on a low bluff overlooking the ocean. And it's massive. Like your Big House, only it was never converted into anything. It's still just a massive house. Ten bedrooms, nine bathrooms, a wrap-around porch, pool house, guest house, croquet on the front lawn."

"Sounds idyllic."

Her sharp laugh held a bitter undertone. "The house was, the show most definitely was not. Daphne and I were roommates straight away. Instant besties. I think because we're both creative types. I love cake decorating and she loves baking. Plus, she makes jewelry, the beaded kind. Used to have an Etsy shop." She tossed away our cupcake wrappers and wiped the counter with a paper towel.

I finished licking the last of the tart frosting from my fingers, then slathered on a healthy helping of hand-sani and let her ruminate.

"Anyway, long story short, *Isle* worked just like every other dating show. The girls had dates with Tucker, in large groups at first, then as we dwindled in numbers, individual dates. We had daytrips and games and competitions. Daphne and I both had a great time with Tucker, and as other girls were eliminated, we stayed in the competition. In the end, Tucker picked me. He proposed in the finale, and now we're getting married. Daphne was genuinely happy for me. She was never really serious about him, you know? Just something to break out of Nashville. But we were all really good friends. Super tight."

"You, Tucker, and Daphne?"

"Yeah, we needed to stick together. It was the *Hunger Games* in that house. We were more tributes than contestants. There were mean girls, sure, lots of shade, but some were straight up nasty. I blame Jona."

"Jona?"

"Yeah, Jona Jerome. She's the producer on the show. More like puppetmaster. Makes great tv, though. But me and Daph stuck together, and Tucker knew we were like, real. Now he and I are getting married, and Daph is my maid of honor. I hated that show. It was so toxic. God, the worst. But at the same time, it wasn't a total disaster. I got a fiancé and a best friend."

"Daphne wasn't disappointed when Tucker picked you?"

"Not at all," she said. "Daphne's mother wanted her on that show more than she did. Thought it could help her launch her bead business. Talked her into it. That's the reason most of those girls even audition. Exposure. Daphne liked Tucker, sure, but only because she was my friend, you know? Tucker kept her until the end so I'd have an ally. I knew he loved me, but I still had to compete." She shrugged. "That's the show."

I smiled and nodded knowingly, as if competing on national tv for a boyfriend was a natural courtship ritual. "Do you mind if I look around? Check out Daphne's bedroom?"

"It's down the hall. The room on the left. Take your time. Whatever you need, if you think it'll help find her."

Daphne was a neatnik with a bohemian vibe. A vibrant, handmade quilt covered her bed, itself adorned with beautiful overstuffed silk pillows embellished with beads and braids. So very many beaded and braided things. From the oversized throw to the macramé wall hanging to the tall jewelry tree holding at least a dozen necklaces. Everything ultra-organized. Patchworked, but lovingly done. A bulletin board hung over the dresser. Colorful postcards from several US cities pinned to the cork, photos of Daphne and friends wedged into the frame. I recognized Juliette and Tucker, along with some of the people who showed up to search.

"That's her brother, Bo." Juliette stood in the doorframe and pointed to a tall man in a scruffy beard. He held a guitar, while others in different photos held drumsticks and a fiddle. "He's in a band. Moonshine. They play country. Mostly originals. They're on tour right now." She looked around the tidy room, then left me to search.

Two recent boarding passes, SPI (Sea Pine Island) to BNA (Nashville's airport), were stuck to the corkboard, as were concert tickets and magazine pages featuring beaded bracelets and earrings.

I gingerly inspected inside the dresser drawers, under the mattress and bed frame, checked the closet and hanging clothes. I looked in her shoes (both pair) and her boots (both pair). It was sparse, but I couldn't tell if it was because Daphne had packed a bag or because she lived small. For all the beautiful beaded boho belongings, there weren't actually that many tangible things.

I was about to stop when I noticed the wood pole holding the macramé wall hanging. It was two inches in diameter with ornate endcaps. I first twisted the right side. Or at least attempted to twist. No amount of pulling or turning loosened it. I tried the left end. While it also was stuck on good, it had the slightest bit of give.

A combination twist/pull and it popped free. Something was rolled inside, almost too far for my fingertips to find purchase. With delicate fingernail scratching and tugging, I coaxed it from the tube. The bottom half of a car rental receipt from the Charlotte airport. Nothing special about it I could see, other than someone had circled the total amount due, underlined the return time, and the space where the date should be was blank. Perhaps a billing mistake? Why hide a billing mistake? I snapped a quick picture with my phone, then re-rolled the receipt and returned it to its tubular home.

Juliette was waiting for me in the living room, fast-typing on her cell phone.

"You had said Daphne's purse and phone weren't here," I said. "How about her backpack? Tucker said she sometimes loaded her pack in the car and left town."

"It's not here," Juliette said. "But that doesn't mean she took off."

"It doesn't mean she didn't," I said as gently as I could.

Juliette hesitated, then seemed to acquiesce to some inner debate. "She left a note." She went down the hall and returned a few seconds later.

The words "Be happy and shine bright" were scrawled in loopy handwriting on a single sheet of stationery decorated with butterflies.

"Where was this?"

"Attached to the garment bag covering my gown and headpiece. She must have finished the beading and hung it on my bedroom door after I left Saturday night. But it doesn't mean she left. She's wishing me well for my wedding. A keepsake note, not a goodbye note. She'd have more to say, right? I mean, not just our friendship and my life-changing wedding week. We have the Cake & Shake. She wouldn't just abandon that, too."

"You own it together?"

"No, it's mine," she said. "Well, mine and Millie Poppy's—she's a silent partner. Daphne works for me part-time. I couldn't have opened it without her, that's for sure. I mean, she's so much more than a temp. She really wants to open a bead boutique. I respect that."

"Here or in Nashville?"

"I thought here," she said, then waved at the note in my hand. "But maybe not. I thought I knew her. Maybe we can't really know someone, you know?"

"Her mother thinks she went home," I said. "Though I doubt it takes two days to drive to Nashville."

"Yeah, I talked to Zanna, too. She said Daph probably drove to Phoenix, or maybe it was Sedona? That's where Moonshine is playing next. We didn't talk long. She wanted to track down Bo. I'll call her later today."

"I'd like to talk to her, too. I'd appreciate her phone number."

Before Juliette could look it up on her cell, the sound of a key scraping the lock came from the front door.

For the briefest of seconds, we exchanged a surprised glance, then the handle twisted and it flew open.

"Well, a good Goddamn, Juliette," the woman said. She had choppy black and gray hair, flowy clothes, and more beaded jewelry than a gypsy. "Why'd you ever befriend my daughter?"

"Zanna, you're here," Juliette said.

"No shit, Sherlock," she said and turned to me. "Who're you?"

"I'm Elliott Lisbon with the Ballantyne Foundation," I said with my hand extended. A ritual that made my germ-conscious countenance itch, but one I'd yet to find a polite way to avoid.

She avoided it for me, barely glancing at my hand before continuing her bite at Juliette. "It's about time my girl got loose of you. Dragging me down to hillbilly country."

"I take it you weren't planning on attending the wedding this weekend?" I asked.

"It's a small affair—" Juliette said.

"Affair is right, isn't it? And definitely too small for the three of us. You, me, and that awful Tucker Turnbull." She turned to me. "He broke my daughter's heart on national television. Deserted my sweet Daphne for Juliette. On camera!" She glared at Juliette. "You two deserve each other. Hope my baby is on the road getting far away from you." She marched down the hall into Daphne's room and I followed.

"You're not surprised Daphne isn't here?" I asked.

"Why the hell would she stay?" She gathered clothes from the dresser. "Her brother, Bo, is on tour. I've been telling her to join him." She moved over to the closet, stuffing clothes into a duffle I hadn't noticed before. "Bo's opening for a comedian. He's pretty well-known. Gotta big tour bus motorhome with his whole family. It's a huge entourage and all, but they're good people." She talked and stuffed at random, never slowing to make eye contact. "There's a guy who sells the merch, for the whole tour, Bo included. He's adorable. Perfect for Daphne."

"But she hasn't called you?" I said. "Or anyone, right? That's not normal for a missing person."

"Obviously, she doesn't know she's missing. Look, I spoke to Bo. He talked to her last week. Told her to get the hell out of here and stay with him awhile. The tour's playing there a full two weeks. I think she did just that. Packed her bag, turned her phone off, and is driving to Sedona right now."

"And you don't like Alex."

At Zanna's look, her eyebrow raised, hand mid-stuff, I said, "You said the merch man is perfect for Daphne, but she's not single. She has Alex."

"That idiot is nothing but a rebound." Her phone buzzed and she whipped it from her back pocket. After a quick scroll, she grabbed the duffle and brushed past me.

"Is that your son calling? Or maybe Daphne?"

"My ex-husband," she said absently. "He hasn't heard from Daphne, either. He's trying to figure the route she'd take to

Sedona, what stops she'd make. She'd never drive straight through. Too much to experience." She tapped a reply, shoved it into her pocket, then turned to me, completely ignoring Juliette. "I'm at the Summerton Motor Inn off Cabana. Where's the central search center? Who's running point? You got enough flyers?"

"I'm running point," I said.

"We're meeting at the Cake & Shake right after this," Juliette said. "We have about five thousand flyers there now."

I'm pretty sure Zanna harrumphed as she left.

"You know, it really wasn't as dramatic as Zanna makes it out to be," Juliette said. "Daphne still visits Isle House. Not daily or anything, but she found it peaceful. Now that it's empty."

"The house is still there? I mean, unoccupied. They didn't sell it?"

"They're not going to sell it. They film every season there."

"How many seasons so far?"

"Just the two."

"You said she visits the house. Do you also visit it?"

She laughed, again with the bitter undertone. "That show was toxic. I know I just said it wasn't a disaster. But I only meant between me and Daph and Tucker." She placed her face in her hands, then breathed deep again and looked up at me.

"We'll find her," I said.

"I really thought she might have gone home. I mean, I really actually thought she'd help me with the wedding this week. Be in the wedding. And help with the cakes. And the shop. Maybe it was too much?"

"Don't give up yet. She might be on tour with her brother."

"Sure, sure. That's why her mother is here organizing a search party, not on the road to Sedona."

\*    \*    \*

Zanna's arrival in Summerton definitely undermined her assertion that Daphne was on the road to Arizona, escaping her life in South Carolina. And part of that life included a boyfriend. Certainly he would've received a note. Or a text. Or a something.

It was a quick drive from Summerton to Sugar Hill Plantation. One of the island's larger plantations, the local name for residential communities, it was located mid-island and offered a handful of amenities along the road to its guarded gates. One didn't need to be a resident to access the fire station, two restaurants, and the local bike rental shop, Island Rentals. The building resembled a hut, one you might find in Adventureland, with a thatched roof, bamboo poles, and hand-painted wood signs. A long row of beach bikes was lined up out front, and angled ATVs were parked along the side.

Alex Sanders was busy behind the counter helping a customer, handing two bicycle helmets to a woman. Another guy, about the same age as Alex, perhaps late in college, maybe graduated, spoke to a couple near a side door. I waited for Alex to finish, then reintroduced myself.

"You have a minute to talk?" I asked.

"Brad, I'm gonna check the locks on the cruisers," Alex said to the other guy, who gave a chin tilt in return.

I followed Alex through the shop and out the way I came in. We stood near the row of bikes. Blue beach cruisers with wire baskets were chained to a steel rack. Sunshine filtered through the heavy shade from the old oak trees. Lazy traffic rolled by, headed to the Sugar Hill Plantation gates.

"You don't seem overly worried about Daphne," I said.

"It's not unusual for her to go out of town," he said. "She's been visiting Nashville regularly. Like every week almost. She really misses it. Plus, buying trips for more beads and, I don't know, whatever. She just had to finish that dress. And the head veil thing. And jewelry. She was way stressed out."

"About the wedding?"

"About everything. Juliette asked a lot to help her make all those cakes for your party. She's only part-time. Juliette expects way too much from her. I don't think she really understands what makes that girl tick. Wouldn't be surprised if Daphne went to see Bo. She's always looking for reasons to get away."

"Did it bother you she traveled so much?"

He glanced at me. A slight hesitation, then answered anyway. "No. I go to Charlotte all the time to our corporate office. It's the perfect time for her to go to Nashville."

"Because she gets so lonely without you? So she leaves when you leave?"

He fiddled with a lock, then moved on to the next beach cruiser. He squeezed the plump white-walled tires, then continued down the line. "Yeah, I guess. You'd have to ask her. Truth is, it's not so surprising she left. She was acting funny these last couple weeks. This whole wedding is messing with her head."

"When did you last speak to her?"

He finished examining tires and locks, one cruiser after another, then stalled on the last bike before finally standing. "Saturday afternoon. But only for a minute to say I couldn't talk. Look, we haven't been talking much, and when we did, well, it's just that I don't know where it's all going. She texted me later that day, and then I didn't answer her last call. I just ignored it. Didn't want to deal with more wedding drama."

"She didn't text you or leave a note? Anything to say she was leaving, if only for the week? Certainly you must think it odd she packed up her car and left without a word to anyone, especially you?"

He brushed past me to the shack entrance, then turned

back. "Maybe that's why she called me. I'm sorry I didn't answer. I'm sorry she didn't leave a voicemail saying she was outta here. She's with her brother. It makes sense. I mean, it's Sedona. That has to be the homemade jewelry capital of the Southwest. I'm sure she'll call or text someone, but I doubt it'll be me."

# FIVE

(Day #4: Tuesday Morning)

The flyer hanging team grew to about thirty people, including Zanna. We hung posters until after ten, which went pretty much exactly how it sounded. A large stack of bright white papers, each depicting a large photo of Daphne, plus one of her car and a close up of her license plate (a Photoshop mock, courtesy of her friend, Tess). In smaller print, the details of her last known whereabouts, where she might be headed, the $10,000 reward for information, and a contact number. We'd divvied up target areas, covering all roads from Savannah to Charleston, and then up and down I-95. We taped them to poles, windows and doors (with permission), and posts. Several volunteers passed them out at shopping center entrances, whether mall, grocery, or big box retailer. Afterward, we regrouped at the Cake & Shake. Four more Bankers Boxes of flyers, plus two cases of packing tape, would be delivered by eight a.m.

I spent Tuesday morning the same as I had done the day before: A bowl of cereal and my notebook on the patio. I'd spoken to Daphne's friends, all of whom showed up to search. To a person, they all conveyed the same push/pull: Yes, she often took off on her own; yes, it was slightly strange she wouldn't tell at least one of them she was leaving. They were worried, but not panicked. They launched a Find Daphne Fischer webpage and posted links on every online social site they knew of, half of which I'd never even heard of.

With Daphne now missing sixty hours, I felt a slight shift in the urgency. The initial "Daphne's missing!" had melded into a "Where could she be?" and was currently teetering on "Did she want to be found?"

As someone who required a significant amount of sanctuary time to recharge, I fully understood the latter and wanted to respect it. However, there wasn't much wiggle room between going off the grid and being taken off the grid. I simply didn't know which situation applied to Daphne. Only she knew. As long as she was still alive. And I wasn't sure if it was too early to entertain that thought or too late.

I needed to talk to the Sheriff. Which felt wrong. I usually needed Ransom or even Parker. This case being outside their jurisdiction put me outside my bubble. Ransom and I had both worked late the last several days. Our relationship had become a series of random texts. I missed him. I missed his voice, his touch, his laugh. It was disconcerting and it unsettled me. I liked to be settled, ensconced in a routine I could count on.

Though I didn't like counting on Ransom. A faint old fear of him disappearing in the night still lingered.

I called the Sheriff.

A brief two-minute conversation later, I knew that an additional investigator had been assigned, bringing it to three, plus Sheriff Hill himself. They'd also begun notifying various highway patrol departments from South Carolina to Arizona, distributing detailed bulletins and the scanned flyer. Her license plate number became a BOLO notice that morning.

Alex had sounded earnest when we spoke at the bike rental shop. Perhaps almost too much so? But he did admit their recent troubles and that he had ignored her calls.

All the texting and calling made me think of phone records. Not the cell tower pings Sheriff Hill tracked, but the actual calls.

I hit a drive-thru cheeseburger (ketchup only), fries, BBQ sauce, and Coke (though I always preferred Pepsi) on my way to Juliette's. As I gobbled my perfectly delicious first lunch, I called Ransom. I received a text in return.

Ransom: *In a meeting. All good?*

Me: *Nothing new. Can't call it good.*

Ransom: *Can I help?*

Me: *Not sure. I feel disconnected.*

Ransom: *I'm here. Me, Parker, the DEA.*

Me: *Showoff.*

My phone rang.

"No progress, huh, Red?" Ransom said.

"It's now been two solid days since she missed the brunch. Her mother, who was so insistent to the Sheriff, and to me, that Daphne absolutely drove to Arizona, had flown here, not there. At this point, I fear any news is likely to be bad news."

"I'm meeting with the Sheriff sometime this week. Perhaps I'll find out something I can share."

"I met with him yesterday."

"How'd that go?"

"I think he likes me being in the middle of a case as much as you do."

He laughed. "I bet. Where you off to now?"

"Let's just leave it at you won't like it any more than I do."

I tossed the wrappers in the parking lot trashcan and sped the five miles to Daphne's apartment complex. Once inside, I drove around until I located a pair of commercial dumpsters near one side of her building. In the last ten years, I'd gone dumpster diving twelve separate times in search of evidence in ten different cases. Two of those twelve dives netted me something useful. Not the best odds, but enough that I continued considering it a resource. Much as I loathed to do so.

With my Mini sufficiently parked in the loading zone, I

reached into my trunk to don my standard garbage gear. First, a plastic poncho, complete with a hood tied tight with a string tab. Second, knee-high rubber rain boots with thick soles. Third, a pair of welder's goggles, ski style. Fourth, a high-end medical mask. Finally, and most importantly, yellow gloves. Not the kind for washing dishes. These were nuclear waste grade. So thick they stood up on their own.

Like I said, I'd done this before.

I waddled over to a concrete block carelessly tossed near a low brick wall bordering the dumpster enclosure pad. I dragged it over, only having to rest twice. It was late September, which in the South still meant summer weather. The sun was climbing toward high noon and warmed the air to a perfect beach-ready seventy-seven degrees. But I wasn't at the beach. I was covered in non-breathable plastic surrounded by heat waves radiating from thick metal, gritty asphalt, and oven-roasting brick.

The concrete block booster gave me just enough additional height to be able to see inside. I flipped the ridiculously heavy lid. A powerful stench hit me full in the face. Sour and pungent. Rotted food meets decaying animal. I peered inside. It was empty save for random disgusting food glops stuck to the bottom panel and side ridges. Trash pick-up must have been earlier that day. I dropped the lid with a clank and returned to the Mini.

As I sprayed my gloves with industrial-strength cleaner from a spray bottle, I contemplated the original theory that led me to dive the dumpster. Neatniks, like Daphne, become neatniks by throwing things away. However, maybe neatniks who feared hoarding didn't bother getting things mailed to them in the first place. They probably conducted a majority of their transactions online.

I stowed the protective gear in its large duffle and drove around to the front of the building. I texted Juliette, asking if she could meet me at her apartment, or perhaps she had a hide-a-key I could use. She replied immediately that she was already here changing her shoes, so I ran up the stairs.

"Great timing." She finished tying her running sneaks. "Finally had to ditch the sandals. These are way hotter, but my feet can't handle all the endless walking."

"I'll make it quick," I said. "Did Daphne have a laptop? I don't remember seeing it earlier."

"It's more of a tablet."

"Do you mind if I take a minute to look through it?"

Juliette hesitated and I understood. She probably felt the same unbalanced shifts in the urgency as I did. "Go ahead," she said. "But you better not take it. Daphne'll kill me if I let a stranger take her tablet." She opened a wicker basket doubling as a table next to the sofa and pulled out a slim black leather zippered case. She turned her back and typed on the screen. "She knows I know her password. It's not a secret. From me, anyway. She knows mine."

"Isn't it unusual she'd leave town without her tablet?"

"Maybe? She didn't use it all the time. Like not every day or anything. She has her phone, right?" She bounced in her shoes, then sighed. "Listen, I'm going to change again real quick. I think I need socks. Maybe cargoes, not shorts? No-see-ums are getting to me. Then I'm heading out. Me and Tess are going to drive out to Isle House, look around. Maybe she's crashing there?"

I tapped on the tablet's browser icon and checked the web history. There was none. "Great, a history-conscious web surfer."

"Did you say something?" Juliette hollered from her room down the hall.

"Just to myself," I hollered back.

I understood password-protecting access to the tablet itself, but clearing her browser history? Who'd she think would snoop? Alex? Juliette? Let's see if Daphne really was texting and calling Alex that night, I thought. I typed different phone carrier names into the search bar, checking each site's home page. On the third one, a local carrier with cheap rates, the login information was partially pre-filled. Daphne's username was saved, but not the password. I snapped a quick pic of the screen, then clicked the settings in the browser menu to check for saved passwords. A long list of saved sites appeared. I saw all the usernames, but the coordinating passwords were strings of asterisks. I clicked the little eyeball symbol to reveal the hidden data. Another window popped up requiring the master browser password to view them.

I closed that window, then quickly scanned the long list of saved websites, trying to find one that belonged to a smaller company, one that might be less secure. Man, that girl saved every website she'd ever logged into. I opted for two mom-and-pop bead wholesalers and got lucky on the second one. The login name was auto-filled, along with the password. It was hidden behind asterisks, but there was also a little eyeball symbol to show the password. I clicked it. The asterisks spelled out "pearlknot," with a zero for the "o."

Another quick snap from my camera phone of the password from the bead website, then another of the browser menu's master list of websites and usernames. I closed all of the browser windows and returned to the tablet's home screen.

I pushed my luck and it continued to hold. The email icon on the bottom row opened without issue. Only a handful of messages, some spam, and three generic email blasts from bead sites. All unread since Thursday afternoon. I took a pic of the inbox and turned off the screen. When I hit the button to turn it back on, it was locked. I quickly entered the password I'd discovered. It worked. Looked like Daphne used a master password for everything. Convenient for us both.

"The tablet's back in the basket," I hollered. "Thank you, and I'll see you later at the Cake & Shake."


I drove to the Big House. I needed to dig and I wanted to do it on my own turf. The search was beginning to feel a little fruitless. Three days since the last cell phone ping and no calls. Well, there had been plenty of calls. The reward made sure of that. But none of the calls led to Daphne. And none from Daphne herself.

The Ballantyne Beach BBQ was Saturday. In five days. As I was a peripheral planner and not central to the event, it left me plenty of time to concentrate on Daphne and my investigation.

In my office, I transferred the phone photos I'd taken of her tablet to my laptop so I could see them properly. My screen was too small to see with my forty-year-old eyesight. I peered close and zoomed large. My first search was of the phone carrier website. I entered the master password from the mom-and-pop bead site, pearlknot, and I was in.

Three clicks later, I saw her latest phone activity. Nothing beyond Saturday evening at 10:47, around the time of the last ping, according to Sheriff Hill. Though it wasn't listed on the activity report as a call, it was data. It didn't tell me what type of data, like an app or internet search, only her usage.

From a different screen, I saw her call list with inbound/outbound numbers, and her messaging list with sent/received numbers.

It didn't take long to create a directory of sorts. It was shamefully easy to determine who owned what number when you belonged to the right databases and knew the wrong kind of people. And I did, via Milo Hickey—CEO of a prestigious asset management firm, proprietor of underground poker games, and Sid's adoring beau.

I recognized the names of Daphne's family, friends from the search, beading companies, the Cake & Shake, and even Jona Jerome, *Down the Isle* producer. The directory I'd created was crazy long. Daphne made more calls than I did, and I ran events for a billion-dollar charity.

Even so, nothing unusual popped, save two things:

Two phone numbers, one of which recurred daily, were nearly sequential and untraceable to any owners; and a third number belonged to the same Charlotte rental car company from the receipt hidden in the macramé tube.

Pressing *67 to block my own number from appearing on Caller ID, I dialed the two nearly sequential numbers. I received two identical voicemails. An automated female voice informing me I'd reached a voicemail box (in case I'd time-traveled and didn't understand what was happening) and instructing me to leave a message after the tone (on the chance I'd be confused as to what to do when I heard it).

Rather than leave messages on the mysterious voicemail boxes, I made a note to investigate them further, along with the rental car company. Though I did leave one message. With Jona Jerome. I'd heard Juliette's take on *Down the Isle*, and because she was showrunner, I needed to hear Jona's.

Next, I scanned Daphne's social media. At least the major ones I'd heard of. Plenty of pretty cake pictures, beautiful beaded things, Daphne and Juliette at the Cake & Shake—though that particular photo had been posted a while ago. The most recent was a comment on Daphne's Insta about needing to get away.

Again the pull. Missing on purpose or missing in danger?

It was closing in on seventy-two hours, and no one in her family or circle of friends had heard from her.

I called Sheriff Hill.

Expecting to leave another message, I was surprised when

he came on the line three minutes later.

"Elliott, how are you?" he said. "Your ears must've been burning."

"Oh?"

"We're organizing an official search party for this afternoon. We'll start small. Take a portion of the people meeting at the Cake & Shake."

"Yeah, don't want everyone panicking over the word 'search,'" I said. "Do her parents know?"

"I'll talk to Mrs. Fischer when I get there. Explain we're exercising an extra layer of attention is all. We're not expecting to find her, just looking for information."

"At least, that's what you're telling the family, right?"

"Will I see you there?" he asked.

"I'll be on my way shortly. And Sheriff—"

"Right, you called me. I dove right in."

"You answered my question."

"Which was?"

"Is it time to pick a side?"

He paused. The faint sound of papers shuffling filtered through the phone. "I reckon it's time to pick a side. We could still be wrong. A good chance we will be wrong. She could be rolling into Sedona when the sun goes down."

I nodded, knowing full well he couldn't see me. "Thanks for taking my call."

"Any time, Elliott. Any time."

I wrapped up my Big House business, stuck my notes inside my faded jean messenger bag, and trotted out to the Mini. I'd barely fastened my seatbelt when my phone rang.

"Elliott, honey, you on your way over to the Cake & Shake?" Millie Poppy asked.

"I am. What's up?" Ready to hear her question the Sheriff's search party plan and what it really meant for Daphne's disappearance.

"We called the Sheriff," she said. "Farrah Something, I don't know her family, is here raising holy hell over Daphne's beads."

"I'll be speeding over the bridge in five," I said.

"I'm not sure what you can do for us, but other than the Sheriff, you're the only person I thought to call."

"Of course. I'm here for you, Millie Poppy."

The Cake & Shake occupied a refurbished Victorian house on Cabana about a mile north of Juliette's apartment complex in Summerton. Its black shutters popped against the toasted almond clapboard siding. A sign with the hand-painted logo hung over the railing of a wraparound porch.

The inside décor was whimsy meets diner. Turquoise vinyl enveloped booth bottoms and stool tops. Bright yellow ceramic pendant lamps hung from the beadboard ceiling, and the most luscious cakes formed a decadent parade in a wide glass case. A chalkboard menu covered the entire right entry wall, detailing coordinating shakes properly paired with each cake flavor.

It was mid-afternoon and it was packed. Two college-aged kids in aprons worked the front, while two more worked the shake machines behind them on the counter. Every table, booth, and square foot of floor space held people. Most in Find Daphne t-shirts. Millie Poppy, Sam, and Tucker were talking to a group near the front window with Alex standing off to the side.

A woman, six feet tall with a mile of flowing dark brown hair, blocked the swinging door to the kitchen. Her voice was loud and her pitch high.

"Tess, you better get back out here, I'm not even close to being done," she yelled. "You're a witness. Stop being such a coward."

Millie Poppy grabbed my hand and pulled me toward the woman. "That's Farrah," she said. "She was on *Isle* with the girls. She's hotter than a wet cat been sprayed by the hose. Though I can barely keep up as to why."

Farrah turned toward us. "I'll tell you why. Juliette and Daphne knocked off my beading technique and my braiding technique, and chickenshit Tess knows it. And if she doesn't come clean, I will sue her and Juliette and the Cake & Shake and anyone else I can think of."

The kitchen door opened into Farrah, and Juliette pushed through. "Well, get out of the way if you want someone to come out." She held a two-tiered pink cake topped with strawberries and glaze. "We didn't knock anything off, and you know it. It's my dress and her beads and you can't sue."

"Her beads?" she said. "Your dress? No. Just no. Tess, stop hiding in the kitchen. Tell her it's my design. If you think I'll let you leave me out of this, Juliette, you're as dumb as you are blind. I've spoken to Jona. My name will be listed in that magazine whether you like it or not."

"Does your drama have an intermission?" Juliette said. "I'm losing interest and can't follow along."

"Oh really? Follow this: Your bridal gown is a rip off. I'll sue for damages if I'm not named as the designer. You and Daphne used my technique without permission. I'm getting the credit."

"You can't own a technique," Juliette said. "There aren't that many ways to bead something."

"What? You think baking is complicated? Anyone can bake a cake. I mean, seriously, they sell boxes of your stale ass mix at the 7-11. You're nothing special."

A woman in line gestured to the cash register. "Are you going to order?"

"Are you under the impression I'm speaking to you?" Farrah said. "Because I am not."

"I'm only asking—"

"Worry about yourself right now," Farrah said.

Zanna Fischer pushed into the room, ignoring the shouting Farrah. She zoomed in on Alex, raising her voice above Farrah's. "Hey, what the hell? I been calling you for two days."

"I haven't had my phone—"

"You don't have a phone?" Zanna said. "Your girlfriend is missing and you don't have a phone?"

"I didn't say that," Alex said. "I just don't have it with me. But she obviously left town."

"Not without telling me," Zanna said.

"She didn't tell you everything," Alex said.

"Well, she sure as shinola didn't tell you everything," Zanna said. "How could you let her get caught up in this wedding?"

Alex turned away from Zanna to face the counter. "Daphne was happy for you, Juliette."

"Daphne would've rather been in Iraq than at your wedding," Zanna snapped at Juliette.

"So no word from Bo?" I interjected.

"Wait, I'm not done," Farrah yelled over Zanna's head. "Juliette, I'm calling the magazine."

"Don't you yell at me," Zanna replied. "If you're not here to hang flyers for Daphne, then you can get out."

Farrah glanced at the crowd, perhaps noticing the folks in Daphne t-shirts outnumbered her, limiting her sympathetic appeal, and whipped her hair around like a professional. Luckily, all cakes were covered. "You know what? I can't. Nope. This is so not over," she called over her shoulder and stormed out.

"It's been almost three days," Zanna said. Her eyes were painted in shadows and highlighted with worry lines. "She should've been to Sedona by now. She would've called by now. I'd think she'da called someone by now. We should be doing more by now."

"We are," I said. "Let's take this to the parking lot."

"Yes, agreed," Juliette said. "Everyone, please, stay inside only if you need to place an order. We'll run shakes out to you."

The Sheriff had just pulled open the door when he heard her announcement. He held it wide as people streamed onto the porch.

"I'll call the women's league, get them and their grandkids over here," Millie Poppy said. "We need the help."

"What was that about?" I pulled Juliette to a corner of the porch. "With Farrah?"

"My dress, her beads, she's jealous, I'm exhausted."

"And the magazine? She sounds pretty upset with you and Daphne."

"Me and my wedding dress will be featured in a magazine, and she can't stand that she's not included. On the *Isle*, she wanted to be in every shot. Every conversation, every date. Watch, by the end of today, she'll be Daphne's best friend crying on the news devasted over her disappearance."

"Do you have her number?" I asked. "I should talk to her about Daphne."

"She's a liar and an opportunist. Talk to Jona first. Though take that with a tub of salt, too."

Zanna's phone rang and she answered it in a rush, hurrying down the porch steps. "Bob, I can't hear you, hold on a sec."

"Noted," I said to Juliette, then followed Zanna to the sidewalk.

She put the call on speaker. "Okay, I'm here, is she there? Is Daph with Bo?"

"Zanna, daggummit, calm down," he said, his gruff voice filled with the exasperation one only used with an ex. "You're getting all hot and bothered over nothing."

"Nothing!" Zanna screamed. "Your daughter is missing, you old fool. I need your half of the reward money."

"Reward money? Zanna, it's embarrassing enough that

Daph's love life was splashed all over the tv. This is just making it worse. The girl's humiliated. Now it's time to give her some space."

"Space? Have you lost your damn mind? No one has heard from her. She's missing. You're supposed to be tracing her route to Sedona. We're trying everything to find her."

"Don't I know it. Daggum news keeps re-running the story of her getting jilted at the altar. Girl's spirit is as fine as frog's hair split four ways after that. You leave it be. She only wanted to get away."

"Not from me!" Zanna hit the red hangup button with so much force, I thought she might crack the screen.

"Zanna, don't worry about the reward money," I said. "We're putting it up."

"I'm not taking your money." She marched over to the crowd gathering on the front lawn, and I thought about Daphne's Insta post wanting to get away. For a breath, I wanted to get away.

Parker arrived in a Sea Pine Island Police cruiser. Definitely not her jurisdiction here in Summerton, but neither Sheriff Hill nor his two deputies seemed bothered. They nodded briefly in greeting as she joined me at the edge of the pack of mostly twenty-somethings. They leaned against thick tree trunks and painted porch railings, sunglasses perched on heads, phones clutched in hands.

"We need about fifteen volunteers to keep hanging flyers," Sheriff Hill said. "The rest will split into teams to begin a cursory search."

"About time we go door to door," Zanna said.

I didn't dissuade her of her assumption. We were not going door-to-door. We were going tree to tree, shrub to shrub, grass patch to grass patch. Parker must have agreed with my silence because she led Zanna away from the search group and over to the flyer group to map out new destinations.

The rest of us were divided into teams and handed reflector vests. Juliette, Tucker, Millie Poppy, Sam, and Alex gathered near the front.

"We'll need a phone tree," the Sheriff continued.

"I can handle that," Juliette said. "I'll put a sign-up sheet on the counter inside for names and numbers."

"And we'll need a base," the Sheriff said. "A place where we can centralize efforts. Needs to have easy access and be able to accommodate, well, a growing amount of people."

"Why not here?" Alex said. "Everyone already knows to meet at the Cake & Shake."

"The fire marshal will shut us down we get much larger," Juliette said. She bit her lip. "Might even today. We're definitely over capacity."

"We can use our house," Millie Poppy said.

"It might be a little tight, honey," Sam said.

"Yeah, and it's kind of far away," Tucker said. "Almost clear at the end of the island."

As murmurs rumbled through the crowd, talk flitted from library branches and golf course clubhouses. But then I realized I already knew the perfect place. "Let's use the Big House."

"Isn't that kind of far away, too?" Juliette said.

"The Ballantyne is close enough," Sheriff Hill said. "We'll consider Daphne's apartment ground zero. We've got a CSI team headed there. I'm meeting them in thirty minutes. You all start with the grids around her apartment. We'll slowly expand toward the island on one side and the highway to the other."

"I'll go to the Big House later and let Tod know to set up."

"Sounds like a plan," Sheriff Hill said. "We'll get the word out to meet there starting tomorrow morning."

Parker passed me as the flyer brigade headed to their cars. "All set. I think Zanna knows what y'all are doing, but just didn't want to talk about it. Not yet, anyway."

Sheriff Hill told the remaining search teams how to tag evidence and how to call it in. While he did that, I pulled Juliette aside.

"Daphne drives a silver Camry, right?" I asked. "Anything else you can tell me about it? Dents, crack in the windshield, decal on the bumper?"

"No dents, but she has a 'There Is No Planet B' sticker in the back window," Juliette said. "Oh crap, we didn't put that on the flyer."

"It's okay. Call Tod and he'll add it to the next batch."

"You want to ride with us to the first search zone?" Juliette asked.

"I'll catch up with you this afternoon. There's something I need to do first."

# SIX

Just because everyone thought Daphne drove to Sedona, didn't mean she did. According to Alex, she often flew to Nashville. Perhaps in wanting to get out of town quick, she flew to Arizona. Or Tahiti or Canada or anywhere but here.

Sea Pine's airport was located down the road from Oyster Cove Plantation. Like everything else on the island, its relaxed vibe lent an air of vacation even when traveling for business. One waited for arriving flights on white Adirondack rockers inside an unhurried terminal. A counter with a handful of check-in stations to the right, a single security lane in the center, and a baggage claim area to the left, it no bigger than a living room.

The secured parking lot was unattended. An automated machine spit out a ticket. Once retrieved, the barrier arm lifted and I drove along the drive to the main surface lot. A treed lane divided two public sections, long-term and short-term, each with six rows of spaces. Covered in leafy oaks and tall pines, it would be difficult to see any of the parked cars from a Google satellite map.

I weaved the Mini around cars and planters, circling each aisle. Having the top down made it seem as if I was just passing the time, cruising along with nothing but a seaside breeze on my mind.

With so few cars to inspect, it didn't take but ten minutes to spot Daphne's Camry in the second to last row. I double-checked the license plate against the flyer, then found my own parking spot in short-term near the airport entrance.

The recognizable sound of plane engines roared overhead as a jet lowered itself over the ocean and onto the airstrip behind the main building. Several people idly rocked along the window while security personnel unlocked the doors to the ticketed area.

"Excuse me," I said, approaching one of the security agents. "May I speak to someone about your parking surveillance?"

"You can report damages or lost and found articles to any airline agent," she replied. "Up at the main counter or at the gate."

"Thank you, but I'm here regarding a missing person." I showed her my credentials. A PI permit with the Sea Pine Police seal on one side of a leather bifold and my Ballantyne business card and driver's license on the other. A quick flash was usually all that was necessary. Quick enough not to read the words "permit" and "training" in red print.

She eyeballed me to the point I figured she'd read the small print, but then told me where to find her supervisor.

I heard her click the mic attached to her shoulder radio and announce me as I walked along a hallway near the secured gate area exit. I passed the vending machines, restrooms, three unmarked doors, one door marked Department of Homeland Security, and finally reached the last on the left. A simple brass plate was screwed to the front with "security" spelled out in block letters. A man answered my knock, his hair long gone, though mostly due to a razor, and his skin tanned from a lifetime of summers in the sun.

"Yes, ma'am?" he said. "I'm Sergeant Whistler."

"I'm Elliott Lisbon with the Ballantyne Foundation," I said. "Can we talk inside your office?"

He stepped aside and indicated a worn chair across from his equally worn desk. "How can I help you, Ms. Lisbon? Officer Yates mentioned a missing person?"

"Yes, Daphne Fischer, from Summerton. Her car is parked in your lot."

He sat up straighter, reaching for his phone. "You sure?"

"It's the silver Camry in the fifth row of long-term. A 'There's No Planet B' sticker on her bumper." I pulled a folded flyer from my messenger and placed it on the desk in front of him.

"Bring in the bulletin on that missing girl out of Summerton," he said into the handset, then replaced the receiver. "Sheriff's bulletin didn't say she'd be at the airport. Said something about state highways."

"Yeah, I think the general consensus has been that she likely left town, but by car. That she drove to Sedona."

"But her car's here," he said. "Well, I'll be dipped."

"Can we look at the security footage? She probably arrived Saturday night. After eleven, maybe."

He hesitated, no doubt considering how much to share with me, a civilian.

"I'm not sure if you're familiar with the Ballantynes—"

"Course I know Ed and Vivi," he interrupted. "Their jet is parked here most days. And you can see their Big House 'bout the same time you see the runway overhead. And I know you. Seen you in their Rolls more than a few times."

"I'm the Foundation Director. Tod Hayes and I usually pick them up. I'm also a consultant with the Sea Pine Island Police under Captain Sullivan." A slight embellishment, but I held his gaze, letting my confidence win the upper hand in his internal battle.

"I guess I need to look at it anyway," he finally said. "Can't hurt to have you in the room. As long as you stay out of the way."

We used a side door from his office I hadn't noticed earlier and entered a compact command center. A large oval table with six chairs and three phones overlooked a wide wall with video screens. Just below them was a long metal desk with keyboard/mouse combinations every few feet. Two officers wearing uniforms and handguns watched the video screens as various images blinked and shifted.

Sergeant Whistler spoke to the man sitting closest. "Bring up the feed from Saturday night. Give us three views of parking: Long-term, ticket booth, front entrance." He turned to me. "You said before midnight, right?"

"Yes, most likely," I said. "Her cell phone pinged on the island, or nearby, right before eleven. Turned off about an hour later. It's a silver Camry."

"Last flights of the day already landed by that time," he said. "Nothing departing."

Took three minutes to get the feeds up on the screens and another five to locate the proper timeframe for each. The sergeant made calls while I watched streaming video race by.

The quality was outstanding. Not the grainy footage one saw when watching reality crime shows replaying liquor store robbery films. This was state-of-the-art. Crisp, high-def digital material, and in color.

It was late night. Tall high-pressure sodium lights cast shadows against the wide leafy branches spread throughout the lot. Like the sergeant said, because of the late hour, the last flight had already landed. Its crew and the airport's staff, along with two remaining passengers, straggled from the building entrance to various parked cars. The officer manning the video sped through the images, stopping when oncoming headlights entered the frame.

Daphne's Camry stopped at the ticket booth at 23:37,

according to the timestamp. Almost midnight. An arm reached out the driver's side window, pulled the ticket from the dispenser. The security arm lifted. Switching screens, I watched as the Camry circled, then slid into a space next to a planter, where it was still parked. The car's front end was partially obscured by low-hanging branches and billowing Spanish moss. Strategic parking choice or happenstance?

A figure wearing a hoodie ducked from the driver's side and jogged away—from the lot and from the camera. No other cars entered or exited. The leaves rustled and the shadows danced in the quiet night.

The officer repeatedly replayed the footage on a loop.

"I can't tell who it is," I said. "It's dark and there are a million trees."

The officer's fingers flew along the keyboard. "I'll grab stills. Might help with traffic cams."

"I'll call Sheriff Hill," I said.

"Already did," Sergeant Whistler said, heading for the door. "Probably arriving about now. We'll go meet him."

"Thank you," I said.

We left the command center, quickly making time to the sliding exit doors in the terminal near baggage claim. We stepped into the warm sunlight. It was early afternoon as we continued walking through the lot to the second to last row.

By the time we arrived, three police black and whites were approaching the barrier arm at the parking lot entrance. It lifted automatically. Close behind them, as if in a processional, I recognized cars. Juliette's, Millie Poppy's, several from the search party at the Cake & Shake.

"Clarence," Sheriff Hill said, his hand extended to the sergeant.

"Will," he said in return. "Thanks for getting here so quick."

"I'd checked every flight departing through Sea Pine,

Savannah, hell, even Charleston and Jacksonville. She wasn't booked on a single one."

"Makes sense," I said. "Because whoever drove this car here, left it and jogged away."

"That so?" Sheriff Hill said.

"We watched the footage," Sergeant Whistler said. "Got some stills we're printing. I'll email 'em to you, too."

"Footage of what?" Zanna said. "Oh my God, that's her car." She stopped as if her soles had been superglued to the asphalt. She seemed to be experiencing the second half of fight or flight. Freeze or faint.

"What's happening?" Juliette said, running up quick to grab my arm. "Is she here? What did you find?"

Tucker, Alex, Millie Poppy, and Sam jogged up behind them. Zanna stood firm, refusing to come closer.

Tucker reached for the driver's door. He'd nearly touched the handle before an officer stopped him. He whipped his hand back. "What are you doing? Open the door."

Juliette peered inside the passenger window. An officer approached her. "I'm not touching, just looking. It's locked. That's good, right? I have keys."

"You have her keys?" Tucker asked.

"Ma'am, how is it you possess her car keys?" Sheriff Hill said.

"I mean, her spare key, obviously," Juliette said. "We swapped, like, forever ago. But I've kept it on me since Sunday. In case she calls. You know, from the side of the road with a flat."

"May I have the key?" Sheriff Hill asked.

Juliette handed it to him, and Zanna found her voice along with her feet. She marched over to the passenger side. "You better hand me that key," she said. "I'll know if something's missing. I'm her mother."

"You can't know what's missing," Juliette said. "You haven't been in her car in, well, ever? I mean, you never come down here."

"Doesn't mean I won't know something when I see it."

"Well, I can see inside, Zanna," Juliette said. "There's nothing in there, so back off already. We'll handle this."

Sheriff Hill kept the key in his hand and spoke calmly. "Law enforcement will be the only ones inspecting the car. We'll need full access, and it's best if you all wait on the walkway up near the entrance."

I noticed two officers standing at the ready near the trunk. Sheriff Hill didn't want to inspect the car as much he needed to check the trunk.

"I'm not leaving," Zanna said.

"No one's leaving," Juliette said. "Look, wait, there," she pointed to a small dent near the rear bumper. An officer semi-blocked her from getting closer. "Open the trunk," she said. Her voice shook slightly as her face paled.

Zanna seemed to realize what the Sheriff was really waiting for. "You think she's in the trunk? Oh my word." She stepped backward onto Sam's foot and nearly stumbled over.

"Sweetie," Millie Poppy said. "Let's go on up and sit in a rocker. These gentlemen need to handle this."

"If my daughter is here, then I need to be, too," Zanna said.

"Me, too," Juliette said. "We can't abandon her."

"Zanna, Juliette," I said. "Millie Poppy is right. Let's give them space." I turned to Tucker and lowered my voice. "They will never open that trunk with the family standing here. Convince them to wait up on the walk."

Four more cars pulled into short-term. The occupants spilled into the lot wearing Find Daphne shirts.

"Folks, really, I know you want to find her," Sheriff Hill said. "But we're going to consider this an active crime scene, and we need you waiting on the walkway."

"Come on, Jules," Tucker said. "You know it's right." He held her hand and gently pulled her away.

Millie Poppy looped her arm through Zanna's. "It'll be okay. We'll just wait up there. We can see the car from the rockers."

The crowd around the Camry slowly thinned until the only person next to it not in uniform was me.

"Oh, I'm staying," I said to Sheriff Hill.

"She has credentials," Parker said wryly.

I hadn't seen her arrive, but having her close somehow reassured me. Because I did not want to see them open that trunk. With Daphne missing a solid three days, the scales had tipped in favor of her being in that trunk.

The officers, both Sea Pine and Sheriff's Office, started their search with the main interior. They wore gloves, carefully touching as little as possible. It was as tidy as her bedroom. Not a tossed wrapper or crumpled anything, and the manuals were neatly stacked in the glovebox.

An officer clicked the trunk button on the key fob. The latch released and the lid slowly rose. The officer shook his head quickly.

I didn't realize I was holding my breath until it came out in a swoosh. I stepped over to peer inside. It was spic and span and practically empty. A red first aid bag on the left. A spare tire beneath the gray carpet. Hard to tell if it had been freshly vacuumed immediately before being parked here, or if Daphne simply kept it that way.

A tow truck rambled up to the security arm, which lifted automatically.

"We'll finish processing the car here, then take it to the main station," Sheriff Hill said. "We'll take possession, as it's our case. But keep Sea Pine involved. The lab will start analyzing today."

"I'll tell the family," I said.

He returned to his deputies and Parker, calmly giving orders, while I walked to the friends and family on the sidewalk.

"The trunk's clean and empty, like the rest of the car," I said. "The evidence team will analyze it taillight to headlight this afternoon in Summerton."

Zanna stared straight toward the Camry. A thousand-yard stare. Tears streamed down both cheeks. "She didn't drive to Sedona. I thought for sure."

"Finding her car doesn't mean anything," Alex said. "Maybe she Uber'd."

"To Arizona?" Juliette said.

Parker eventually joined us. We numbered close to twenty-five. She encouraged the teams, both search and flyer-hangers, to return to their zones. With a squeeze to my arm, she left.

I spent the long afternoon hours with Zanna and Juliette and Millie Poppy. The four of us waiting and watching. The evidence team arrived. Uniformed technicians collected and swabbed and sealed the tiniest bits into bags. The entire Sea Pine Island Airport's lot was thoroughly examined. It gave up its own selection of random detritus. Hard to know what would be important. Better to simply collect it all.

As the sun's rays faded, the tow truck driver loaded the Camry onto the truck's flatbed. Loud clanging of metal and cables, along with the officers' soft murmurs, floated across the lot to accompany our silence. No one spoke. There wasn't much to say, and I'm sure we were all thinking the same thing.

What the hell was Daphne's car doing at the airport without her?

It only meant one thing. The shift in urgency had picked a side.

Daphne Fischer was truly missing now. Not missing on purpose, but missing in danger.

# SEVEN

A pair of bright red fire engines, one a ladder truck, the other search and rescue, were parked in the circular drive of the Big House. Three police cruisers, two belonging to the Summerton Sheriff's office and the other Sea Pine Island Police, were street side, all facing the Oyster Cove Plantation security gates.

Tod, Carla, Jane, and I had met late the night before to discuss using the Big House as the search base headquarters. It was a quick discussion with nary a complaint nor objection from any of us. Nor a recrimination about the timing. As in, why wasn't this done three days ago? At least, none of us said it out loud.

By the time I arrived Wednesday morning, more than fifty people filled the foyer. Zibby manned a makeshift registration station. She'd converted the antique sofa table into a provisional desk and positioned it at the bottom of the wide staircase. After people registered with Zibby, they moved to the library where Find Daphne tees were folded and stacked according to size. Then the line streamed down the hall, past my office, to the sunroom for search instructions and zone assignments.

I slipped my messenger bag into the bottom drawer of my desk just as Tate Keating slipped into my office.

"*Ballantyne To The Rescue, Three Days Late,*" he said.

"Great headline. A real catcher. You know I always do right by you."

"Right by us? *Pot Luck Means Bad Luck at the Ballantyne* is not right by anyone's measure, and most assuredly not mine."

Tate Keating, the *Islander Post*'s top columnist, fancied himself a cross between Walter Cronkite and Edward R. Murrow. He was more like Walter Winchell meets Hedda Hopper. His jaunty newsboy cap, askew no less, proved it. "Let's talk Alex Sanders," he said. "Will the search focus on his apartment now? *Ballantyne Beau Becomes Prime Perpetrator.* Such an alliterational ring!"

"That's not a word, and what are you talking about?"

"Mr. Sanders stopped cooperating. Do I need to spell it out? Innocent people cooperate with the authorities in times of crisis. What? Am I breaking news to you, the Ballantyne's very own Trixie Belden?"

This was indeed news to me. "It's not news to me. I'm simply surprised you heard. And so we're on the same page, exactly how did Alex stop cooperating, according to your unrevealed sources?"

"His phone is off-limits. Privacy concerns, he says, but more importantly," Tate dramatically waved an arm through the doorway, "do you see him here? One doesn't need a source to use their own eyeballs. But alas, he's not at the police station either. Probably at his attorney's office. And for that, I did use a source."

That was not good.

"Ta-ta," Tate said. "Unless you have a comm—"

"I have no comment."

"Then you shall read about it like everyone else on the morrow."

I waited two minutes, giving him time to ta-ta out of the Big House, then went in search of Sheriff Hill. His lead investigator was briefing volunteers in the sunroom, and Parker was assisting Zibby at her makeshift desk. Registration was vital to this investigation. The police needed to track who showed up to search and who didn't. Something I should've already done myself. I hadn't realized I'd need a gossip columnist to tell me what I should've noticed in my own house.

"Alex Sanders check-in today?" I asked softly over Parker's shoulder.

She shook her head. "Sheriff Hill isn't here either."

I peered into the library, then the sunroom. I recognized many of the faces, but not one belonged to Alex Sanders. I returned to my office, closed the door, then dialed Sheriff Keep It All To Himself.

"What's going on with Alex Sanders?" I said when he answered on the second ring. "I've been informed by a reliable source that he's stopped cooperating and won't let you look at his phone. Also, you're not here leading the ground search. Tell me what's happening."

"Elliott, always nice to hear from you," he said.

"Thank you, Sheriff," I said. "I'm feeling a little left out. How about you share some of the most vital bits of your investigation?"

"You calling from the Big House? How's it going there?"

"Daphne's still missing," I said. "Alex is noticeably absent. As are you. You almost here? Perhaps we could chat. You can catch me up."

"Not today," he said.

Silence stretched as I waited for him to explain why he wasn't participating in a search he arranged. Apparently, he was waiting for me to figure out he wasn't going to answer me.

"What did you find?" I asked. "Or more specifically, what did you find, and how does it connect to Alex? Something with Daphne's car? We agreed to cooperate with one another, remember? I'm the family's liaison, and we'd appreciate an update."

"Some things can't be shared, you know that. But you're a smart one, Elliott Lisbon. I have no doubt you figure it out soon enough."

"Yes, but wouldn't it be sooner if you told me?" The question turned out to be rhetorical, as he'd already disconnected.

I called Ransom. If I wanted a police detective to keep things from me, I had my own.

"It's always the boyfriend," I said.

"Ah, you heard about Sanders," he said. "You already at the Big House? It's like eight thirty. A bit early for you."

"Yes, I'm here. And it's a good thing, because the second I turnaround, something happens. I'm telling you, it's always the boyfriend. Or husband."

"Or girlfriend. Or wife. But El, ask yourself this: Has that always been your experience?"

I thought about my cases. The first serious one, the murder of Leo Hirschorn, was eighteen months earlier. I'd investigated three additional major cases in the intervening months. It certainly wasn't always the spouse. "I concede the point."

"See, your own investigative history pokes holes in your boyfriend theory. You may be barking up the wrong tree."

"But the Sheriff knows more than he's sharing."

"You think?"

Tod and Carla walked in with a tray of food. "I gotta go," I said to Ransom. "Priority is being given to those who know me best."

"Carla brought food?" he said.

"Exactly."

The three of us ate warm raspberry white chocolate scones with sweet clotted cream and homemade jam. I sipped Pepsi while they gulped coffee.

"I made fifty to-go bags with scones," Carla said. "Ran out in the first thirty minutes."

"Yeah, cars spilled out into the auxiliary valet lot first thing this morning," Tod said. "Girl has some friends."

"That she does," I said. "I peeked at her phone bill, and she made at least a dozen calls a day. That's more than I make. But she had two odd ones. They were nearly consecutive numbers. Off by like two digits."

"Maybe she was calling a help center or something?" Carla said. "Those calls roll."

"These calls were both incoming and outgoing," I said. "And when I called the voicemails, there were identical, non-committal messages for each. Identical. Message verbiage and voice."

"Sounds like Burner," Tod said.

"A burner phone?" I said. "I Googled the numbers and checked every database I could find. The carriers weren't listed. It's as if they don't exist. Burner phones would at least have a carrier attached."

"Not a burner phone, Burner the app," Tod said. "Or maybe HushHush or Cover Me. You download the app and use your own phone to make secret calls and texts. That way you don't need a second phone."

"Like FaceTime?" Carla asked.

"What's FaceTime?" I asked.

"It's an Apple thing," Tod said. "And not exactly. That's for video calling, when you want to see the person while you're talking. A burner phone app is about private calling and texting, so they don't show up on your phone bill."

"It was only calls, no texting," I said. "Her monthly statements didn't show any texts to or from either of those numbers."

"Messaging is done inside the app," Tod said. "You don't use your phone's messaging app, you use the Burner app."

"How do you know so much?" Carla asked.

"It's the twenty-first century?" he said.

"Is it normal to have two separate Burner accounts?" I asked.

"She probably didn't have separate accounts, just different numbers," he said. "It's not overly common, but it's one way to keep things completely independent. What about her credit cards? Can you take a peek at those, too? You should see recurring payments. Something small like $4.99 or $7.99 a month."

"Man, that's good stuff, Tod." I opened the lid to my laptop and clicked my way to the magic Google machine. Using Daphne's global login and password, I checked all the big banks: Chase, Citi, Bank of America. No hits. I went wider and regional and got lucky with a local bank on the island. "Here's her checking account. It looks like she has a debit card and a credit card."

"I don't even want to know how," Carla said.

"No you do not," I replied. "She has a large credit line and matching large credit balance." I clicked and scrolled, then stopped. "There's a recurring charge for $5.99 for the last three months for a corporation called Smithson."

"That could be it," Tod says. "Or something like that. The company would keep the billing name generic to protect privacy. And people who use burner apps want privacy. Clearly, they fear someone will snoop their phone and their phone bill. Can't have a recognizable burner app name show up on the monthly statement."

While I scrolled, I noticed multiple airline purchases. All the same airline. "She seemed to fly a lot," I said. "Let's look at her frequent flyer history." From a new browser window, I tried to log into the airline, but Daphne's global username and password combo didn't work. Interesting. So the one website where she added an extra layer of protection was the airline. And almost literally the only one. "Note to self," I said. "Make sure every website has a different login name and password."

"Or don't even get on that thing," Carla said. "I don't have a single account anywhere."

Tod mumbled something that sounded distinctly like "amateurs" as he cleaned up the scone tray.

"Amateur nothing," I said and clicked my laptop lid shut. "How's this: Where's the parking ticket?"

"Daphne got a parking ticket?" Carla asked.

"When you park at the airport, you have to take a ticket to enter the lot," I said. "Someone took a ticket when they entered with Daphne's car, and I want to know where it is."

# EIGHT

While the search teams headed to Summerton, I headed to Sea Pine's airport. I parked in the same spot and walked down the same hall as the day before. Sergeant Whistler wasn't on duty, or at least his door was locked, so I approached Officer Yates. She stood at her post next to the gate area exit.

"I'm not sure if you can help me," I said. "I'm Elliott Lisbon with the Ballantyne. I was here yesterday looking for a missing person. You directed me to Sergeant Whistler. Is he in by chance?"

"No, ma'am," she said.

"Will he be available later? Or perhaps there's someone else I could speak to. It's about Daphne Fischer."

"Crazy that girl's car was here for three days," she said with a slow head shake. "You're welcome to wait for the sergeant, over on a rocker, but it'll be a while."

"Maybe you can help," I said. "You know anything about the tickets for parking? The ones you need to enter the gate?"

"Only that the Summerton Sheriff took them."

"All of them?"

"All of them," she said. "Including the container. About took all last night to remove it and install a new one."

"Interesting. Though I guess it only matters if the driver had driven her car out of the lot, not left it here, right? You need to insert the ticket into the container to pay the toll when leaving?"

"Yep," she said. "Unless the driver had been here earlier that day. Or week, since that's about how long those tickets been in the box. Maybe scoping out the lot?"

Or a frequent flier.

"Can you help with flight information?" I asked.

"I cannot," she said. "Barely able to help you with those tickets." Her stoic look revealed more than her words. Our chitchat was over.

I thanked her and walked outside to a row of rockers, all unoccupied. The next flight wouldn't arrive for at least an hour. Which meant most people wouldn't need to leave their beachfront homes and seaside condos to retrieve inbound guests for another forty-five minutes. Even Tod and I usually didn't head to the airport to pick up the Ballantynes until we heard the plane approach the runway.

I needed access to flight information, and after a few minutes running through my mental Rolodex, I landed on Milo Hickey. He'd long since provided me with introduction to various nefarious underground groups. I assumed he knew a guy who knew a guy who could access a passenger manifest without needing official documents. Like police badges and search warrants.

"Milo, it's Elliott," I said. "You have a minute?"

"For you and the Ballantyne, of course," he said. "Though I'm walking into a shareholder's meeting. You'll need to be quick."

"As a rabbit," I said. "You know anyone who can show me airline records? Specifically, flights?"

He paused for the briefest of seconds. "Air traffic is strictly regulated. Inquiries may be flagged."

"I'm not planning anything, Milo," I said. "I'm at the Sea

Pine airport investigating the disappearance of a local girl. Woman. Girl woman. She was booked on a flight to Tennessee last week, and I want to see if she had booked any other flights."

"Ah," he said. "Give me a moment."

I listened to cars in the distance. The rhythmic hum of tires on pavement over on Cabana. A mile of brush and trees and blankets of pine needles muffled their thrum. The lunchtime rush as visitors and residents scattered to local eateries and hotels, markets and shops. If I strained, I could probably even hear the ocean. It was closer than the highway, but the waves were lazier in their travel.

"Elliott," Milo said. "Speak with Jeanine Gurly at the ticket counter. She's working now. She'll assist with passenger and flight information."

"Thank you, Milo," I said. "I appreciate it. And I owe you."

"No reciprocity required," he said and clicked off the line.

Fifteen steps later, I was inside the terminal. Jeanine Gurly greeted me with a corporately trained smile when I stopped at the end of the counter.

"I'm Elliott Lisbon, and I really appreciate this," I said. My voice was low, but indoor voice low, not conspiratorial whisper low. "It's about Daphne Fischer."

"I heard about her car," she said. "Right there this whole time. Been the talk of the airport all day."

"Can you provide a list of the flights she was booked on? I'm not even sure which airline she used or her exact destination."

"Not a problem. Let me see what I can find. I'll start with a general search for the month." Her fingers clicked and clacked on keys at a speed that made me question her accuracy. "Here we go...Thursday. That's this Thursday, tomorrow. Our airline, by the way. To Nashville with a layover in Atlanta."

"She's listed as a passenger on a flight leaving tomorrow?"

My voice was a pitch higher than normal as surprise leaked in. I distinctly remember the Sheriff saying he'd checked all departing flights. Perhaps he didn't check this far in advance?

"Yes, ma'am," Jeanine said. "The 7:12 to Atlanta. First flight off the island."

"Anything for last Saturday?" I asked. "The day her car drove into the lot?"

"Nope. Her previous flight was the week before. A two-day turnaround. Flew out Thursday, returned Friday."

"What time again on Thursday, the one tomorrow? You said early?"

She handed me a slip of paper with the flight numbers and departure times. Though with only about six flights a day through a single gate, I didn't actually need the flight numbers for the Sea Pine Island departures.

"This is weird," she said. "Huh." Her fingers clacked and clicked at gamer speed. "She reserved a seat through to Nashville, but..."

"But what?"

"She never boards the second leg," she said. "She lands in Atlanta. She's supposed to connect. About a seventy-minute window to catch the leg to the Nashville, but she doesn't check-in for it." Five hundred clicks later. "Not for her previous four trips. Weird, right? And I verified. The initial flights landed with plenty of time to make the connection."

"She only flies to Atlanta, not Nashville?"

"Looks like. Why pay for Nashville if you're not going there? Each trip, she's booked and paid in full."

"Does she fly to Charlotte?" I asked.

"She doesn't fly anywhere. Just boards the return flight in Atlanta the next day."

"Can you check one more name for me? Alex Sanders? He travels to Charlotte, and I think he flies about the same time as

Daphne. Maybe check the same weeks that she flew."

Clickety-clack. "Well, isn't this something?" Tappity-tap-tap. "Not about the same time, nearly the exact same time on the same day. She took the earlier flight. It leaves for Atlanta ninety minutes before his flight to Charlotte."

"That's weird."

"It's all weird. And he's also got a flight booked tomorrow." She handed me a postie with Alex's flight info on it.

I thanked her and returned to my Mini in the front row. Even though Alex had told me all about it, it still seemed odd Daphne would travel the same day he did. Precisely the same day. Maybe he thought it odd, too. But only in hindsight?

Well, I thought, Alex has a flight tomorrow. Just like Daphne. It was weird and odd and coincidental, and at this point, maybe Ransom was right, and I was barking up the wrong tree. Then again, maybe I wasn't. Either way, the maybes were starting to get to me.

Jona Jerome returned my call as I sailed over the Palmetto Bridge from Sea Pine Island onto mainland South Carolina. Rather than talk on the phone, which with the top down was more like yelling on the phone, she agreed to meet me at the Cake & Shake, since she was already there and I was but a handful of minutes away.

She was easy to identify. She leaned against a sporty two-seater, its top also down. Black oversized sunglasses square on her face, a frothy milkshake in her hand, and a *Down the Isle* press badge hanging from her waist.

I parked in the spot next to hers, then walked around to join her, leaning against my passenger side, facing her. "You here for the search? It starts over at the Big House."

"Cute," she said with a sip of her shake. "I'd heard Daphne

was missing."

"You don't seem concerned," I said. "Or even mildly surprised."

"That girl marches to the beat of her own tambourine. She was not long for this shake shop. I bet she's already in Seattle or Portland or some northern town like Eureka."

"We found her car abandoned at the airport."

Jona tilted her head. "Seriously?"

"Yesterday," I said.

"Dang," she said. "I did not see that coming. Well, I'm here now. What is it you need from me?"

"Tell me about *Down the Isle*. The season with Daphne and Juliette."

"Best season of tv ever," she said. "And I don't just mean for us. I mean on all of tv. Network and cable. It was batshit wild. That's why I love reality. You simply cannot script something that good."

"But you can plan something that good, right? You had to know Tucker and Juliette knew of each other prior to filming. That they were basically related, right?"

"Absolutely," she said. "That's the only reason we selected Juliette to be on the show. You have any idea how many twenty-two-year-old blonde aspiring somethings apply? It's a shortcut to fame. Or a husband. It'd make your independent female backbone bend."

"Oh?" I said, my brow semi-raised.

"I know who you are," she said. "Research is how I make my living. And I'm very good at it." She sipped her shake. "We vet all the contestants. We knew Tucker and Juliette were basically strangers. Thought it could be an interesting angle that their grandparents were married, yet they'd never met."

"Interesting? You mean you were counting on bad blood. Like the Montagues and Capulets."

"Perhaps. It got even better when Tucker was more attracted to Daphne."

"Really? 'More attracted,' as in he was more attracted to Daphne than he was to Juliette?"

"Look at you," she said. "Smart and independent."

"I was under the impression Tucker and Daphne were only friends, and only because of Juliette."

She snorted. "Not any kind of friendship I've ever had. Those two were hot and heavy. Tucker and Daphne had phenomenal chemistry. I swore it was love. Like actual love. Certainly looked like the real thing, and I had a front row seat to watch the whole relationship blossom."

"Or a back-room advantage. You're the producer. I imagine it's your job to make it look like the real thing."

"Those two didn't need much producing. Those three, really. Don't get me wrong, he and Juliette had no trouble steaming up the camera lens. Dang, that Tucker could work it. For those last couple episodes, Daphne and Juliette were neck-and-neck for his affections. My money was on Daphne. But in a twist I woulda sold my soul for, he dumped Daphne and picked Juliette."

"On camera?"

"On the finale shoot. Brilliant." She leaned over and tossed her empty shake into a nearby trashcan. "It's been almost two years, and I still remember it like yesterday. It was magic."

"True love won out?"

"Something did."

"Do you keep in touch?"

"Are you kidding? Absolutely. Having Eligible marry his true love that he found on the show after dumping her best friend? And now she works for the bride? Ratings gold. Platinum. Titanium. I set up a photo shoot for the wedding with a spread in a national magazine. The whole ceremony will be shown on prime time tv. Network tv."

"But not live, because I would've heard about it."

"Not live. Though I tried everything to get them to agree. But I'm filming it, exclusively. Those girls know it'll blow up the Cake & Shake with that kind of national coverage. Even help Daphne launch her bead boutique. That's what sold her."

"You had to sell her on it?"

"She and Juliette may have been bffs, but she was ready to stop taking her leftovers. We're going to photograph all of Daphne's bead work on Juliette's wedding gown and bridesmaid jewelry, and all of Juliette's cakes from your BBQ and her wedding. Win-win."

"That's what Farrah was hollering about at the Cake & Shake. Raising all kinds of holy everything that Daphne and Juliette were getting all the attention."

"I wasn't there, but that sounds about right," she said. "The contestants get a bad rap. Everyone thinks all the girls are backstabbing, clawing, marriage-obsessed drama queens. Some of them are genuinely good girls. Farrah? She's the ruler of the backstabbing, clawing drama queens."

"She threatened to sue Juliette, the Cake & Shake, maybe even you."

"She's all bark. I'll toss her a mention about bead collaboration or some such whatever. She'll calm down."

"And the new season of *Down the Isle*? Is that already filming?"

She opened the driver's door and slid into her roadster. "Not yet, but soon."

"Oh? I thought the show was a huge hit. Wasn't it renewed?"

Her smile was more sardonic than social. "It will be now."

# NINE

Isle House was situated on the highest point of Thatch Island, South Carolina, twenty miles from Summerton if traveling by motorized watercraft. When traveling by Mini Coop convertible, one had to drive around Port Summerton Sound to reach it.

Folklore held that Thatch Island was named for Edward Thatch, more commonly known as the pirate Blackbeard, after he traveled to the barrier island aboard *The Queen Anne's Revenge* sometime in the very early 1700s. It ran aground on a sandbar, forcing Blackbeard to bury his treasure nearby.

It was not lost on me that batshit wild *Down the Isle* was filmed on an island named for a dastardly pirate who captained a ship called *Revenge*. Talk about bad juju.

Island hoodoo aside, the house itself was quite grand. An antebellum plantation manor, its block columns spanned a full two and a half stories. Thick iron railings bordered the wraparound porches. Black shutters adorned every door-sized window, and a gallery or bedroom wing jutted from one side. Ornate corbels supported the cornice across the roofline with four stately chimneys standing tall. The front faced the ocean across a wide lawn, overgrown gardens, and intermittent spots of ranch fencing. Far across the lawn, an ornamental railing faded into tall marsh grass. Likely a stairway to the rocky beach below.

Isle House was empty, forgotten, left behind. This close to the beach, the light winds brushed the sand and dust into mini drifts across the porch. It made it hard to identify individual footprints and determine when they might have been left there. Juliette said Daphne liked to visit the house, and I wondered if Daphne sat on the sand-swept steps, pondering what might have been or what could still be. Juliette and Tess had been here searching for her, and I didn't really know what I was searching for, other than answers to vague questions.

The front doors and windows were bolted tight. I followed the porch along the side wing, then a path around to an iron gate blocking access to the rear of the house. A wide chain held the latch to a post. It creaked when I pushed it, its chain stretching far enough to create an opening at least a foot wide. I scrunched down and sucked in my stomach, my back scraping and bumping against the unforgiving metal. I was halfway through before I realized nothing was actually attached to the chain to lock it to the post. It was merely looped. I unlooped it and walked through the open gate like a normal person.

Whilst the front of the property told the story of Southern wealth established long before the Civil War, the back spoke nouveau riche. A pool worthy of a five-star Las Vegas resort covered nearly half the grounds. Tiered sunning lounges, two swim-up bars, a tiki bar, and a fire pit peninsula. It probably once looked decadent and sparkling and refreshing in the summer sun, but now it was sans water and sans sparkle and surrounded by a low chain link fence dotted with faded warning signs.

The wraparound porch picked up again behind the side wing. I stepped onto it. All rear-facing windows were locked and bolted like their front-facing counterparts, including the double-wide entry French doors. Scratches on the metal lock indicated tampering. Perhaps by Daphne? I added my own set of scratches until the lock clicked and the handle cranked downward.

I expected the house to be empty, and it was. I thought it might be wrecked from vagrants and hoodlums who used its massive expanse as a flop house. It wasn't.

My footsteps fell against the solid wide plank floors, echoing throughout the cavernous rooms. Chandeliers still hung from high ceilings nearing eighteen feet tall. A handful of rugs remained. Some scattered, some rolled. Elegance and grandeur exuded from the architecture with tasteful updates mixed in. Granite countertops in the kitchens (plural, there were two) with stainless appliances, and the baths (nine) each with jetted ceramic bathtubs. The master suite was larger than my cottage, even if you put the upper and lower floors side-by-side, included the garage, driveway, deck, and beach frontage.

I spent an hour touring the interior. Only the ghosts of residents past lingered inside. A single call sheet from an early *Down the Isle* taping, its edges curled from the humidity, rested on the floor of the butler's pantry. No other evidence of the home's prior occupants, including Daphne Fischer, one-time contestant, and perhaps dreamer of a Prince Charming. Or a new life, one outside the borders of Tennessee.

Awash in melancholy, I slipped out the rear French doors, shutting them with a soft click.

"We call that breaking and entering way out here on Thatch Island," Sheriff Hill said. "Not sure how it runs over on that island of yours."

"Who me? I was just testing the door handle." I gave it a good rattle.

"I've been here ten minutes."

I had no answer for that.

He half-sat on the wide veranda ledge. One leg bent, the other stretched. "You find anything?"

"You mean like an arrest warrant for Alex Sanders or notes

indicating he's a person of interest for the local sheriff? Nope, nothing like that. Tell me this, since you waited for me and clearly want to talk to me, how long you been focused on him?"

"You sound a little chapped," Sheriff Hill said. "I can respect that. I'm happy to answer your questions. Sanders has been on our radar since Sunday morning."

"Sunday morning, as in the day before I sat in your office and specifically asked about Daphne Fischer and you said she probably left town because she wanted to?"

"Yep, that's the day."

"You didn't tell me about Alex Sanders being 'on our radar.'"

"It's an ongoing investigation."

"What am I, if not an investigator?"

"Not an investigator."

"So it's like that?" My melancholy fully evaporated, I tipped my head in a short nod. "You have a fine day, Sheriff."

"Stay awhile, Elliott," he said, his voice stopping me as I hit the third wide porch step to the pool.

"I'm chapped, remember?"

"An arrest warrant for Alex Sanders can't be the reason you're really here," Sheriff Hill said.

"Why are you really here?"

"Like I said, happy to answer questions. But as you noticed, you might not always like the answers."

I waited.

"Patrol called in a pale blue Mini convertible in the Isle House drive without a driver."

"Patrol called the actual Sheriff to pop on over and see what's what? Man, it's pretty slow on this island of yours."

He smiled at that. "You're on a list."

"Of what?"

"People associated with the disappearance of Daphne

Fischer. And this house. I like to stay personally involved. It's a major case."

The ocean air blew in soft puffs, swirling the blooming wisteria that ran wild through the trees. The air smelled of sweet jasmine and salty seaweed. I leaned against the rail and gazed over the empty pool.

"They put that fence up last summer when the house sat vacant too long. Too much of a liability. May need to fill in the pool soon or at least cover it."

"I heard you took the parking tickets from the Sea Pine airport exit. An entire container's worth."

"We did," he said. "Before you ask, about all we know is that someone took a ticket to enter the lot. The rest is just evidence gathering in case something comes up."

"Would you actually tell me if you knew more?"

"The machine recorded issuing a ticket at the same time the parking lot camera recorded Daphne's car entering at the security gate. Guess if we find that particular ticket, we might be able to tie it to the driver. Good call on the stub. I shouldn't underestimate you."

"No you should not. And you don't need to be butter me up. I saw it on *Dateline*. A convoluted story about a guy who reluctantly reported his girlfriend missing. He had all this proof she left town, but they discovered her abandoned car at the airport. They later tied him to it."

"With the parking stub?"

"They used cell towers to track his phone to the airport parking lot. However, in his case, he fed the ticket into the machine to pay the toll and exit the lot. I don't remember the whole thing, but they found that parking ticket, and her body buried in his backyard."

"We're doing the same thing. Tracking, and you know, checking each ticket left in the container. Even though the driver didn't leave it behind, it's possible the driver did a trial run earlier."

"You keep saying driver, but you mean Alex. You think he planned this in advance. And so much in advance, he did a trial run. That's calculated. Premeditated. And definitely makes him more than a person of interest."

Sheriff Hill stood, brushed the front of his pants. "Time to get back to it."

We walked in silence down the garden path and around the side wing to the circular driveway. His department black and white SUV snuggled up tight to my pale blue Mini.

"Daphne may not have been happy about this particular walk down the aisle." He opened his driver's side door, leaned on the frame. "Seemed like that poor girl got way more than she bargained for. It was a crazy show, that's for sure."

"You watched *Down the Isle*?

"When I could. Never live, though, just recorded. Hard not to be curious, what with it filming right here in my backyard."

"You have a copy of any of the episodes? I'd love to watch the season."

"A copy? You mean like a VHS tape? You can stream it. Didn't take you for a Luddite."

"I'm not a Luddite, Sheriff. I can stream."

"Next time you want inside Isle House, let me know. I have the key." He tipped his hat and climbed inside, then drove away.

I called Sid. "Do you stream?"

"*Killing Eve, Goliath, Bosch, Ozark—*"

"I need to stream *Down the Isle* episodes. Everyone keeps saying it was a crazy season, and maybe I should see just how crazy."

"Isn't that a little shut-the-barn-door-after-the-horse?"

"Very possibly," I said with a sigh. "How's the search?"

"Good or bad, depending on your perspective. We've found

nothing. And I mean nothing. Another forty people registered to search, so now we number over a hundred."

"Alex ever show up?"

"Nope. Neither did your Sheriff."

"Not my Sheriff. And no surprise. He just left me at Isle House."

"He tell you anything useful?"

"He alluded they were checking cell tower records. In a roundabout way, he glossed on about tracking and checking tickets for 'the driver.' I don't think he intended to tell me about the cell towers, or for me to find out."

"Because?"

"One needs to know whose cell phone to track. He already looked at Daphne's. I'm thinking he's now looking at Alex's. Hard. Something's up with Alex, and I want to know what." I started the Mini and slowly drove down the long drive. "You busy tonight?"

"Noooooo," she said slowly. "Why?"

"Meet me at my house at ten. No, wait, it's too close to the Big House and search headquarters. We need to be more covert. Meet me at the Mariposa."

"Clandestine margaritas, perchance?"

"Yes, definitely," I said. "After."

She sighed the sigh only a best friend can. Two parts love, one part I'm-not-going-to-like-this-but-I'll-do-it-anyway.


The Mariposa was located mid-island in Locke Harbor, a one hundred boat marina with a bustling boardwalk of restaurant and shops. As close to genuine Mexican food one could find in a region known for its Lowcountry Boils and shrimp grits, they made tart margaritas and chunky guacamole. Unfortunately, the closest I planned to get to that palate-pleasing pairing was the parking lot.

Sid was waiting for me in the very last row, far from the entrance, close to Cabana Boulevard. Before debating which car to take—I liked my Mini, she liked her Mercedes; mine had sass, hers had everything else—I hopped out of mine and into hers. She was doing me a favor, and I appreciated it as much as I appreciated her.

"We're going to Island Rentals," I said. "That's where Alex Sanders works. It's after hours, and I need to take a peek at a few things they won't allow me to peek at during business hours."

"I'm waiting in the car," she said.

"Of course," I said. "You're the lookout."

She eased onto Cabana. The traffic was light for the late hour. Island life was a quiet life. Vacationers and retirees spent their days golfing and lunching in the sun, their evenings tucked in early to get up and do it all over again.

Sid turned onto Sugar Hill Drive, then drove two miles along the winding road to the Island Rentals hut. She slowed as we approached. "You said it was after hours, right?"

"Huh," I said in reply. The overhead lights still shone inside the squat building, highlighting both customers and staff. "How late does one need to rent a boogie board?"

Sid tapped on her phone, clearly using her handheld Google machine to type and scroll. "Open until midnight seven days a week."

"This must be the only thing on the entire island open until midnight."

"The Mariposa is open 'til midnight."

"Please do not name everything that's open late."

"You want to wait until they close?"

"For two hours? Um, no."

Sid started to reverse out of the space when I stopped her.

"What are you doing?"

"Leaving?"

"I meant, let's not wait two hours, let's go inside now and Plan B this sucker."

"Which sucker? What exactly do you need?"

"Alex Sanders isn't participating in the search for Daphne. He also isn't cooperating with the authorities, and the Sheriff isn't cooperating with me. He was quite open in the beginning, but now he's watching me more than talking to me. Which means if I want to know about Alex, I need to find out for myself."

"Uh-huh."

"I want to see Alex's travel records. It's thin, but Alex said he travels for business, and this is his business. I want to know where he was going. Daphne certainly wasn't going to Nashville, so maybe Alex wasn't going to Charlotte. He said he goes to corporate, but really, why? Training? Expansion? Was he planning a move?"

"He kidnapped Daphne because he's moving from one Carolina to the other?"

"I said it was thin. Alex has probably said all of thirty-two words to me, and those are the ones that stood out." I leaned over the passenger seat and rummaged the space behind us. "You have a hat back here? A scarf? Sunglasses, maybe?"

"It's nighttime."

"I'm aware," I said, ditching my backseat search. "Never mind, I have one." I pulled a floppy hat from my messenger bag and handed it to her.

"I'll look more suspicious wearing this thing. I'm six feet tall."

"Calm down. You'll look like a tourist. It'll be great."

"Me? What are you doing?"

"Going to take a look in that office." I pulled another hat out of my messenger bag and ensconced it firmly over my slightly frizzy hair.

"How many do you carry with you?"

"Not nearly enough." I slipped my slim lockpick case and phone into one pocket, my hand-sani and thin surgical gloves into the other.

We formulated a decent plan in the thirteen-second stroll to the entrance. We walked inside, me lagging ten steps behind, and to my great satisfaction, every patron wore a hat. Most were of the baseball variety, but still. Two couples left through the side door, leaving a lone staff member inside, the one I'd seen earlier when I questioned Alex. I wasn't surprised Alex wasn't there. He was probably being read his rights.

"Excuse me," Sid said. "I have an issue with one of your ATVs."

"Sure," he said. "What's up?"

"I strapped my boogie board to the rack and rode to the beach—"

"You rent them here?" he said. "You have your driver's license? I can look it up."

"Oh, sure, but I'm not...let me finish. I actually got cut off by an ATV, and it had one of your stickers on the back. Snapped my board in half."

"The one strapped to the back?"

"It happened so fast."

Sid continued to coat her story with an extra layer of varnish. She led him to the window overlooking the ATVs parked along the side. "Swiped right in front me and I skidded. This guy was driving recklessly, probably drinking. I'm sure y'all don't allow that. These things all look the same, but perhaps up close..."

I quickly ducked behind the counter and crossed into a short hallway. Every step squeaked. The floor was a bit bouncy, as if it floated. Probably nothing more than plywood subflooring covered in thin carpet.

I passed the door marked "restroom" and chose the door marked "private."

It was unlocked and empty. The overhead light was on. I looked for cameras, keeping my expression peppy and innocent, one hand on the knob. Just a tourist looking for a restroom.

No cameras.

I entered fully and closed the door behind me. I leaned against it, scoping the room and forming a search plan.

A crowded bookshelf hung over a heavily marred wood desk. It butted up against one wall, while dented file cabinets lined another. Receipts, forms, invoices, all in a rainbow of triplicate shades, were crinkled and stapled, stacked and tilted, on every surface, including the floor. Folders indicated a haphazard filing system. Filing, because they leaned against the dusty filing cabinets; haphazard because they were overstuffed with papers and had no labels.

My OCD germ-conscious palms began to itch.

I slipped on the thin surgical gloves without a pre-hand-sani rinse. It would have to wait. Sid's boozy beach tale was being told on the fly, and I didn't know how long her audience would stay engaged.

The only thing a quick rummage into the floor files, metal cabinets, and desk clutter netted me was a face full of dust and a concern the owner of Island Rentals had an audit in his future.

Unsure if there was an order to the various stacks of paperwork on the desk, I gingerly shifted and re-shifted them until I found a large calendar, or maybe it was a blotter. Something tacky stuck the whole thing to the wood surface. I pried a corner. It rippled with a deep zipper sound. I imagined a long-since spilled sugary drink hardening into the cardboard backer. It was a desk calendar dated two years earlier filled with doodles and scribbles and random food splots. Nothing useful.

Above the messy desktop, binders of vehicle catalogs and user manuals, along with office supplies and dirty coffee mugs filled a pair of ramshackle shelves. I flipped through a couple binders, but nothing fell out other than dusty microscopic mold spores. I couldn't see them, but I could smell them.

Below the ramshackle shelves and above the messy desktop, additional papers were thumbtacked directly into the drywall. On the far left, a schedule. I pulled out my phone to check it against the dates of Alex's flights. Alex was marked off for those particular dates. Nothing about a trip to the corporate office or team meetings or an industry conference on the schedule. It simply said, "Alex off."

The only place left to inspect was the space beneath the table opposite the desk. On the floor. I first crouched, then remembered I wasn't twenty-two and would never be able to stand back up if I knelt longer than three seconds. I sat instead. Fine spider webbing and fluffy dust bunnies kept me company while I scrabbled through the stacks of ancient boxes. The air reeked of old corned beef and mustard. The plastic wastebasket behind me overflowed with crumbled containers and half-eaten food.

From outside the office, floorboards creaked. Heavy. Steps moving quick. Faint at first, then right at the door.

I pushed the wheeled office chair aside and squeezed under the desk, wedged between the plastic garbage pail and the solid side panel of the desk. I had just reached for the chair's swivel leg to pull it toward me to use as cover when the door handled squeaked.

I whipped my hand back and held my breath.

"Wait, Brad, I haven't told you about the turtles," Sid said, her voice three octaves higher than normal. "There are nests everywhere on that beach."

Papers shuffled on the desktop. "We're good," he said. "I know who you're talking about."

More papers shuffled. Closer this time. Right above my head.

If he stepped farther into the office, he'd see me.

I closed my eyes.

A floorboard squeaked as his weight shifted.

"Really, it's important," Sid said. "The turtles—"

"It's here somewhere," he said.

I held my breath.

"The dust is horrible back here," she said, her voice another octave higher. "I have asthma. Chronic, we really—"

"You can wait up—"

"I wanted to show you another angle of the damage," Sid said. "I have it on my phone."

"Give me a minute," he said. "It's here someplace. Unless he filed it."

"It's vital you look at it," Sid nearly screeched.

"Found it," he said.

Papers rustled above me as they shifted. A paperclipped sheet floated down and settled onto the desk chair.

"Let's see that photo," he said.

"My phone's up front," she said. "Was that the door? Sounded like a bell."

Floorboards squeaked and the door shut with a thud.

I exhaled as if I'd been drowning and rested against the desk's inner side panel. The hallway foot squeaks slowly faded.

I crawled out and smacked my head on the desk drawer. It rattled open, slammed into the chair. I slapped my hand over my mouth out of instinct and gagged. I needed better instincts.

Hunched between standing, sitting, and injured, I waited.

The hallway remained silent. Brad didn't return.

I quietly snapped off my gloves, brushed dust and webs and

bleck from my face, then opened the door with the same innocent ditzy face I entered with. Ready to exclaim a whoops, not the bathroom.

No one was in the hall.

I walked straight to the front, caught Sid's eye. She distracted Brad with a friendly shoulder shove for doing such a great job as I slipped under the counter, sneaking my way toward the door.

"Well, isn't that something," Sid said. "I'd have sworn it was one of your ATVs. But thanks anyway."

"Wait, you're sure," Brad said. "I have the—"

"Positive. Now that we're talking, I think it was more of a Jeep. Like an actual Jeep. Probably the lifeguard. It was red. I'll call them. You have a good night, now."

Two guys with snorkel gear held the door open for Sid as they were entering and she was leaving. I followed her out.

We had parked in a remote spot on the far side of the lot, almost next door. We debriefed while I bathed in hand-sani beside her car.

"Sorry about that," Sid said. "He was fast on his feet. I blinked and he started down the hall."

"I'm good." After my bottle was nearly empty, I brushed and patted away as much grime from my clothes as possible, then re-bathed my hands, arms, and face.

"There's no corporate office, right?" Sid said.

I stopped washing my hands.

"I asked if I needed to file a complaint with the corporate office and he laughed. Said this is it. One shop. His shop."

"Good to know," I said. "I'd figured as much, since every single sheet of the two thousand papers I just handled all had this Sugar Hill address on them. Nothing about a chain or other locations."

"So what's next? I know you well enough to know a simple

office search will not suffice."

"We go to Charlotte. Alex lied about a corporate office. Definitely to me. Maybe to Daphne. He's flying there for some reason, and I'm guessing it's an important one."

# TEN

(Day #6: Thursday Morning)

In order to properly recreate the Daphne/Alex travel tour, I needed to take Daphne's same scheduled flight to Atlanta, look around, see if anything popped as important, then switch gears and beat Alex to Charlotte to pick up his trail. Which meant waking before the sun shone over the Atlantic to catch the 7:12 to Atlanta. As I'm not one prone to rise before the roosters, I required a double Pepsi with a Pepsi chaser to fully embrace the bright side: I didn't have to pack a single garment, and the airport was less than seven minutes from my cottage.

Sid waited for me in an Adirondack rocker, a grande something in her hand, a beautiful travel satchel at her feet. I parked in short-term, pulled my messenger from the passenger seat, and joined her. We checked-in at the counter. The agent, Jeanine Gurly, handed us boarding passes, and other than a friendly hello and a wink, she didn't acknowledge our previous discussion regarding this particular flight.

"Sheriff Hill is acting suspiciously," I said to Sid as I settled into a cushioned chair near the boarding gate. There were only two, marked Gate 1 and Gate 2, on opposite sides of a room measuring about twenty-five feet wide. "He's being all cagey and friendly. Helpful in a distinctly not very helpful way."

"Maybe he's flirting with you," Sid said.

"Flirting? That's absurd. I have Ransom."

"He doesn't know that. You don't wear a ring."

"A ring isn't necessary," I said. "It's not normal to assume just because I don't wear a ring, I don't have a life partner."

"Life partner?"

"Boyfriend sounds silly over forty."

"Do you want a ring?"

"I want a Post-it. You know, like Derek and Meredith. Can't we just commit our vows to each other? We say them and keep them, but we don't need to go to the courthouse. It makes it messy. I like clean."

"Maybe you shouldn't live your life according to an episode of *Grey's Anatomy*," she said. "As for me, I want it all. The romance, the engagement, the wedding on the sand, and the always-be-my-person ending."

"I'm your person."

"I need a backup. One who isn't afraid to go all in and doesn't settle for a Post-it."

Before I could reply, the agent announced our flight. We followed the line of people through the doorway directly onto the runway. Outside was breezy and bright and smelled of oceany air and oily fuel. A small jet, loud and rumbly, waited with its built-in stairway lowered and its uniformed attendant greeting us as we ducked inside. We took our seats in turn, me at the window, Sid on the aisle. It was a tight fit, and once we took to the sky, nearly impossible for either of us to be heard over the engine without shouting.

Our hour-long flight was entirely uneventful. Usually how one hoped to travel. But as I said, I'd also been hoping for something to pop. The plane taxied to the gate in Atlanta. We deplaned, used the facilities, and sat in the waiting area for the connection to Charlotte.

"Where did Daphne go when she was here?" Sid asked.

I leaned in close, keeping my voice low to match hers. "I

wouldn't even know where to start looking."

The airport buzzed with activity. Early commuters, vacationing families, tour groups, random strangers, all in various stages of hustle. To gates, to coffee, to places exotic, familiar and unknown.

"You think she stayed inside the terminal?" Sid said.

"Why would she? She wasn't flying anywhere. That's what Jeanine Gurly told me, that Daphne landed in Atlanta, never connected, then flew home from Atlanta the next day. This is a monster huge airport, and she could move freely between terminals. Maybe she didn't need to fly anywhere."

"Let's assume she wasn't interested in shopping for overpriced snacks and neck pillows and actually left the building. But why? To visit friends? Why keep it a secret? Why not just tell Alex she's visiting friends in Atlanta?"

"Excellent point. He specifically said she flew to Nashville, which we know she did not. Was he lying?"

"Was she?"

"Maybe she had another boyfriend here in Atlanta," I said. "One she could only see when Alex was out of town."

"Which assumes he knew of the Atlanta connection, right? Like, he would've put it together she was seeing another guy in Atlanta. Otherwise, why disguise it with a trip to Nashville?"

"Right," I said. "And that's a lot of assuming. She could've grabbed a local bus to anywhere or met someone inside the terminal or at a hotel nearby."

"Or at the convention center, the aquarium, or simply took in a baseball game."

"Exactly. Which is why we're heading to Charlotte. It's a solid lead."

"By solid, you mean what?"

"It's all we have. Alex visited Charlotte on the same days Daphne flew to Atlanta. Without direction with Daphne in

Atlanta, we follow Alex to Charlotte."

"But there's no corporate office, so we don't know where he's going?"

"Yep," I said, and blew out a hefty sigh. "I know this is wild goose territory. We'll spend a day searching for I don't even know what a hundred miles from Daphne's ground zero, two days before the Ballantyne BBQ. But my gut says to go. Things are swirling around Alex right now, and this feels like I'm taking action."

"I'm with you, El," Sid said. "How do we do this, exactly?"

"With our connection time and Alex's direct flight, we land in Charlotte about twenty minutes before he does. I'll hit the rental car agency, you watch the exit near baggage claim—"

"If he brought baggage," Sid said.

"Charlotte's airport may be larger than Sea Pine's, but it's relative. He'll be funneled through baggage claim to get outside. We just need to get the car rented and to the curb before he exits the airport, or he'll disappear into a wave of traffic."

The universe continued to shine upon us as our flight boarded on time and landed two minutes early. Without bags to slow us, we hustled to the lower level. I left Sid at the curb and continued at a fair clip across the street to the rental car lobby.

That's when the universe's shine took on cloud cover.

I stood between a pair of stanchions, the front of a line of one. A friendly placard requested I wait for the next representative to assist me. There was only one representative. A salesperson in a grass green vest with a large plastic nametag bearing the word "Micah." He was wrapping up a rental agreement with a gentleman traveler whose external foot tapping egged on my internal hurry-up hand-waving as minutes ticked loudly by, both internally and externally. The clock on the wall was comically loud.

The traveler scribbled on the bottom of a contract and

hurried off, and I quickly moved to the counter, my driver's license in hand. Micah didn't raise his head. He gathered additional paperwork from the desktop and turned to the door behind him, casually ditching me at the counter.

"Excuse me," I hollered. "Hello?"

I checked my watch. Nine minutes until Alex landed.

No response and no return.

Two more minutes ticked by. I searched for a bell to ring or a buzzer to push. I leaned over the counter toward the door and hollered again.

Another minute before Micah returned. "Hello, how may I assist you today?"

"Reservation for Elliott Lisbon." I passed him my driver's license along with Daphne's missing person flyer. "Have you seen this girl? Her name is Daphne Fischer, and I believe she rented a car from you about two weeks ago or maybe two months ago. I'm not sure when, perhaps you could look it up?"

He didn't so much as glimpse at the flyer. He continued his slow-tap on the keyboard. "I just started last Saturday."

"May I speak with a manager? Perhaps another associate?" I checked my watch. Five minutes until wheels down.

"I'm the only one here," he said.

I felt relief. I wanted to know more about Daphne and her hidden rental receipt, but I knew I could check again when I returned the car. I scribbled my phone number on the flyer and asked him to ask his associates, and then post it on the desk for customers to see.

He agreed, but his assurance underwhelmed me. He rattled off a monotone speech about gas and insurance and where to return the car.

"Sounds like you've said that a thousand times. Aren't you new?"

"I worked at Piedmont-Triad for four years until they made

me manager here." He placed a pink contract in front of me. "Just sign here. Car will be in space twelve in about fifteen minutes. It was just returned, so realistically, maybe twenty before it's out of inspection and wash. You can also wait inside."

"Twenty minutes? I need it now. Like a literal now, not a twenty-minutes now." If I missed Alex at the curb, I might as well fly home.

"It's all we have—"

"You have to have something else. There's not another soul in this building renting a car."

He slow-tapped the keyboard again. "I have one gassed and ready, but it'll cost you. You sure you don't want to wait? There's a bench."

"Positive," I said. "Just give me the keys."

With my signed contract in hand, I found the car in space one. It was available because who spent nine hundred dollars to rent a convertible Ferrari Portofino at the Charlotte International Airport? Per day. The rental counter was off-brand, not a chain, and I realized as I perused their aisle that they specialized in unusual. I'd simply booked a "standard" car when I'd called. I figured a standard car was a compact sedan. Turned out it actually meant a Hummer. Did Daphne rent a Hummer? What the heck was Daphne doing in Charlotte with a Hummer? And with whom? Unless it wasn't actually her car rental receipt.

The Portofino fired up like a dragster behind the line, reminding me of Ransom's sleek McLaren Roadster. All power and elegance and ready to race. I didn't disappoint it.

Once curbside, Sid hopped in. "Go, go, go! He's in a black Camaro. Newer, souped-up. Not vintage."

I barely glanced over my shoulder, then zipped into the darting traffic of pickups and drop-offs.

"So you were going for conspicuous?" Sid said. "Interesting

tailing tactic choosing an orange racecar."

"I was going for available. This sucker cost more than both our plane tickets combined. Also, it's on the red side of orange. And I'll keep the top up."

"There he is," Sid said. "Up on the right, maybe ten cars?"

"What did he have with him? Roller bag? Pet carrier? New girlfriend?"

"Tan backpack slung over one shoulder. That's it. He's alone. And the car was waiting for him at the curb without a driver. He walked straight to it and drove away."

"That's weird."

"Def."

"And strange he didn't bring anything with him. He's booked on the afternoon flight leaving at 6:22. That's about eight hours to do whatever he's doing."

The most difficult part of driving a Ferrari was keeping the speedometer below 100 mph. I was making myself carsick with the constant ebb and flow required to maintain a reasonable distance without being seen. Conspicuous is right. Though one doesn't suspect a Ferrari would be used for a tail. At least I hoped not.

For the next thirty minutes, we wound around various freeways. Majestic oaks and tall pines bordered our scenic drive on the outskirts of downtown Charlotte. Alex finally slowed when he reached the Kings Drive exit off highway 277. A large sign indicated Freedom Park was up ahead.

"What do you think?" Sid asked. "The park?"

"Definitely. And he has to be meeting someone, right?"

Sid used her phone internet skills to give us the birds-eye. "Ninety-eight acres of parkland with a lake, playground, bandshell. Multiple bridges and covered picnic areas. Your basic massive citywide park serving a community of hundreds of thousands of people."

The Camaro pulled into the front row of spaces near the sidewalk, so I chose a spot in the third row, nestled between a minivan and a family sedan.

"You think we blend?" Sid asked.

"We don't need to." I pointed to Alex getting out of his car.

"I'll follow," Sid said. "You wait here."

"No, I follow. I'm the PI."

"The recognizable PI."

"You're six feet tall, remember? And you've been at all the search meetings. You're much more recognizable." I slipped a canvas floppy hat out of my bag and popped on oversized sunglasses before she could reply. "Be right back."

The park was busy for a weekday afternoon in September. A yoga group stretched and breathed while kindergarteners circled around monkey bars and swing sets. Little tail-waggers chased squeaky toys and large ones leapt for frisbees. I surreptitiously glanced around for the camera crews filming this idyllic scene scripted for a meet cute in a romcom.

Alex and his low-slung backpack meandered along a brick path. I meandered about forty feet behind. He passed the bandshell and peaceful Tai Chi practitioners. He eventually stopped at the playground section with a sandbox, choosing a bench on the outer rim. Assorted toddlers waddled with buckets and shovels, their mothers bunched in twos and threes, one eye on kids, the other their phones.

I remained out of his sightline by sitting several yards behind him beneath a shady oak tree. I slipped a paperback from my bag and tilted my head toward the page while keeping my sunglass-covered eyes on Alex.

He dug into his bag and pulled out an apple. By the weight of the pack, I figured that apple may have been the only thing in there. It was flat and slumpy. He finished the apple, tossed it into the metal trash bin, returned to his bench. Arms splayed wide across the top, enjoying a leisurely afternoon at the park.

I was thinking Sid and I really needed a pair of walkie talkie earbuds for our next stakeout. Perhaps something was happening back at the Camaro, because nothing was happening here. I was contemplating texting her when a guy approached Alex with his hand extended.

"Hey, man," he said. "What's up?"

"Dude," Alex said, doing the whole hand grip, half hug, back pat greeting. "Just hangin'."

It was hard to tell the newcomer's age. Perhaps a little older than Alex? Maybe younger? College buddies? Colleagues? He matched Alex's outdoor adventure vibe with his faded tee and cargo shorts—and backpack. Same color, same size. But his was full. They'd each set it on their insides, so both packs rested between them on the bench.

The ole switcheroo was in play.

They talked lazily. No rush. Just two buds kickin' it in the park. Their voices drifted in the languid early afternoon breeze, but I couldn't fully follow the conversation. Only random words floated my way. Bits about surfing and cycling, waves and winds, girlfriends and families. These two had nothing but time.

I noticed a man on a bench to the left of Alex, but near the other side of the sandpit. If Alex was at six, this guy was at ten. He must have been there before we arrived. He was large, bald, and bulky. Almost thuggish. He wore an ill-fitted suit and carried a brown bag lunch, very office worker on a break. But something seemed off. Like the fact he looked thuggish.

I thought he might be watching Alex's exchange. He lifted his phone a smidge too high at times. Secretly snapping pictures? Certainly not frequent enough or obvious enough for Alex to notice. But I did. And he didn't actually eat anything from the brown bag on his lap.

A girl with blue spiked hair and a face chain of some sort

stopped and asked the suit a question. He looked at his watch, looked at her, said something, and she moved on. All very deliberate. Anyone watching could easily follow their exaggerated pantomime. A casual parkgoer asking for the time. But a millennial without a cell phone or a smart watch?

I didn't think the suit noticed me, and Alex and his friend didn't so much as tense a shoulder during their chat. Easy breezy, those two.

I continued to randomly turn pages, my expression engrossed. Blue hair punk girl was at the very edge of my peripheral. To get a better look, I'd have to swing my head with a fake stretch or something. I didn't risk it. There seemed to be a lot of people watching a couple of laid-back guys hanging on a park bench, and I didn't want anyone to notice me.

"My mom's—ill, so I gotta cut—short," the friend said, his words hit me in batches. "I'd say visit sooner, but—let's see how—out."

Alex bumped him a fist. "No worries—I totally—it."

They each picked a backpack, slung it single shoulder-wise, and walked down different paths.

Except they had chosen their own packs from the bench. Had I missed the switcheroo?

I followed Alex, though I was tempted to follow his friend. Alex's pack was still empty. His friend's still full.

I walked in the grass until I found a brick path that mirrored Alex's. I grabbed my phone. The sun glare made it difficult to see the screen, so I just started talking. "I'm almost there," I said with a laugh into the mouthpiece. "I'm hurrying. I got lost in my book. They'll hold our reservation."

As I babbled on my call to no one, Alex's pace picked up. His casual stroll quickly escalated to mall-walker speed.

We were nearing the parking lot.

The suit thug was also nearing the parking lot. He must

have taken the long way 'round the sandpit, then hustled along a different route to arrive when Alex did. He had a whole watch ruse playing out, frantically checking the time. It seems he, too, was late for a very important date.

Alex didn't seem to notice either of us. Without a backward glance, he simply unlocked his Camaro, started the engine, and darted out of his space.

Sid sat behind the wheel of the Ferrari. She started the engine as soon as I hit the passenger side. "Buckle up."

I'd barely snapped it into place when she whipped into the aisle.

We passed the suit hurrying into a slick black coupe. "We may have company," I said.

"Who?"

"No one I want to meet in a dark alley."

Alex zipped onto Kings Drive, but didn't stay there long. He had his muscle car pushed to maximum, hightailing it toward the highway.

It was no match for Sid and the Ferrari. Though we still kept a reasonable distance behind as Alex sped as fast as his rumbler let him.

"What happened at the park?" Sid asked. "Kidnapping? Stabbing? Jewel heist?"

"Nothing. A twenty-minute chat with a dude who looked like Alex. Same surfer outdoorsy vibe and an identical backpack. Same color, size, everything. I swear they talked about the weather. I thought they'd at least swap packs. Maybe it was a silent handoff during the handshake? Maybe one of them got spooked and called it off?"

"Good call on spooked because someone is chasing him. That coupe is right behind us, one lane over, and gaining. But who is that guy? Drug dealer?"

"That expensive car he's driving suggests he'd be higher in a drug dealing food chain than a street dealer. Maybe manufacturer? Though even that doesn't seem quite right. Like he should be chasing Alex in an SUV with machine guns out the window."

"Watch tv much?"

"What about corporate intelligence?" I said. "He could be a hired fixer. Maybe we're dealing with a smuggled flash drive loaded with stolen trade secrets? That'd be a quick handoff."

The thug suit's coupe blasted past us, tailing Alex two cars behind. I couldn't tell if Alex saw him or us. His speed continued to climb, but he didn't make any overt evasive maneuvers. Simply flying fast down the highway in a souped-up muscle car, changing lanes as speed limit abiding citizens got in his way.

"We have company," Sid said with a pointed look in the rearview.

"More?"

I pulled my sun visor down and clicked open the mirror cover. Blue hair punk girl was behind us in a black Hummer.

She changed lanes. She rode to our right, staying a car's length behind. Another SUV, long and black with dark windows, stayed close to her bumper.

Alex's Camaro continued to race, but had begun to weave and bob.

"Must be some kind of corporate secret to bring this heat," I said. "We're all over ninety miles an hour now. But he works at a beach rental hut."

"A hundred, but who's watching? Then it has to be espionage? From a bike shop? Oooh, maybe money laundering?"

"Whistleblower!" We shouted at the same time.

"Which makes him a good guy, right?" Sid said.

"And makes these guys chasing him very bad," I said. "His flight is in six hours. Let's say he'll need forty-five minutes to get to the airport, depending on where he's headed. That gives him about five hours."

"You think he has another stop?"

"There's plenty of time for one," I said. "I mean, how long could've that park conversation actually lasted, had it all gone well? Assuming, of course, that it hadn't gone well? Another ten minutes? Alex had to have planned another stop today."

The thug floored it. He raced up to the Camaro, and I thought he was going to slam into his bumper.

Alex may have, too.

The Camaro made a hard right. He crossed two lanes and missed the water barrels at the exit by a paint chip.

The coupe's brake lights flashed red, but it was too late for him to make the exit. He swerved before he hit the water barrels and missed his chance.

We did not.

Sid switched the engine to manual mode with a flick. She downshifted and punched it.

My head thumped into the headrest. My hands gripped the door.

We flew across multiple white lines.

She shifted again and we flew down the exit.

The Camaro turned left onto the cross street, running the red at the bottom of the ramp.

Sid kept her foot to the floor. "Hang on."

"I've been hanging on," I said. "I don't want to fly out when you take this turn."

"I'm less concerned with the turn, more concerned the Hummer is going to ram us."

Our tires screeched—in protest or in conquest.

I checked the side mirror. "Shit. The girl is still on us."

"Us or Alex?"

"Us and Alex?"

The Camaro hit a curb on the right. It bounced over, then skidded into a turn Starsky and Hutch style.

"How bad do you want to know where Alex is headed right now?"

Another black SUV, like a twelve-passenger Yukon, swerved into our lane. It nearly overtook us.

"Not this bad," I said.

Sid flicked the gearshift and we launched. The Ferrari shot down the center lane like a racehorse out of the gate. An Italian one with a turbocharged V8.

Sid turned left on a yellow, then a quick right down an alley. The park's idyllic movie scene had morphed into an action film.

We burst onto a side street.

Sid slammed her foot to the floorboard and we flew.

I dared a glance in the side mirror. The SUV turned the corner three blocks back.

At the next light, Sid hollered to hang on.

I'd been hanging on so tight, my knuckles cramped.

We whipped right, then an instant left.

Four turns and five minutes later, we skidded into a hospital's multi-level garage. Sid slipped the Ferrari behind a delivery truck on the first floor.

We were both shaking. One from adrenaline and the other from terror. Silence enveloped us. The engine ticked. A car honked in the distance.

I rested my hands in my lap. My meditation app guided me through slow inhales and exhales.

"You okay?" Sid asked.

"I'm great."

"Tell your face."

I gave her a side eye.

"I'd kill for a dash cam right now," Sid said. "Milo will never believe this."

"Oh, he'll believe it."

"Yeah, he will." Sid stretched her arms, rotated her neck.

"I can't believe we lost them," I said.

"Who were they?"

"Hired security? Organized crime? Alex is mixed up in something, that's for sure." I slipped my hat from my head and put it in my messenger. "We can do a better job next time. Rent something non-descript. And we need a set of earpieces."

"Next time?"

"Alex flies to Charlotte monthly, if not weekly," I said. "I think he's got a reservation for next Thursday."

Sid ignored me.

We waited another fifteen minutes before she drove conservatively to the airport, using a dozen different side streets, turns, parking lot crisscrosses, and slowdowns. We monitored the mirrors constantly.

With Alex on the run or hiding out, we decided to fly stand-by on an earlier nonstop flight to the island, rather than spend the afternoon re-routing ourselves through Atlanta as originally planned. Under no circumstances could I miss this flight to Sea Pine. The BBQ was in two days, and while I wasn't central to the planning, I was central to the not wanting to drive four hours back to the island chased by the mob.

Micah was still on duty at the rental counter. "You're returning early. Did the Portofino meet your needs?" His smile was bland, but I detected a note of smugness, like I should've waited for the standard.

"It exceeded all of my expectations, and I can't imagine how I could've survived the day without it," I said. "While I'm here, did you have a chance to ask your co-workers about Daphne Fischer?"

Bland turned to blank.

"The flyer I left earlier," I said. "She's a missing girl who used your rental services frequently." A teensy embellish.

"I've never seen her," he said.

"Is it possible to look her up in your system? See when she rented?"

"Our records are confidential. If you'd like to return with a warrant, I'd be happy to forward it to our corporate office."

No amount of me imploring, canoodling, or explaining changed his position. And he was truly the only one at the counter. He had dramatically opened the office door for verification.

"Last question," I said. "Is there any significance to a rental receipt timestamped at 11:27 p.m.?"

"We close at eleven," he said with a shrug. "Any return after that is auto-processed. You take a ticket, put the keys in the lockbox, and you're mailed a receipt."

I thanked him and left the rental car building. As I waited at the crosswalk signal, I checked each parked and passing car, their drivers and passengers. No one looked familiar. No thug in a suit or a girl with blue hair. But that didn't mean those chasing Alex earlier were the only teams assigned to him.

Sid and I raided the terminal newsstand for airport snacks, then tucked into a corner at the departure gate.

"Feel like we're being watched?" I asked.

"The thug in the coupe or the girl in the Hummer or the unknowns in the SUVs?"

"I don't know, but at least it's a small plane, and we'll see who boards before us."

I didn't notice any strangers lurking behind unfolded newspapers or peering around load-bearing posts. But I maintained a stealthy and consistent watch until the gate agent announced pre-boarding.

We remained seated until general boarding was nearly complete. Passenger after passenger scanned their pass beneath the mounted laser reader. The gate agent never really looked up. Just scan, "have a nice flight," scan, "have a nice flight."

"Oh shit," I said.

Alex Sanders approached the gate agent, his boarding pass in hand. He wore a baseball cap low over dark sunglasses, but was recognizable enough in the same tee and cargoes he'd been wearing earlier.

"We still boarding?" Sid asked.

"Definitely," I said. "Keep your head down and don't make eye contact with any passengers. When was the last time you noticed anyone on a flight?"

Sid slumped down the walkway, her shoulders slightly humped over, and I kept my ticket close to my face. We hurried onto the tarmac, wind blowing steadily. We hunched our way up the steps into the plane.

I snuck a glance once inside. Alex sat on the single seat side of the aircraft, the row in front of us. He never looked up. Kept his own face snug behind the inflight magazine, as if engrossed in the airport diagram provided in the seatback pocket.

With the engine roaring and humming at peak altitude, Sid and I leaned close to talk. When it proved too difficult, especially with Alex so close in the cabin, we switched to writing notes on our cocktail napkin squares.

Me: *He didn't make another stop. Thugs stayed on him?*

Sid: *Drove like it. Maybe better to leave town?*

Me: *Word.*

I drew a line, then wrote beneath it.

Me: *I think Daphne flew from Atlanta to Charlotte.*

Sid: *Agent said no, tho?*

The plane bumped as it vibrated toward Sea Pine Island. I elbowed her and nodded toward the bathroom.

Sid raised a brow, so I nudged her and half-stood, urging her toward the cramped quarters by the galley near the tail section. The bathroom door lock had a green unoccupied placard in place. I opened the door and squeezed inside, waving frantically until Sid joined me.

"I can't write all this out on a napkin," I said straight into her throat.

"Clearly this is the only solution," she said into my forehead.

"What if Daphne did what we did and followed Alex? He said she was acting funny. Maybe she thought he was acting funny."

"He's definitely up to something."

"Right!" My hands flew up in excitement and I jammed my wrist into her hipbone. "Oof, sorry."

"How does she get to Charlotte if she doesn't fly? We barely picked up his trail, and our flight was early. No way she could take a train or a bus."

"Daphne flew, just like us. But she tricked the system. She took the same connecting flight we did, but she flew under a different name."

"Say again?"

"We didn't have to show ID to board this flight, right?"

"Riiiiight," she said slowly. "Only a boarding pass."

"So she books the first leg to Atlanta under her own name," I said. "She goes through security on Sea Pine, shows her ID. It's all legal and logged. However, once she's in Atlanta, she doesn't need to show any of that. She only needs a boarding pass to catch the connection to Charlotte. No ID required."

"Ah, tricky. She must have another credit card in a different name or one of those you get at the Piggly Wiggly."

"Yep. She books two separate flights. First a flight from Sea Pine to Atlanta in her name, then a round-trip from Atlanta to Charlotte under whatever name. She prints the second pass and keeps it in her bag. I figure it took her once or twice to nail down the timing with a rental car to follow Alex, like we did. Probably why she was renting a Hummer. It's all they had ready, and she needed to get down to the exit."

"Dang, girl had some skills," Sid said.

The cardboard door rattled as someone knocked.

I pressed the faucet and wiggled closer to slap on some soap.

"What are you doing?" Sid whispered.

"I touched the door handle to get in this germ box. I'm not leaving until I wash."

"How are we supposed to exit?"

"Carefully and casually."

The bifold opened and Sid poured out with a bump, me on her heels.

I simply smiled at the man waiting. Some things didn't require an explanation.

We dutifully fastened our seatbelts as the plane began its descent over the Atlantic. The ocean glittered in the late afternoon. Speed boats and catamarans catching gentle waves. The beachfront was dotted with people and umbrellas. The sun was visible across the horizon as we lined up to the runway, the ocean behind us.

The short runway rushed up quick as we landed. We passed a plane near the maintenance hangar with several cars parked haphazardly close. Chatter inside the cabin grew louder, more animated. The terminal was surrounded by lush palm trees, airline personnel, and baggage carts. Along with two fire trucks, the paramedic unit, four police cars, and three unmarked SUVs. All with their lights flashing.

Alex scooted down in his seat.

"I think your investigation just ended," Sid whispered.

Once the pilot stationed the plane along the appropriate white line, he cut the engines and made an announcement to remain seated until the seatbelt sign had been turned off. The flight attendant unlatched the door and lowered the staircase.

But before passengers could disembark, an officer wearing heavy gear and a tactical helmet boarded. He counted passengers, checked the restroom and galley, then stood guard at the very back. He nodded to the flight attendant.

She welcomed us to Sea Pine Island, told us the local time, and wished us a pleasant stay.

Two officers, wearing identical tactical gear as the man still on board, checked each person as they stepped onto the asphalt.

"SWAT," Sid whispered. "Making sure we all exit?"

"Yeah, but they're not local, and not from the Sheriff's office either," I said. "I'm more interested in the men not in uniform."

Three men in sunglasses waited with additional SWAT officers near the opposite gate door. Passengers from our flight were filing through Gate 1, but the G-men manned Gate 2.

"Sir," the officer on the left side of the stairway said to Alex. "Can you come with us?"

Alex seemed fairly cool. He didn't run, and he didn't look panicked.

I wondered where they were taking him and why. And if I could hang around the security offices to find out.

"Ma'am," a different officer said to Sid. "Go with him."

"You, too, ma'am," he said to me.

A two-member SWAT team escorted us to Gate 2.

"This can't be good," Sid said.

"No it cannot."

# ELEVEN

The four-man tactical squad led Sid and me into the airport via the Gate 2 entry door. Waiting passengers watched as we walked in formation straight through the exit and past the security checkpoint. People stared, holding their belongings close and their loved ones closer, as the armed men directed us to the hallway I'd discovered a few days earlier. We passed the vending machines and restrooms and Sergeant Whistler's office, finally arriving at the door marked Homeland Security.

Once inside, they relieved us of our handbags. Politely, officially, and definitely not friendly. Sid was directed into one room and me another, each door unmarked.

"Ask for an attorney first thing," I said to Sid before her door swung shut.

"No shit," came her fading reply.

My room was windowless and cramped. A single battered metal table sat center with two padded office chairs on one side, a metal folding chair on the other. The officer indicated the metal chair with the briefest of gestures and left.

Minutes past. First five, then ten. The door swung open and one of the sunglasses from the runway entered. "Good afternoon, Ms. Lisbon, I'm Agent Hunter. Thank you for waiting."

"Good afternoon," I said.

"I have a few questions. Simply answer honestly, and we'll get you on your way."

"Of course. Whatever I can do to help."

"What took you to Charlotte today?"

"Business," I said.

"And your business is?" He kept his pen poised over a short notebook.

"I'm Director of the Ballantyne Foundation," I said. "Here on Sea Pine Island."

"And what," he said, looking at his notes, "Ballantyne Foundation business took you to Charlotte this morning?"

"I'm guessing you're asking about Alex Sanders," I said.

"What makes you guess that?"

"I saw your men pull him out of line, right before they pulled me."

"How well do you know Mr. Sanders?"

"Not well at all," I said.

"But well enough to accompany him to Charlotte," he said. "Can you explain? Is he part of the Ballantyne Foundation?"

"You misunderstand, Agent Hunter," I said. "While we happened to be on the same returning flight, I actually don't know when he arrived in Charlotte." A stretch, but since I wasn't at his arriving gate, I really didn't know exactly.

"Fair enough," he said. "Let's skip the arrival segment of your trip and pick it up in Charlotte. You met him at Freedom Park. What was the purpose of this meetup?"

It was one thing for Agent Hunter to surmise Alex and I had been on the same outbound flight to Charlotte as we returned together, but how did he know about Freedom Park? I'd wondered why they'd chosen Sid and me from the deplaning passengers. Clearly, it wasn't because of a random security check. This line of questioning indicated something much larger.

"Ms. Lisbon?"

"Is this about Daphne Fischer?" I paused a breath. "Did you find her?"

"I'm asking about Alex Sanders."

"Is he under arrest? You must have found something."

"What was the nature of your meeting with him at Freedom Park? Him and the other man?"

"Wait, am I?"

"Are you what?"

"Under arrest," I said.

"If you'll answer my questions, we'll be able to move this along."

"Which agency?" I said.

"Pardon?"

"You said your name is Agent Hunter," I said. "It implies an agency."

"Drug Enforcement," he said.

"I guess we were wrong about the whistleblower," I said.

"Excuse me?"

"Agent Hunter, always go with your first instinct."

"I'm sorry? I don't follow."

"I'd like to speak to my attorney," I said.

He started to speak, but I put my hand up to stop him.

"I respect you have a job to do, and you need information. I appreciate your service, truly. But I won't answer any questions without my attorney." I smiled. Well, part smile, part remorseful grimace.

He waited as my so-so-sorry grimace held firm. He nodded once with a glare and without any part of a smile, and left me alone in the tiny room.

Being alone never bothered me, even as a child. And now as an adult who was surrounded by eccentric board members and their screwball antics and lively parties, I welcomed moments of silence. Though I mostly preferred to welcome the silence from my patio beachside, I often drove without music or sat in my quiet cottage without entertainment.

The presence of the DEA meant Alex was involved with drug dealers. Bringing that much fire power to a tiny airport to apprehend a single suspect, a kid armed with an empty-ish backpack and Jesus sandals, indicated a connection to something much larger. Even larger than a manufacturing operation like Sid and I first speculated. Perhaps a cartel?

If Alex was in DEA custody, and he and Daphne were tied to a cartel, Sid was right. My investigation was over. And after the car chase earlier, I'd happily relinquish it.

The door opened and Ransom walked in.

"You my attorney?" I asked.

"We're all on the same side," he said.

"Uh-huh. That's why they sent you to talk to me, right?"

"How'd you know to go to Charlotte?"

"Oh no, Good Cop, not in this room," I said. "I'll answer questions in here with an attorney or outside without. Your call."

He waited a beat, then stood aside so I could pass him.

"Sid, too?" I asked.

"She's already been released."

An officer handed me my messenger bag, and I helped myself to a generous dose of hand-sani. Between the airports, planes, and interrogation room, I contemplated investing in something stronger than a mini-pump of hand-sanitizer. Like a bottle of tequila.

Sid waited by her car, facing the Mini in the adjacent spot, Ransom's McLaren adjacent to that.

"Seems the security offices at Sea Pine Island Airport hold the majority of the terminal space," Sid said. "All those private interrogations rooms. Who knew?"

"Seriously," I said. "Next time let's pack a lunch. Airport pretzels aren't enough. Maybe we can go to dinner? I'm starving."

"I'd love to stay, but Milo is taking me out."

"I'm really sorry we were held up."

"No worries, it happens. And Milo doesn't know yet. But he will, and it'll be fancy. After today, I need something fancy." She opened her door and climbed in. "We'll catch up tomorrow. I have to be at a hospital board meeting until mid-day, but I can join the search teams after that." She turned to Ransom. "Officer, go easy on her. You know how she gets when she's on a case."

"You were the one driving the Ferrari."

She smiled and waved and drove away.

"How do you know she was the one driving?" I asked. "And that it was a Ferrari?"

He pulled me into a hug and kissed my forehead. "That was DEA surveillance you were evading in Charlotte. Why were you running?"

"The thugs? All of them? They were DEA?"

"Thugs?"

"Yeah, the bulky guy with the sport coupe and blue haired punk girl in the Hummer and the two black extra-large SUVs. Though I didn't get a good look at those drivers."

"Three SUVs, and they were undercover agents, not thugs. Now tell me, why were you running?"

I pulled back and looked up at him. "We weren't running. We were simply following a whistleblower who was accused of corporate espionage and he had hitmen on his tail. We only needed evasive maneuvers when they got in the middle of our surveillance."

"Evasive maneuvers from the DEA? They were following Sanders, but then started chasing you when it became obvious you were also chasing Sanders. They couldn't use the sirens and risk spooking him."

"It went sideways pretty fast," I said. "I'll give you that."

He stood close as we leaned against the car. His thigh against mine, his shoulder against my shoulder.

I loved feeling him next to me. Strong and protective, curious and encouraging. "Sorry they called you down here. I know you're on a big case."

"I've been here all day," he said. "Since you arrived at Freedom Park, anyway."

I pushed up from the car. "You knew I was in Charlotte? Being chased by federal agents? Why didn't you call me if you knew? At least send a text. Give a girl the heads up."

"Because it's against the law."

"We were scared shitless those thugs would run us off the road. Fire machine guns out their windows. Hunt us through the Charlotte airport. Track us to Sea Pine Island."

"There were two marshals at the airport, and one on the flight. I knew you were safe. And also, they weren't thugs."

"Is this your case? Your DEA task force? Damn, Ransom."

"Damn is right, woman," he said. "You two could've flipped that Ferrari. Sid took that last turn and my heart nearly stopped."

"You could see us? How? Satellite? Drone? Oh my good Lord, dash cam?"

"Satellite."

"Did they find Daphne? Did they arrest Alex?"

He stayed silent so I punched him in the arm. "You tell me right now, Nick Ransom. My day is not over unless my investigation is over."

"On Daphne, not yet. On Sanders, yes, he was."

"For kidnapping or, well, or worse?"

"For drug dealing."

"And Daphne?"

"It's an active investigation."

"Not your investigation," I said. "Or is it now?"

"Talk to Sheriff Hill."

"Why didn't you tell me all this earlier? Before I went to Charlotte?"

"All what? Did I know you were dragging Sid to Charlotte to follow Sanders into a drug deal, which would lead to a high-speed car chase with the DEA?"

"You could've guessed that last part." I pushed him out of the way of the door with a swift hip check.

He held the door open, making sure I tucked in properly. "Elli, I know you're good at what you do. But you've got the Summerton Sheriff's Office, the Sea Pine Police, and the DEA on this case."

"Yes, I know. And what I take from that is Alex's drug dealing is tied to Daphne's murder."

"Disappearance."

I sighed, hit the button to put the top down. "Right. But we both know there must be some kind serious of evidence to bring Alex in, and so spectacularly."

"They have plenty."

"And you're not going to tell me?"

He leaned into me, his hand on my chin. He smiled low, his eyes crinkling. He kissed me. Softly, then deeply. He smelled of sandalwood and vanilla soap. Ransom never cared who saw his public affection. He only had eyes for me. He rested his forehead on mine. "I'm happy you're home. I wish I could see you tonight, but this case will go late."

"I know," I said. "Mine, too. Here's hoping Sheriff Hill plays nicer than you."

By the time I drove down Spy Hop Lane to my cottage, it was past dusk. I decided to get something fancy for dinner, too.

I called John's Pizza for a double sausage and black olive with a side of cannoli. Hey, it was fancier than cereal. And I needed the extra carbs to restock my nerves from a mostly harrowing day.

With Alex under arrest and Daphne still missing, where did that leave me and my investigation?

Square uno.

# TWEL♥VE

Here's what I knew about Daphne Fischer's disappearance: Her cell phone pinged on the island Saturday night.

The end.

Here's what I knew about Daphne Fischer: She participated in a batshit wild season of *Down the Isle* where she met her best friend and/or fell in love and was jilted on national tv. Also, her boyfriend Alex dealt drugs via Charlotte, North Carolina, and Daphne knew about it or maybe just simply liked to visit the Atlanta airport. She enjoyed beading and may or may not have stolen a beading technique developed by a fellow contestant who threw a hissy fit for not getting credit in a magazine. She worked part-time at the Cake & Shake with the aforementioned best friend who'd asked Daphne to a) be her maid of honor and b) bead her wedding gown. Lastly, Jona Jerome, producer slash pot-stirrer, promised to film, photograph, and promote said beading, cakes, and wedding to launch Daphne's new business, which as far as I could tell was a dream not a reality.

The only illegal bit in the bunch belonged to Alex Sanders. He was an alleged drug dealer currently in the custody of the Drug Enforcement Administration. He'd also been a significant person of interest to the Sheriff's Office in Daphne's disappearance starting the morning after that fated final cell phone ping. The hidden car rental receipt implied Daphne knew about Alex's nefarious extracurriculars (Note to self: Add the hidden car rental receipt to the list of things I knew about Daphne).

Had she confronted Alex about his drug dealing? Had he reacted poorly? Or perhaps one of his associates had?

As I drove to the Big House that morning, I realized I'd started thinking of Daphne less as missing and more as gone. With Alex's arrest, the energy had shifted again. And with no police agency sharing information with me, my investigation was definitely not over.

Another day with fire trucks and police cruisers in the circular drive. The uniformed personnel directed volunteers into the Big House in the morning and sometimes assisted those same volunteers in the afternoon. As the sun rose hot and humidity thickened the air, the risk of heat stroke and exhaustion intensified. I was grateful for their presence, but seeing so many emergency vehicles parked in front of the literal structure of my stability was unsettling.

Volunteers jammed the foyer from library to staircase, and the registration desk had been moved to the second-floor landing. People wore bright pink Find Daphne shirts, but had long swapped bare feet in flip-flops for sneakers with socks. I, too, had forgone flowing linen in favor of heavy shorty pant cargoes and traded my messenger for a backpack.

"We're in the ballroom now," Tod said. He wore a trim plaid blazer over his pink tee. "Carla made egg wraps and about two hundred gallons of fresh squeezed everything."

"Thanks, Tod, to you both, and really, everyone," I said, glancing up at Zibby. She handed clipboards and pens to those in line, guiding people through the gallery landing. She'd dyed her hair fuchsia to match her tee.

"I'll grab Carla," he said. "You can update us—"

"Elliott!" Zanna Fischer pushed through the crowd. She

clutched my arms when she found me. "Did he tell you where she is? Where is he keeping her? Why did he take her? Where is she?"

"I haven't spoken to Alex," I said.

"But he was arrested right?" Zanna said. "He took her? Is that what they're saying? Where is she? Oh my mercy, he really took her?" Her voice rose with each word, vibrating and breaking with each passing syllable.

"You know it ain't kidnapping, Zanna," a man said. His beard was as big as his belly, and a buxom redhead walked by his side. They approached us mid-foyer, the crowd parting as they rambled into the Big House.

"Don't you tell me what I know, Bob," Zanna said.

"You must be Bob Fischer," I said. "When did—"

"We're not cutting a deal." He stuck his finger toward my face as if I was personally handling interagency negotiations. "We'll find her first, before he can cut a deal. You can take that to the bank."

"A deal?" Zanna didn't even toss him a glance. She kept her back to him and her gaze intent on me. "What deal, Elliott?"

"You know what deal," he said. "He tells us where he buried Daphne, and he gets a lesser sentence."

"You shut your mouth!" she said, and clutched me tighter. "Don't you dare say those words."

I placed my hands on Zanna's arms, my reassuring grip firm to match her desperation. "Alex was arrested on a drug charge, not kidnapping," I said. "He's not talking about Daphne."

"That's them bargaining," Bob said. "Police think we don't know no better. But we're going to find her. Today."

"Oh, so now you're going to help?" Zanna said. "You and Lulu over there? Finally decide to drag yourselves away from that country bar on Fifth to look for your own daughter? She'll be thrilled when she comes home and finds out y'all didn't start lookin' 'til you felt like it. What? The press finally guilt you into it?"

"Don't you go gettin' snide, Zanna," he said. "Bo says she ain't in Sedona, you know that. If she ain't home and she ain't in Sedona, well, only leaves one thing. Now that Sanders kid's about to strike a trade, it's time we face facts. Bring my girl home."

"What the hell you think I been trying to do for a week?" Zanna said. "What we're all trying to do. Look at this place. You think we ain't been trying to find her? How do you go from thinking she needs space to—to—this?"

"Never you mind," Bob said. "We're here now. Where do we check-in?"

"Up the stairs," I said. "Zibby, in the pink—hair, hat, pants—she'll show you where to go, what to do." I waved up at Zibby and she returned a thumbs up.

Bob and Lulu lumbered up the stairs, and I turned to Zanna. "We will find her."

"I don't want to find her," Zanna said. Forceful, irritated, completely deflated. Tears streamed down her face. "I do not want to find her out there." She let me go, then slogged up the wide staircase, her shoulders hunched, her will nearly broken.

"I'll take care of Zanna," Tod said and jogged to meet her on the steps.

I spotted Corporal Parker's blonde ponytail above the throng and inched and pardoned my way to greet her. She wore hiker gear, not her usual uniform. Heavy shorts with pockets front and back, side to side, and a wide utility belt.

"Can we talk?" I asked.

She nodded and followed me into the hall outside of my office.

"Look, I know you can't tell me what's going on with Alex—"

"Then don't ask me," she said.

"You know I have to ask," I said. "Look at this family. All of her friends. Daphne obviously suspected Alex of something. She probably figured out his whole Charlotte drug dealing scam. Maybe he knew she had? Did he hurt Daphne? Is he cutting a deal?"

"All I can tell you is we keep searching for her. It's not easy, but she's a missing person, and we simply keep looking."

"Can I talk to him?"

"He's with the DEA now," she said. "You'd have to ask them, but I wouldn't advise it. They'll tell you even less than I'm telling you now."

"Is that why the Sheriff isn't here? He's with the DEA? I was hoping he'd give me something."

"I'm giving you something," Parker said.

"I need more, Parker," I said. "Daphne's father is convinced Alex is cutting a deal, and her mother is convinced she's locked in a basement somewhere. And I have nothing to go on. At least tell me if this is still a search and rescue. Or is it recovery?"

"Keep looking for her," she said.

"Elli," Carla said over Parker's shoulder. "Mr. B is on the phone."

"Okay, two seconds," I said, but Parker was already walking away.

I exhaled slowly. I'd been holding my breath a lot lately. The burden of anxiety faced with the unknown was manifesting as bated breath. I retreated to the quiet of my office, the streaming sunlight warming the interior in complete contrast with the chill I'd started to feel.

"Mr. Ballantyne," I said. "How happy I am to hear your voice. How are you both?"

"We're well, my dear," he said. "It's been a rough one for you. You holding up strong?"

"Yes, sir," I said. "Mostly. The air feels heavier with each day that passes. The number of volunteers is growing, but without any news, concern is evolving into dread."

"We'll be home tomorrow morning," he said. "Perhaps we can ease some of the weight."

"We put a $10,000 reward on the flyer for Daphne. I hope that's okay."

"Let's up it. Doesn't seem to be doing the trick. Double it— no, triple it. And we can discuss other options when I land."

"Thank you," I said. "Her family thanks you, too. Using the Big House has made all the difference."

"Not all the difference, my dear," he said.

He was right. There was barely a difference between the minute Juliette said Daphne was missing until now. "Alex Sanders, Daphne's boyfriend, was arrested."

"Yes, yes, I heard. But I also heard he'd stopped assisting in the search for Daphne."

"I think he's using it as leverage," I said. "Which is terrible on so many fronts. The DEA has a big drug case. I almost blew the whole sting in Charlotte. Inadvertently, of course. For not having much to go on, this entire case seems to be getting away from me. I'm sorry for any trouble, especially for you."

He boomed his hearty laugh. "You keep doing what you're doing, my dear. Daphne is our priority."

"Thank you," I said. "I cannot wait to see you tomorrow."

He sent his love, along with Vivi's, and I felt better than I had in days. His warmth and kindness and generosity enveloped me, restored me.


I joined the search team briefing in the second-floor ballroom. Wide crystal chandeliers graced the painted ceiling and polished parquet covered the floors. Thick white linen covered long tables in rows, like an elegant executive classroom. In the far corner, a dozen people surrounded a poster station with vibrant papers, markers, flyers, and photos.

Carla's egg wraps were the highlight of a protein breakfast station. Fluffy scrambles, hearty sausage and bacon, fresh chopped veggies, and a tortilla press. Another buffet table held filled water bottles, the good kind with sippy straws and carabineer hooks.

"Divide by color code," Parker instructed the room. "If you didn't receive your team tag, please see Zibby Archibald in the gallery. That's right here on the second-floor landing. Each color coordinates to a grid zone. Follow it carefully and stay in your own zone."

I slid a water bottle into the side netting of my backpack, then asked Zibby for a team assignment.

"We'll give you blue to match your car," she said. "It's the Cabana Boulevard zone, dear, in Summerton. Check the crisscross for essentials."

"Set your phone ringers on high," Parker said, her voice fading as I descended the stairs. "Call your zone leader if you see anything and remember to mark everything."

The car procession stretched across Palmetto bridge into Summerton. Most of the vehicles had Find Daphne flyers taped to their car doors and trunks. Light poles and stop signs along the route all bore the same Find Daphne flyers, blowing and fraying as traffic zipped past. Did anyone even look at them?

My grid section of the blue zone started a mile beyond the Cake & Shake. Its own lot overflowed with cars and people and signs. The shift in energy, specifically ignited by the news of Alex Sanders' arrest, seemed to have sounded the call, galvanizing locals beyond friends and family, to find Daphne.

I arrived at my zone and parked on the shoulder on the right side of Cabana next to a row of orange cones. I kept the top down and popped the trunk to retrieve my largest brimmed hat and a walking stick.

Juliette's car bumped onto the grassy shoulder ten feet in front of me. She climbed out with a weak wave.

"Hey," I called. "You alone?"

"Yeah," she said. "Divide and conquer, right?"

"You're supposed to be in a team," I said.

"Tucker had to work. Finish a job at his grandfather's shop before the wedding. Which is in two days." She choked on the last word, then cleared her throat. "This isn't how this week was supposed to go, you know? We planned that he'd work all week so we could have a honeymoon, and me and Daphne would bake cakes so we could have a wedding."

She fell into my offered hug and cried into my shoulder. "I know, it's not about my wedding," she said. "It's just, I don't understand why this is happening. I want her here with me baking cakes and drinking martinis and gossiping about Farrah and Jona and Alex and Tucker."

With a soft touch to her shoulders, I pulled back. "It'll be okay. We'll find her."

"I'm with Zanna," she said and wiped her tears with the back of her hand. "I do not want to find her out here."

We each checked our backpacks. Secured and tightened, we entered the grove of thick scrub pines. It ran for miles. Thousands of trees—loblollies, sweet gums, oaks, wax myrtles—bordered the road from the bottom tip of Sea Pine Island all the way to the highway and beyond.

Juliette stayed close to me, and we could see and hear other people walking through brush stretching west and north.

"How is Millie Poppy doing?" I asked.

"She's built pretty tough," Juliette said. "Plus, she has Sam. He's been by her side almost constantly. She doesn't always know when to lean on people, but he's there when she does."

Dry pine needles crunched softly beneath her steps. "I can't believe it's been a week."

"Only a few days," I said. "There's still plenty of time—"

"No, I mean, we were just getting ready for my bridesmaid brunch. It's seems like forever ago I delivered cakes to the Big House for your tasting party, and Daphne was finishing the beads on my veil." Her voice sounded flat, almost numb. "How did it all go so wrong? So fast?"

I didn't have an answer for that, and it was frustrating. Her family asked me specifically to find out, and I'd yet to uncover anything useful.

"I want my phone to ring and her brother to say, 'Hey Jules, she's here. Got caught up in Texas, you know how she loves those farmer's markets.'" She laughed, sort of. "God, she'd be mortified to find out every person she knows is on the side of the road looking for her."

A clear plastic cup poked out from beneath a scraggly bush. A matching lid and straw were tossed nearby.

"How do we know what to mark?" Juliette asked. "It's all so random."

"We mark it all." I placed of colored paper slip near the cup and took a photo. Did the same for the lid and straw. "We let the investigators decide what matters."

It was hot, summer hot. The dense forestry began to thin. We ambled farther from the highway, closer to Loggerhead Bluff, a golf community in the distance. She spotted another cup while I tagged a torn fast food wrapper.

My phone vibrated.

A text from Parker: *Call me.*

I dialed her number and held the phone tight against my ear. As it rang, Juliette noticed I'd stopped walking and backtracked to meet me.

"We found someone," Parker said. "Green zone, about two

miles from your grid."

"What is it?" Juliette asked.

I kept my face as neutral as I could and held up a finger.

"You alone?" Parker asked.

"No, Juliette's right here," I said.

"What's going on?" Juliette asked and grabbed my arm. "Tell me."

"I hear her," Parker said. "Okay, keep it quiet as you can, but head this way. Quickly. News will spread as the emergency vehicles arrive. I'm just down Piedmont Lane, off Glen Falls. Bring Juliette. She might be able to help."

The words "identify the body" went unsaid.

"We gotta go," I said.

I jogged atop the pad of pine needles and tangled shrub vines, Juliette at my shoulder. We had traveled farther from the road than I'd realized. About a half mile. The heat made it difficult to move swiftly. We arrived at the orange cones sticky and red-faced.

Juliette ran to her car and whipped open the door.

"Wait," I said. "Drink your water first."

"But—"

"Take care of yourself," I said. "It's hot out here. And I'll drive. You're in no shape."

Her shaking hands tilted the sippy straw, and she gulped a third of the water. She locked her car and strode to the Mini. "They found her, right?"

"I don't know."

"You know something. They found something. They found her? Oh God, just tell me."

"Juliette, I don't know. You're right. They found something. Parker wants me to come help, that's all I know."

It was the longest two-mile drive in all my life. We passed dozens of cars and search teams. We turned right onto Glen

Falls, then another right onto Piedmont. The volunteers in this zone had thinned out, but the police presence had recently increased.

Police vehicles, both cruisers and SUVs, were parked caddywhompus along the shoulder. Two fire trucks rolled up behind us, one ladder truck, one search and rescue.

"Why are there no sirens?" Juliette asked. Her voice shook. "That's not a good sign. Means she's not alive, right? If she was alive, they'd have sirens."

I put my hand over hers. "Slow down. It only means they don't want to alert every person within a five-mile radius. The use of sirens doesn't change their speed. They can still drive fast."

Parker emerged from the brush and Juliette flung herself out of the car. She abruptly stopped and dirt flew. "What am I doing? I don't want to know. I don't want to know. I can't go in there."

I put my arm around her and walked her back to the Mini. She leaned against the hood.

"It's okay," I said. "I'll find out what's going on. You wait here." I pulled her water bottle from the side of her pack. "Keep drinking."

Parker led me a hundred feet into the brush. It wasn't as dense as the border along Cabana Boulevard, and I could still see Juliette by the car.

Parker stopped before a wider clearing where evidence techs were stringing yellow crime scene tape. Other techs placed squat numbered cones in various spots. Cameras clicked and flashed.

"Is it Daphne?" I asked.

"We're not sure," Parker said.

I looked at her. She looked at me.

"I see."

"There's a beaded earring, like Daphne makes. I think. It's near the body of a woman. About her age. But she hasn't been here long."

In the space of our five-minute walk and talk, cars had raced down Piedmont and skidded to a stop in the dusty grass. Car doors slammed and thumped as voices grew louder.

Zanna, Bob, and Lulu ran toward us. Then Millie Poppy and Sam. Then Tucker, and finally Juliette, her water bottle still clutched in her hand.

Parker and I jogged toward them. We stretched our arms wide to form a human blockade. One built more of will than physicality.

"Where is she?" Bob yelled.

"Oh my mercy," Zanna cried. "Please tell me. Please tell me. Just tell me."

"Stop, everyone, please stay back," Parker said, then she hollered over her shoulder. "Get some help here?"

"Wait," I said to Daphne's family. "You'll ruin the integrity of the scene. There's evidence out here. You'll make it worse, not better." I found Millie's gaze as the family continued to shout. "Please, Millie Poppy. Help them understand. They cannot go back there."

"We gotta see," Bob said.

"We gotta know," a male voice from the crowd yelled. "We have a right to be here."

"Hey, Tucker," Bob said. "Grab your friend, maybe two. Go 'round the other side. Take the brush, through the trees. We'll hit it this way."

"Who has binoculars?" another voice shouted.

"Please, please, please," Zanna begged. "I know I said I don't want to find her, but I have to know. I have to find her." She clung to Millie Poppy on one side and Sam on the other.

"You can't keep us away!" Bob shouted. "This is ri-

Goddamn-diculous! It's a free country and that's my daughter!"

Sheriff Hill arrived mere seconds before Ransom. They jogged up to the throng scattered midway between the car line and the clearing.

"I brought barricades," Sheriff Hill said to Parker. "We'll get this moved back."

Several officers formed a half-circle on both sides of Parker and me. Their arms spread wide like ours.

Ransom approached my side, leaned in close. "You okay?"

"Yeah," I said. For all the shouting and yelling to run 'round the other side, no one had actually moved. "Zanna, honey," I said, leaving the protective line. "I promise I'll tell you. I promise." I eased my arm around her shoulder and gently turned her toward the cars. "Let me do this for you, okay? Just let me do this for you. You wait here. I'll be right back."

"Come on, now," Millie Poppy said, touching Lulu's arm. "You and Bob come on with us over here. It'll be okay."

"If she's out there, she would not want you or any of these people to see her like this," I said. "Let me go instead."

While the crowd never retreated as far as the car line on the shoulder, Sheriff Hill did move them back a solid twenty feet. Exhaustion, fear, and panic colored their faces. Anguish mixed with desperation. They wanted to know, but didn't want to know.

Parker, Ransom, and I walked to the clearing. Once inside the delicate circle encased in yellow tape, I carefully stepped forward another hundred feet. The squat cones marking evidence peppered the ground more freely.

A young woman lay in the center of a grouping of officers and techs. I approached and knelt near her waist.

Her matted brown hair held a streak of pink. Sticks and leaves tangled sideways in her cropped cut. The visible side of her face was bruised and beaten. Smeared blood had dried across her cheeks, neck, and earlobe. An earring of tiny turquoise and gold beads was discarded about a foot from her head. It made it sadder somehow. This girl making herself pretty for someone, for herself, matching her earrings to her outfit. The last one she'd ever wear.

Her t-shirt and flowy skirt were grimy. Filthy and torn. Stained. Several tattoos marked her left calf. An elegant woman holding a sword to her side, the word "Queen" scripted below. And just beneath that, the words "always play The Fool."

This girl looked sturdier than Daphne, or perhaps I'd simply begun to think of Daphne as fragile.

"It's not her," I said and waved to Parker to help me stand.

Ransom rushed to my side. He held my hand, put his arm around my waist, and lifted me from crouched to standing.

"You sure?" Parker said. "Looks like she's been through a lot, and we don't know where Daphne's been for the last few days. Maybe she got a haircut?"

"I hear you," I said. "But it's more than her hair. It's her face, her build. And those tattoos. No one mentioned Daphne had tattoos. and those're pretty prominent."

Dr. Harry Fleet, a meld of Delroy Lindo and Quincy in both appearance and demeanor, lumbered into the clearing. As Summerton County Medical Examiner, he held jurisdiction regardless of the city.

Ransom and Parker waited with me while Harry performed a cursory inspection of the dead girl. He knelt as I had, but he did more than simply look. He and his team used various instruments to take her temperature and to inspect her clothes and body.

"She's probably been her since early morning," Harry finally said. "Fits your time frame, in that she died recently, not prior to last Sunday before Fischer was reported missing. This girl was somewhere else before today. She wasn't killed here. No shoes. Cuts on her feet indicate she'd been running. Maybe a lot longer than since this morning. Possibly days. She's in bad shape."

"How can it not be our missing person?" I asked. "I know it's not Daphne, but how can it not be Daphne?"

"Not terribly unusual to find a body when searching in the brush," Ransom said.

"We'll fingerprint her," Harry said. "Someone might be missing her, too."

Ransom squeezed my hand and I squeezed back.

"I'm not sure if this is good news or bad," I said.

My feet dragged against the dry leaves and pine needles as I crossed the wide clearing, then again through the thicker scrub. I could've been gone a minute or an hour. The crowd of friends and family and locals hadn't moved. I wasn't sure they'd even said a single word in my absence.

"It's not Daphne," I said to Zanna.

"You can't be sure," Zanna said. "What you know about her is a yard wide and an inch deep. It should've been me to look. I should go. Let me go."

"I'll go," Juliette said.

"Does Daphne have any tattoos?" I asked.

"No," Juliette said, along with Tucker, Bob, and random voices in the crowd.

"The girl, the one they found, she has several large tattoos," I said. "Visible and prominent."

"Maybe she just got them," Bob said. "She'd do something like that."

"And didn't tell anyone," Juliette said.

"No, they've been there awhile," I said. "Years, maybe. It's not her. I promise, it's not her."

Zanna cried in relief, or maybe frustration. "We're never going to find her. I can't do this."

Millie Poppy held her while Bob cursed and kicked the dirt. "This ain't right," he said.

The rest of the crowd looked just as frustrated, but also shocked and wounded. And lost. They'd faced the edge of finding Daphne dead. Discarded on the side of the road. It wasn't her, but that didn't make the situation any easier.

Ransom came up behind me. With a gentle hand on my arm, he pulled me aside. "I have to go," he whispered. "It's my case. It just got legs."

"Oh?" I whispered back. "Alex? This girl?"

He kissed my forehead softly. "Call me if you need me." He climbed into his sleek silver racer and sped away.

"We keep searching," Parker said. Her voice projected well over the crowd. "I know this is hard, but Daphne is still out there. We keep going."

As we returned to our respective cars, I asked Juliette to stick with Millie and Sam. "You shouldn't be searching alone. No one should."

"I'll take Zanna, honey," Millie Poppy said to Sam. "I don't want her to be alone either. We'll finish our zone. You take Juliette and finish hers."

"You want to come with us?" Juliette asked me.

I spotted Harry Fleet in the brush and shook my head. "I've got other leads to follow. Keep me posted, okay? And keep drinking your water."

# THIRTEEN

(Day #7: Friday Late Afternoon)

Most of the civilian cars left the roadside, leaving me and my Mini squeezed between a police cruiser and the medical examiner's van. I knew it might be awhile before anyone emerged from the brush with information, so I closed the convertible top for privacy, turned on the a/c, and settled into returning calls.

Tod, Carla, and Sid had all left various texts and voicemails.

I texted Sid: *Not her, still looking.*

Then called Tod at the Big House.

"It wasn't Daphne," I said when he answered. "I'm not sure who it is, but it's not her."

"A different girl?"

"I know. I'm hanging around to find out more. It's too coincidental."

"I'm calling Edward in a few minutes," Tod said. "I'll update him."

"Good idea," I said. "They've probably heard about the body by now."

"They've probably heard it's not Daphne by now."

"True," I said. "Let me know if something comes up at the Big House. I'll be out most of the day."

I scrolled through my recent call list and found the rental counter in Charlotte. "Hi," I said. "I'm Daphne Fischer. I rented one of your cars a while ago. I can't find my receipt and I need it for my taxes."

I'd tried this on a case last year and broke it wide open.

"Yes, ma'am, I can help with that. My name is Yolanda, and this call may be recorded for quality assurance and training purposes."

"No problem," I said, and happy to talk to a different agent other than Micah. "I rented a car several weeks ago. I turned it in late at night. You were closed. It was after hours."

"Of course," she said, faint typing sounded as she hummed. "I don't see a Daphne Fischer."

"It's spelled with a s-c-h, like F-i-s-c-h-e-r."

"Yep, tried it every way possible. There's no record of any rental, customer or driver, under that name. I'm sorry, I wish I could help. Is there anything else?"

"Not today, but thank you for trying."

"Of course," she said, and then there was a click and she lowered her voice. "I hope you all find her."

"Excuse me?"

"We have Caller ID, Ms. Lisbon, and your name is on the flyer you left. Micah researched you after you left here yesterday. Sorry to hear about the missing girl. We all are."

"You'll keep the flyer displayed?" I asked. "Let me know if anyone recognizes her?"

"You bet," she said. "You have a nice day."

She disconnected and I knew I had to up my game. The usual tricks weren't working. Or maybe it was because I'd been using all the old resources.

I started the car, and with a three-point turn, I was back on Piedmont, then Glen Falls, and finally Cabana Boulevard. I didn't need to wait to talk to Harry at the crime scene. As soon as he finished, he'd return to his office at Island Memorial Hospital. Which happened to be mere blocks from the airport.

I parked in short-term in a spot I was beginning to consider my own. Ten seconds later, I entered the airport through the automatic sliding doors. Only a handful of people, all airline and security personnel, roamed the bright room. Sunlight shone through the glass onto the row of empty Adirondack rockers and nearby potted palms. Another flight probably wasn't due for hours.

Jeanine Gurly, airline employee and Milo confidante, stood at the ticket counter behind her terminal. She used a pen to mark pages from a stack of paperwork.

"Jeanine," I said. "You have a minute?"

"Hey, Elliott," she said. "I heard they found a girl out near Loggerhead Bluff."

When midwestern nosy Nellies spoke in watercooler clichés of news traveling fast, our island citizens showed them how it's done.

"Yes, but unfortunately, I don't know much more than that. Other than it was not Daphne Fischer."

"It's a different girl?" she said. "What's this world coming to? I'm joining the search today after my shift. Most of us are. Seems like the best way to help bring her home."

"Actually, helping me will help, too. I think Daphne bought two sets of tickets each time she flew—"

She flipped a switch on the monitor and her fingers drummed a staccato beat against her keyboard. "Only see one set of reservations."

"I think she bought the second set of tickets under a different name."

She raised a single brow, and her hands hovered above the keys.

"Hear me out. Daphne wouldn't need any type of identification once she's inside the terminal, right? She only needs to show security when she first arrives at the airport."

"Mmmm, maybe."

"Here's how I think it could work. I show my ID here at Sea Pine. The security agent checks it. It's me, all good, and I'm waved on to the conveyor belt and body scanner. Once through this security checkpoint, all I need is my boarding pass. It's scanned prior to boarding, and I fly to Atlanta. Now I'm in Atlanta, and I'm already inside the airport. Inside the secure zone, right?"

"Right, right, right," she said. "I follow. You don't need your ID to board the next flight. You only need a valid boarding pass."

"Exactly. Which I could print at home and take with me. I don't need to get it from any airport personnel. I think that's what Daphne did. She didn't want her name to show up on the manifest, probably so it wouldn't show up on her airline account. No boarding pass or record of the flights in her name."

"Meaning she booked the second flight under a different name. Very easy to do online. Can use prepaid credit card or gift card or someone else's credit card."

"Exactly. At first, I thought she bought a credit card at the grocery, but now I'm thinking she used someone else's card. Because once in Charlotte, she needed to rent a car."

"And for that, you definitely need ID."

"I know she didn't rent one under her own name. Well, I mostly know that." I'd need to call every rental car agency in Charlotte to confirm, but it seemed more likely she'd use a different name with the rental car as well. She didn't want her name to show up anywhere in Charlotte.

"Okay, let's see," Jeanine said. "I'll look up her last three flights to get the dates."

I quickly pulled out the list of her flights Jeanine had given me the last time I asked and showed them to her. "We have those dates. Now we need to check the passenger manifests for the flights from Atlanta to Charlotte on those specific days."

Jeanine tapped with purpose, clickety-clacketing, periodically taking notes. She scribbled names, crossed off two. Tapped again.

"Anything?"

"I think so. Let me check one more flight." She scratched off another name. "Does the name Tess Martin mean anything?"

"It does indeed," I said. "Thank you so much for your help. And look, I don't know if Daphne did anything illegal—"

Jeanine pressed a key and turned her screen. She handed me the scrap of paper with Tess's name on it. "You have a nice day now."

It felt good to connect that particular dot about Daphne using Tess's identification. Either Tess lent it to her or Daphne lifted it. They resembled each other. Sort of. Not twins or even sisters. Cousins maybe. Not enough for her to risk showing Tess's ID to a federal TSA agent, but enough to fool a disinterested car rental agent who might glance two seconds at an ID. Micah hadn't even really looked at mine. Just tapped in the numbers and handed it back. I made a mental note to talk to Tess and see if she was missing her driver's license and a credit card.

But first I drove the short distance from the airport to the hospital, parking in a quiet lot on the south side which faced away from the main entrance. This section of the complex looked more like a restored colonial home than a medical center. The building was white with shutters and bunches of geraniums bloomed in the beds. The interior door I wanted was unmarked and unmanned. I rang the bell and waited for an orderly to grant me access.

The security door opened with a buzz, and the emerging doctor in scrubs recognized me. She held the door and let me find my own way to Harry's office.

Dr. Harry Fleet, terse, cranky, and the best in the business, popped a mint from a slim blue bottle. "Nicotine lozenge" was written on the side. "Nerve pills," he said in greeting. "I just got here, Lisbon. Going to be a long while yet. Give it a day. Or better yet, three."

"Is there anything you can tell me now? Anything at all? I said this earlier, but how can this poor girl not be Daphne Fischer? How do you find a girl in the woods while you're looking for a girl in the woods, and it's not the right girl?"

"We have close to two hundred missing persons cases in South Carolina. That's only the ones who been reported. Doesn't include all the homeless and runaways who don't have a soul to file a report. And of the fifty thousand annual deaths in the state, sixteen hundred happen in my county. Put it together and you find a girl while looking for a different girl."

The same doctor in scrubs who met me at the entrance stuck her head in the door. "About to start. Did the prelim. You joining us, Elli?"

I felt my face blanch at the thought of attending the autopsy, and I waited for Harry to kick me out.

He hesitated, likely enjoying my discomfort, then let me off the hook. "She was just leaving."

"Before I go, can I hear the prelim?" I asked.

Harry sighed and waved his hand at the doctor.

"Looks like strangulation," she said. "Best guess is about twelve to eighteen hours ago. We sent her fingerprints to the lab. Ran a missing persons search, but no names popped. Might be too soon."

"So no idea who she is?"

"Hispanic descent likely. Mid-to-late twenties, early thirties at most. Two tattoos. What we think is maybe from *Game of Thrones—*"

"I think it's a tarot queen," I said. "The Queen of Swords,

especially with The Fool reference."

Harry put on his white lab coat, held the door open. "You coming?"

I thanked them both and turned right in the hall while they turned left.

It may seem normal to everyone else to find one girl when looking for another, but to me, it was too coincidental to ignore. I thought it was time to talk to the Sheriff.

Sid phoned as I crossed the lot. I'd forgotten she had board meetings at the hospital all day, so I changed my path, heading away from the palm trees in the lot to the palm trees at the entrance.

"You up for a late lunch?" I asked. "I'm in the parking lot. I've got lots of updates to share."

"It's good you're here," Sid said. "They just brought Juliette to emergency by ambulance."

# FOURTEEN

(Day #7: Friday Late Afternoon)

My sneakers squeaked on the linoleum as I hurried through emergency. Harsh disinfectant with a pungent lemony overtone made the glare of bright industrial overhead lighting more intense. I slowed only to check the posted white board where names of patients and doctors and bay numbers were written in black marker.

"Elliott," Tucker called. He waved from a curtained cubicle across from the nurses' station.

I jogged over, sliding my phone into my pocket with my keys.

Juliette rested in a standard adjustable hospital bed, its top inclined forty-five degrees. Loose bandages were wrapped across her forehead, blood spots stained her pink tee.

"What happened?" I asked.

"A car," she said, twisting her shaking hands. "It came out of nowhere. Like nowhere. It rammed the side, the passenger side. Sam, he got hit worse." Tears rolled unabated down her cheeks, off her chin. "He needs surgery, they said. I think he broke his hip."

"The doctors took him," Tucker said. "Upstairs, maybe?"

"I'll find out exactly what's going on," I said. "Is Millie Poppy with him?"

"Tucker, you go," Juliette said. "Please, check on Millie

Poppy, too. I'm okay, really. He needs you more than I do right now."

"You need me, Jules," he said. He held her twisty shaky hands. "I can't leave you. This shouldn't have happened. I should've been there."

"It happened so fast," Juliette said. "So so fast."

"When?" I said. "I just left you, what, an hour ago?"

"I know, right? It was like fifteen minutes max after...we were...the girl...after we split up...you know." She squeezed Tucker's arm. "Please, be with Millie Poppy. She's alone. Find out about Sam's surgery and when we can visit."

He seemed unsure of what to do. He loosened his hold and leaned on his heels. He looked anguished, confused. His grandfather on one floor, his fiancée on another.

"I'm okay," she insisted. "It's barely a bump. I don't need surgery or anything. And Elliott will stay with me, won't you?"

"Absolutely," I said. "It's a small hospital. We'll be right here. You just keep us informed, okay? The nurse at the desk," I slid the curtain wider to point, "he'll tell you where they moved Sam."

"Okay, I'll go, thanks," he said. "I'll be right back."

We watched the nurse direct Tucker to the elevator, and he passed us with a short wave.

"Close the curtain," Juliette said. "Then sit right here." The rolling hooks hadn't even stopped scraping the metal bar when she continued. "We don't have much time. I know Tucker. And Millie Poppy. They won't leave me for long."

"What's up?" The visitor's chair screeched as I dragged it to the bedside.

"That car purposely ran me off the road," she said.

"Like road rage?"

"No, not quite. Rage, yes. Look, I found something out, but I can't tell you now. Not in the hospital. Later tonight when I'm home."

"I've watched enough movies and read enough books to know when someone says they found out something sinister, but will only talk about it later, that person ends up dead."

She half-laughed. "That's fair. But I don't think I have time to tell you everything, and what if someone is listening?"

"No one's outside this room. We can see beneath the curtain, and with this whispering, no one will hear what we're saying. They may wonder what's so secret, but they won't hear the actual secret. Is this about Tucker? Sam? Is that why you don't want to tell me now?"

"Not exactly," she said. The hand twisting returned. "They already won't leave me alone for three minutes to use the bathroom. Tucker had to beg Millie Poppy to check on Sam, and then you saw, we had to beg him to check on Millie Poppy. They find out I was purposely run off the road, even that little bit of freedom will disappear. I'm not a fool. I don't want to be left completely alone, but I don't need them within four feet of me at all times."

"Then talk fast. Trust me, it's better if you tell me now."

She sat up straighter, then grimaced in pain. "My head hurts. The airbag smacked me right in the face."

I handed her a plastic sippy cup with water from the side table. "Drink, then talk."

After a long swallow, she nodded and leaned closer. "Okay, here goes. It's about Jona and Farrah."

"You think they crashed into you? About the show and Tucker? Why Farrah?"

"It starts with Jona. She always has a secret agenda, or really, multiple agendas. She'd prepared this whole plan for the wedding, the magazine, a tv special."

"She told me," I said. "Highlighting Daphne's beadwork and your cakes."

"Exactly. Then all of a sudden two weeks ago, there's a whole new plan for a season three of *Down the Isle*. She told me it was because of our wedding. A spinoff. She was totally vague. But she lied. Turns out Daphne was to be the next Eligible. Was going to start filming right after my wedding if they could sell it to the network. Farrah thought it should be her. That she deserved to be the next Eligible, not Daphne."

"How do you know all this?"

"Tess called me when I was driving Sam to the blue search zone, right after we left you. Farrah stormed into the Cake & Shake today looking for me. Screaming it was her show, not mine."

"Not yours?"

"Weird right? First, she's mad about me and my dress, and Daphne ends up missing. Then she's mad about Daphne being Eligible, and I get run off the road. And it wasn't my show!"

"Why did Farrah think she should be Eligible?"

"Farrah was cut from our season by the producers. All behind the scenes. Tucker cut her on camera, that's the way the show works. She said Daphne sabotaged her and that's why Jona made Tucker send her home."

"Sabotaged her? How? With Tucker?"

"Daphne caught Farrah stealing her beads and told Jona. Farrah was pissed. Like next level apoplectic. Said it was bullshit, completely fabricated. That Daphne knew Tucker was into her, not me. She claimed Tucker was going to cut me from the show. Farrah said Daphne didn't want to lose her only ally on the show, meaning me, so she made up some story about stolen beads forcing Tucker to cut her, Farrah, instead."

"And you're only telling me all this now?" I said. "You said Farrah was furious at the Cake & Shake the other day because of your wedding dress. Now it sounds like she's had a huge beef with Daphne since the show aired two years ago."

"It wasn't that huge."

"You used the word 'apoplectic.'"

"Yeah, that's a Millie Poppy word. It's just, you know, on the show everything was DEFCON 5 drama."

"DEFCON 1, but I get you."

"The whole thing was, like, half a day. But anyway, before Farrah was furious about me and my dress. Today, Tess said she was losing her shit over Daphne and the show. Fuming she thought she should've gotten the big break. Been the one to get the magazine spread, open her own boutique, be the next Eligible. Maybe it was me who sabotaged her all along. That I wanted her off the show since now I'm getting all the publicity."

I scooched closer. "Daphne never told you Jona proposed season three with her as the next Eligible?"

"No! And I didn't even know there was a season three. You'd think Jona would've said something with all this planning we've been doing. Like I said, she's always hiding multiple agendas." Juliette sipped from her cup. "Anyway," she said, her voice even lower, "Tess never finished talking to me. A car came out of nowhere and ran me off the road. I didn't see who was driving or even notice what the car looked like."

"It was hit and run?"

"Yeah. It could've been Farrah. I mean, look at the timing. We were right by the Cake & Shake, and I think she'd just left."

"You tell the police this?"

"Yes," she said. "But they didn't seem convinced. A detective is going to call me tomorrow. He wanted to come by today, but with Tucker and Millie Poppy here, I said to call me."

The curtain whipped open and we both jumped. Sippy cup water splashed onto both our shirts and the thin blanket covering Juliette's legs.

"You scared me," Juliette said, with a nervous laugh. "What's wrong, Tucker?"

His skin was ashen, his lips drawn tight. "It wasn't a broken hip. It's dislocated."

"That's better, right?" Juliette said.

"Sure, I guess," Tucker said. "We couldn't talk to him. He's getting an MRI. The doctors didn't say much. But they didn't look optimistic. Millie Poppy told me to wait with you, and she'll tell us everything in a minute."

"You left her alone?" Juliette said.

"I'm going to leave you two," I said. "Sid's here in the hospital. She'll fill me in on Sam. Get some rest."

"No rest," Juliette said. "I have to bake all night. They're releasing me any minute, I'm sure. They said there's a concussion protocol, but I'm totally fine."

She looked like crap. Tear stained, blood stained, shaky, jittery, and freaked out.

"Do not worry about the cakes," I said. "We can do without them."

"No," she said, gripping my arm. "We need the cakes. The cakes are everything. Our whole arrangement."

"Juliette, I meant for the BBQ," I said. "You'll still have your wedding. It's okay, really. We'll leave all the beach décor in place for you. It's not a problem."

"But it's your whole party," she said. "The centerpieces for every table."

"You're giving us the beach and the tents and everything, and for no cakes in return?" Tucker said. "We can't accept. With Juliette and Sam in the hospital, how can we get married?"

"You don't want to marry me?"

"I didn't say that, Jules," Tucker said.

"You're definitely getting married," Millie Poppy said from the curtain opening. "Sam already agreed with me. Said we need some happiness this week. If only for a day."

"But without Daphne?" Juliette said. "Shouldn't we wait

until she gets home?"

"Honey," Millie Poppy said. She leaned in from the other side of the bed, brushing Juliette's hair away from her face.

I didn't dare glance at Millie Poppy, in case she thought what I thought. Daphne wasn't coming home.

"I know," Juliette said. "Best case scenario is Daphne didn't want to come to her best friend's wedding. I can't believe I didn't think of canceling earlier. I'm a monster." She cried in her grandmother's arms, soft sobs turning thick, coming from a deep well of pain.

"Let's not give up hope," Millie Poppy said.

"Hope she hates me or hope she's still alive?" Juliette said.

"How about we decide tomorrow after the BBQ?" Millie Poppy said. "This is your future, Juliette. Yours and Tucker's. The wedding and the Cake & Shake. It'll keep us busy, honey."

"What about the catering?" Tucker asked. "Won't waiting until Saturday night to decide be too late to cancel?"

"No later than now," I said. "Your wedding is in less than two days. The food's probably already been bought and prepped. But that's the only big expense. The flowers, décor, beach, tables, almost everything else will already be set from the Beach BBQ."

"See?" Millie Poppy said. "Let's see where we are tomorrow."

"Tucker?" Juliette asked. "What do you think?"

"It doesn't seem right to use all the Ballantyne stuff for free," he said with a head shake. "It doesn't feel right."

"I made all the sketches and details for every cake, down to the last candied pearl," Juliette said. "Really. And they've already been baked. Most of them, I think. We have plenty of others at the Cake & Shake. It's the decorating. I think I can do it. But what about the search? They need me, too. And Sam."

"You need to rest," Millie Poppy said.

"It's too much," Juliette said. "I can't do this. I'm getting married in two days. My best friend is missing. I didn't finish the cakes, and it's for the Ballantyne, the biggest job of my career. And the photographers—"

"It's okay, honey," Millie Poppy said. "It'll be okay. Sit back. Take a deep breath. You're in shock."

"Can Carla decorate your cakes?" I asked. "Using your sketches? They won't be identical, but perhaps if she follows your instructions, it'll be close. Could that work?"

Juliette wiped her face. "Absolutely, I've got drawings, color charts, everything. And she can cut some corners. Simplify them. Tess could help, too."

"Tell me where your drawings are, and I'll recruit Carla tonight."

"Are you sure?" Juliette said. "It's a lot to ask, and the party is tomorrow."

"I'm positive," I said. "We've done more with less, I promise."

"The sketches are at the apartment," Juliette said. "I've got my spare tools there. You can't raid the shop, Tess'll kill me, but it should be enough to finish them. If Carla needs anything, Tess will run it over to her." She reached for a plastic bag next to the hospital bed. "Crap, my purse. I don't know where it is. My keys are inside. My phone, my wallet."

"Here, honey, use mine," Millie Poppy said. She dug inside her own purse and pulled out a ring of keys. She wound one around the metal loop, then handed it to me.

"But how will you get into your house?" Juliette said.

"I'll get Sam's," she said, then turned to me. "Her apartment lock was keyed with our house locks, so the keys open both hers and mine. Easier all the way around."

"Thank you," I said. "I'll give it back tomorrow."

"See, honey," Millie Poppy said. "You have plenty of help

with the cakes, and there are hundreds of people searching for Juliette. You pushing yourself to collapse will not help anything."

"Yeah, Jules," Tucker said. "It's been a tough week." He looked as exhausted as Juliette did. Dark circles under his eyes, pasty skin. Worry lines had formed canals across his forehead and between his brows.

"Get better," I said with a squeeze to Juliette's hand. "And stay positive. Never give up hope."

I'm what's known as a highly sensitive person. Meaning most of the time, every emotion played across my face as I experienced it, sometimes full seconds before I even realized it. I'd spent years trying to perfect a poker face, and I hoped that hope shone through in that moment.

I wasn't sure I agreed with Millie Poppy's insistence of hosting a wedding where the bride and the grandfather of the groom were both in the hospital, and the maid of honor was on the national missing person registry. But it wasn't my place to agree. Or to judge. In my sixteen years at the Ballantyne and thirteen years as an investigator-in-training, I knew every person handled grief, loss, and hope differently. Sometimes clinging to a distraction was the one mechanism that allowed a person to process a difficult, if not devastating, series of emotions.

Besides, I'd been tasked with locating Daphne. It was my priority to worry about her, not the wedding or those getting married. I didn't need a distraction. Her family and friends did. I needed to stay focused and find answers.

By the time I arrived at Juliette's, the early evening twilight had turned the sky pale lavender, blanketing the apartment in soft hues to match its quiet tones. The refrigerator's hum. An upstairs neighbors' footfalls. I appreciated Juliette's contribution to the BBQ with cake sketches and piping tools. I knew Carla and I could pull it together. But more, I appreciated the opportunity to freely comb through the tangles hidden in this compact home.

I spent the first twenty minutes searching Daphne's room. My earlier inspection on Monday had been perfunctory. She'd barely been missing. However, being on the other side of finding her abandoned car at the airport, along with the scare of finding a dead woman in a field, my perspective had shifted.

Unfortunately, it didn't bring clarity or additional evidence like a diary outlining her travel plans or her phone hiding in a shoebox.

Although thinking about her phone gave me new ideas. Daphne had two burner numbers, their users unknown. But now I had an inkling as to her motivation to use a burner app in the first place. Daphne agreed to be the next Eligible on *Down the Isle*. Though why not tell Juliette about it? Embarrassment? Why keep it secret? A confidentiality clause? One of those burner numbers had to belong to Jona. I recalled seeing only a call or two from Jona on Daphne's cell phone bill, and they'd happened months ago, not recently. Arranging for Daphne to be the top-secret star of the new season would've taken lots of private communication.

With complete access to the apartment, I decided to find that burner app on Daphne's tablet.

Only the tablet was no longer in the basket next to the sofa.

I called Juliette, but it rolled to voicemail after a half dozen rings. I left a message, then searched Juliette's room.

It was the apartment yang to Daphne's yin. I don't think Juliette had met a drawer she ever used. Clothes, shoes, journals, remotes, cords, yoga gear—mats, straps, blocks—all semi-stacked on the floor, bed, and cubbies. Photos, albums, scrapbooks, scissors, stickers, and paper occupied one entire corner. I paged through different albums filled with memories.

Of childhood, college, friendships. And at the very bottom of the stack, one from *Down the Isle*.

Candid shots of Juliette with various contestants—Tucker, Daphne, Jona—were glued and stickered to heavy pages. Some pics showed them playing games, some were by the beach. The excellent quality spoke to stills taken by a professional camera crew, not quick snaps from a cell. Probably didn't allow personal phones on the set. The candid shots revealed nothing but happy moments. No drama, no angst.

Until I turned toward the final pages. Torn remnants remained in the binder where two full sheets had been ripped away. I checked the wastebasket in the corner. Beneath a mound of tossed makeup cloths, wrappers, and shopping bags, two scrapbook pages had been slashed and crumpled. The scraps showed three photos of Daphne and Tucker, and two of Juliette, Tucker, and Daphne. The difference in these in the trash versus the ones intact in the scrapbook was in the body language. Tucker's body language. He leaned in toward Daphne, his hand on her shoulder in two of the shots.

Jona said Daphne and Tucker had chemistry. Perhaps Juliette didn't fully grasp its depth until much later. Like this week? Maybe she wasn't so surprised after all that Daphne didn't want to be in her wedding.

My cell vibrated and I eased out of Juliette's room.

"Hey, Juliette," I said. "Thanks for calling me back. You doing okay? How's Sam?"

"I'm the same," she said. "And alone. They both went up to check on Sam. The intern needs to stitch my forehead. Said it's better if they aren't here. What's up?"

"I'll be quick. Did you move Daphne's tablet?"

"Move it? No, not at all. Isn't it there?"

"Nope. At least, not in the basket."

"You think Daphne came back for it? Maybe she snuck in

when we were out searching for her?"

"Possibly," I said slowly. "Who's been here?"

"No one. Me and Tucker. That time Zanna came over, but you were there. The Sheriff showed up once. No, twice."

"The actual Sheriff or the investigation team?"

"Both, I guess, the first time," she said. "But they didn't really investigate. Not like a search or anything. Just fingerprints. Asked for her hairbrush. Sprayed stuff, used a blacklight, but they didn't take anything. The second time, it was just the Sheriff. Oh! And Alex came by once. He needed something. Wanted a picture of Daphne, I think."

"Did you leave either of them alone? Even for a minute? The Sheriff or Alex?"

"Ummmm." She paused a second.

I considered asking her about the torn scrap pages, but didn't want to explain how I knew about them. At least not yet.

"Yes, both of them," she said. "But for only a minute. Like, not even two minutes."

"Okay, thanks. I'll ask the Sheriff about it."

"You don't think Daphne came back? It's possible though, right? Why would someone else take her tablet? It's password-protected."

"It was probably the Sheriff," I said. "For evidence."

What I didn't tell her was that passwords can be broken. I'd done it myself, and on the very tablet we were discussing. The Sheriff would've needed a warrant. But the real question was, if he grabbed the tablet after being in the apartment less than two minutes, how did he know exactly where to find it? The answer: He wouldn't. But Alex would.

After inspecting every drawer, shelf, and cupboard in the apartment, I gave up. The tablet was gone, and there wasn't a single scrap of information on Daphne or her whereabouts.

Using the prep list Juliette gave me earlier, I gathered up

the cake decorating supplies, notes, and tools Carla would need to recreate Juliette's designs. I added seven utensils I couldn't identify but looked important. With two trips to my car, everything jammed in wheel well to wheel well, I then drove to the Cake & Shake.

Their parking lot still overflowed like a 1950s summer hangout. The only thing it needed was a string of carhops roller skating trays of shakes to and fro. Teenagers and college kids in pairs and groups hung outside their cars, sipping, stirring, and talking in the dusky glow of late evening.

I wedged the Mini in an almost legal spot on the sidewalk and wiggled my way through the line, up the porch steps, and into the shop. Find Daphne posters were taped to the walls and cake cases. The staff wore the matching pink Find Daphne tees under their aprons.

"Two Roasted Bananas Foster and a Churro Dulce de Leche," Tess hollered. She ran the register, a red retro one with white paint on the outside, but a digital keypad on the faceplate.

"Hey, Tess," I said. "I know you're swamped, but can we talk?"

She glanced at me, then the next person in line. "It's really not a good time. We close in three hours. Can you wait?"

"It's about Juliette and her car accident," I said.

"She called. Said she was going to be okay." Tess's brow raised with equal parts worry and doubt. "And you're decorating her cakes?"

"She's fine," I said. "And not me personally, but I do have a few questions. I only need a minute."

"Quinn," she hollered over her shoulder. When the kitchen door swung open and a girl leaned out, Tess continued, "Cover me a minute?"

"Sure," she said. The girl wiped her hands on her apron and took the next order.

"Let's go in here," Tess said.

I followed her into the kitchen. It was chilly and smelled of sweet sugar and berries and cinnamon. Pedestal trays held plain cakes next to stainless mixing bowls filled with whipped frosting. Piping bags and rubber spatulas dotted the center table.

She led me to a tiny office, and we sat in the cramped space. "I told the police everything I know."

"I'd like to hear it for myself," I said. "Make sure I don't misunderstand any details. You told Juliette that Farrah came in this morning? Shouting about Daphne and Juliette?"

"She was bananas," Tess said. "Pushing people out of her way. Put her finger in my face. As if I was the next Eligible. She said the show should be hers, that Juliette sabotaged her. Said she probably planned it all along. She demanded to know where Juliette was."

"What did you tell her?"

"That I didn't know," she said. "She was out searching for Daphne with a hundred other people. She could be anywhere."

"Why did she think Juliette sabotaged her? I thought it was Daphne who told the producers about the stolen beads."

"She did," she said. "Well, they both did. Daphne and Juliette. Daphne told Juliette who said they should tell Jona."

"What did Farrah do when she found out?"

"She had a massive meltdown. Threatened she'd go public. Contestants aren't allowed to talk to anyone outside the show. They almost didn't let her finish filming the episode. But Tucker calmed Farrah down. She definitely spilled tea in the confessional. You know, where we tell the audience what we think. The whole show was heavily edited."

"What about today when you told her you didn't know where Juliette was?"

"She called me a liar. Said she'd get what she deserved. I

said I had no doubt she would get exactly that. She tipped over two shakes on the counter and stormed out."

"And you called Juliette right away?"

"Almost right away," she said. "She'd made a huge mess. Ice cream, strawberry sauce, whipped cream. It was all over me. I went in the back, washed my hands, and called Jules. Told her to watch herself, that Farrah was melting down."

"Tell me about Daphne using your credit card and driver's license."

She missed a beat, coughed. Took a sip of water from a bottle on the desk. "I don't know what you mean," she said. "What does this have to do Juliette?"

"I visited the airport earlier," I said. "I checked on Daphne's flights—"

"I should get back," Tess said. "With Juliette gone and me running the shop and now helping Carla Otto with cakes—"

"I'm completely grateful for all of those things, but I'd still like to know about Daphne using your credit card," I waited patiently. Legs crossed, sitting back in the chair. All the time in the world.

A full minute ticked by.

"Are you suggesting Daphne stole my credit card?" she finally said.

"Tess," I said. "I'm not the police. I'm not going to arrest you for allowing Daphne to use your credentials. But I know she didn't steal your card. You let her use it. And your driver's license. What I want to know from you is why. And when."

Another minute ticked by while she fiddled with the string on her apron. It wrapped around her waist and tied with a bow in the front. She bit her lip.

"Cross my heart," I said. "Just tell me why."

She chugged more water. Twisted the cap in place. "About two months ago, Daphne asked if she could borrow my old license. It was from Georgia, where I used to live. When I moved here, to South Carolina, I never surrendered it when I got the new one. Said I lost it. I'd just forgotten to take it with me and didn't want them make me go get it."

"How did Daphne know about it?"

"I don't know how she remembered," Tess said. "It was like two years ago? She had her old license, too. The one from Tennessee."

"Did she say why she needed it? Your Georgia license?"

"She said Alex might be cheating on her with his old girlfriend in Charlotte. She wanted to follow him. She paid me for the charges on my card. It's not like it's illegal to let someone charge on your card when they pay you back."

"You sound skeptical," I said. "You didn't believe her?"

"That it wasn't illegal?"

"No, that Alex was cheating."

"Oh, I definitely thought he was cheating. But that she wanted to stalk him by herself? I don't know. I offered to go with her, but she said she needed to do it alone. I made her promise not to confront him."

"Did she tell anyone else?"

"She made me swear not tell anyone, especially Juliette. She'd go bonkers if she thought Alex cheated on Daphne. After the whole *Down the Isle* mess, Juliette was protective of her."

"Protective from Alex?"

"Daphne was obsessed with Alex cheating on her, even though she didn't think he was, like, 'the one.' But you know, that finale devastated Daphne. Getting left at the altar and all that. Juliette was sensitive to that. I mean, it wasn't Juliette's fault. She was really good to her."

"I thought they were all friends," I said.

"They are. We all are. I mean, it was years ago, right? We all got sent home at some point. Me, Farrah, Daphne. Juliette won, we lost."

"How long were you on the show?"

"For six episodes," Tess said. "I never had a chance. I was Farrah's roommate. Of all the luck. But water under the bridge, right?"

"Tess, can you grab the caramel cream?" a voice called from the front.

"Look, I gotta get back. Juliette's counting on me. I can't let her down. This place will fall apart without me."

Tess offered to send me home with a cake and shake for dinner and I accepted. It had been a long day, and I still had to deliver supplies to the Big House.

My thick Strawberry Shortcake Custard sufficiently depleted, I pulled into the porte-cochere. Carla helped me unload, and I thanked her for graciously accepting this enormous responsibility—decorating twenty plus cakes in eighteen hours—on top of the enormous responsibilities she already committed to—preparing BBQ for three hundred people.

"It'll be a walk in the park," she said. "That poor girl has too much to worry about."

"You're wonderful," I said. "What time you need me here in the morning?"

She laughed right out loud. "You're adorable," she said. "I already called Chef as soon as you called me. He's sending his pastry team first thing. I need to be beachside before sunup to get the brisket in the smoker."

"I can help, Carla," I said. "No need to be impolite."

"Sweetie, you find that missing girl. You leave the food to me. I'll infuse it with so much love, she'll have no choice but to come home."

"If only it were that easy."

# FIFTEEN

(Day #8: Saturday Morning)

After leaving Carla late the night before, I left voicemails for
Jona, Sheriff Hill, and Farrah. It seemed no one was taking my
calls. However, when a knock in the gray of morning rattled me
from an exhaustion-induced sleep, I thought perhaps someone
had finally decided to communicate with me. Which was
fantastic, as long as they didn't mind if I communicated with
freakishly fluffy hair whilst wearing a faded Dodgers tee and
ripped sweatpants.

Sunshine had yet to peek through the skylight as I padded
downstairs. I opened the front door, but the knocking
continued. It was coming from the patio slider.

"Parker?" I said, as it glided open. "Kinda early, don'tcha
think?"

I blame my sleep bubble for taking an extra two seconds to
realize she was in uniform, and then to hear a siren chirp from
the alley that ran between my cottage and Ransom's house.

"Oh my God, you found her," I said. "Out here? On the
beach?"

"No," she said. "Not yet. Can you come outside?"

"Hang on a sec," I said and slid my feet into the flip-flops by
the door. "So you didn't find her? But you found something?"

"It's not about Daphne," she said. "But it's not good news,
either."

Sand crunched against the wood slats as we crossed my patio, then the three steps to the beach. Gorgeous rays of orange burst from the horizon over the deep blue sea. A smattering of clouds reflected hues of pink and yellow as the sky slowly lightened with the early sunrise.

"Where's Ransom?" I asked as we passed his house. No lights shone through the seagrass hedge.

"Down the beach talking to the captain."

"The captain? He's here?"

About a hundred yards away, a crowd had begun to form, and was growing larger, as early morning joggers and dog-walkers ambled over, the police presence interrupting their routine.

"What's happened?" I asked

"Looks like off-roaders rutted the sand," she said. "Like, you could swim in those ruts."

"What? Wait, the captain is here. Let me get dressed and meet you there."

I quickly turned back, ran to my cottage, shaking the sleep from my foggy brain. I figured I had five minutes to make the magic happen. Which allowed for a mostly thorough toothbrushing, real pants, and a hat to cover my crazy sleep hair.

I approached the damaged end of Oyster Cover Beach and stared. Humungous grooves crisscrossed a quarter mile of sand. The seagrass had been either smashed or uprooted, and the wood plank path leading up to the park was broken.

The entire area was a disaster. Right where the Ballantyne Beach BBQ was to be held. Today.

I joined Ransom, Parker, and Captain Finnegan near the epicenter. "You think joyriders did this?" I asked. "Not bulldozers?"

"From the tire treads, it looks like four-wheelers of some

kind," Captain Finnegan said. He stood tall, his gray hair military trim and his slim build runner-ready. "It's good you're here, Elliott. I called the Ballantynes, but couldn't reach them. Didn't want to leave a message."

"They're inflight from Dallas," I said. "Tod's picking them up later this morning. But don't worry about the Ballantynes. We can get this cleaned up before the party." My words conveyed a confidence I did not feel. "We have all day." Nine hours, give or take. We'd need give, not take.

"Well, that's the thing," he said, sounding both apologetic and firm. "We revoked your permit."

"You can't do that," I said. "Sir. Obviously, we'll pay to have this fixed. The BBQ is today. We cannot possibly cancel. We have over three hundred people attending. Sir."

"I know you're good for it, Elliott," he said. "But this is coming from the Mayor. He was awakened by complaints starting at four a.m. He was not happy." He turned to Parker. "Corporal, let's move the tape another foot."

"Wait," I said. "Please. There must be something we can do. A fine? Extra fees? How about we restore the beachfront, but host the party farther down, away from where the damage happened?"

"We cannot allow it," Captain Finnegan said. "It's out of my hands. It'll be the lead story. You know how it'll look granting the Ballantyne special privileges. Not when we're in the middle of our ecotourism campaign. The Loggerheads are endangered, as you well know."

"What if we use the Tidewater Inn? They have permanent facilities set up. We wouldn't need a special permit, and we wouldn't impact any natural resources that aren't already in play."

"Last minute on a Saturday?" Parker said. "They'll have a wedding booked for sure."

"Shit, the wedding," I said. "Captain, our permit carried through the BBQ this afternoon until the end of day tomorrow for the Pete/Turnbull wedding."

"Not anymore," Captain Finnegan said. "Parker, that tape."

Just as they walked over to other officers, Tate Keating jogged up with his camera flashing. A large professional piece with an enormous lens. He clicked and shuttered, taking pictures from every angle, the words "crime scene" on yellow tape I was sure centered in every shot.

Ransom wrapped me in a hug, then kissed my forehead. "The Ballantynes will understand. They've done a lot to protect the turtles. Probably more than anyone."

"I know," I said. "This will break Vivi's heart. Not just the damage, but the lack of humanity. Who would do this?"

"It's too soon to know," he said. "Had to have happened in the middle of the night. I didn't hear it, but it's by the park entrance. We'll check video surveillance, canvas the beachfront homes. See if anyone was out late and saw something."

"I didn't hear it either. How do you quietly destroy a beach like this?"

"And why?"

"To disrupt the BBQ? We've heard from a few mild protestors angry about us using the beach, saying the Ballantynes are afforded too many favors."

"Mild protestors? Is there such a thing?"

"You know, calls, letters, things like that."

"Send a list to me. We'll check them out."

"Thanks," I said. "I'm sure Mr. Ballantyne will want to be involved in the restoration. Even though we won't use it for the BBQ, he'll still want the beach repaired quickly. There could've been Loggerhead nests here."

"You going to be okay? Anything I can do?"

"Yes. You can tell me what Alex has confessed to so far. And if there's a deal on the table."

"You know I can't do that."

"I know nothing of the sort. He's a prime suspect."

"In a drug case, yes, I agree with that statement."

"But not the disappearance?"

The wind off the Atlantic blew in swirls around us. It was refreshingly crisp as the silence grew.

"Not Daphne's disappearance?" I repeated. "Fine, I'll call the Sheriff. Again. Who does not live to return my calls. You want to help? Pull a string and make that man call me."

"How about here?" Ransom asked. "Can I help with the beach?"

"First no cakes, now no beach."

"No cakes?"

"Juliette was run off the road yesterday," I said. "She's in the hospital. She hadn't finished the cakes, and she was panicked last night about us cancelling her wedding."

"I heard about the accident. I'm sorry about your friends. This one hits close to home."

"Weirdly, it's also happening outside of home. Summerton is close, but it's not here. I feel disconnected, like everything is happening right out of reach. There's this big hole. An emptiness in not knowing where Daphne is. And that's just me. Her family is in unthinkable pain and confusion. This blanket of torment. The growing uncertainty, wondering if they'll ever be able to bring her home. Thousands of acres to search. She could be anywhere. In alligator country, she could be nowhere."

We stood on the hard-packed sand, the commotion behind us. I wrapped my arms around him, tucking into his shoulder, and he held me tight. It was warm and comforting and protected.

A high-pitched beeping sounded at the top of the plank walkway near the park entrance. The familiar sound of a truck in reverse.

"Oh crap," I said, quickly pulling back. "That's Sandpiper Rentals. They're here to setup the party. And the Ballantynes land soon. I need a solution before those wheels touch down."

He kissed me, his hands on each side of my face. "You'll figure it out. You're the smartest person I know."

I ran up the broken path to the park, nearly tripping over a split plank. "Rusty," I called, waving. "Wait!"

He climbed out of the driver's side of a plain white Freightliner box truck and met me at the curb overlooking the beach.

"Dang," he said. "What's going on down there? We in the right place?"

"Yes, but no," I said. "Vandals annihilated the beachfront last night. We need to relocate."

"The entire BBQ?"

The Ballantyne golf cart, a tricked-out Garia six-seater, zipped into the lot with Carla behind the wheel. A half dozen stuffed grocery totes jostled as she parked.

I was fully aware that I probably jinxed myself earlier when I had said "centerpieces and setups, a snap" with nary a knock on wood.

"Hey, Elli," Carla said, reaching for a tote. "I should've known you'd show up early to help."

"Change in plans," I said, and nodded toward the sand.

"Bless the heavens," Carla said. "What in the world?"

Rusty, Carla, and I watched transfixed as officers stretched crime scene tape along the shoreline, winding it around wooden spikes every few feet. Tate Keating spoke to the crowd. He jotted notes and took pictures with a peppy step I didn't appreciate.

"I'm calling the Tidewater Inn," I said. "We can use their BBQ facilities."

"What about the beachfront at South Pebble Beach?" Rusty

said.

"Can't use any public beaches," I said. "The city revoked our permit."

"But they're all public beaches," Rusty said.

"Revoked our permit?" Carla said at almost the same time.

"Bad press," I said. "Tate's presence only underlines it. Especially with Captain Finnegan himself organizing the officers. And it's still turtle season, even though there weren't any nests this close to the sound."

I dialed the Tidewater Inn, a quaint boutique hotel located mid-island on over six acres of prime oceanfront real estate. After two transfers, two voicemails, and three re-dials, I spoke with the on-duty manager. They didn't have one wedding scheduled later today, they had two.

"Sweetie," Carla said. "I have to get this brisket in the smoker if we're to serve it this afternoon."

"Let's regroup at the Big House," I said. "Rusty, just hang with us. We'll find a new location. I have an idea. I'll meet you both there in fifteen."

After the quickest shower my OCD-driven brain could manage, I dressed and drove the two miles from my cottage to the Big House. Golf carts putted along the path bordering Spy Hop Lane. Twosomes and foursomes hitting the links, enjoying the early autumn temperatures and dewy grass and clear skies. The easy life.

Easy stopped at the driveway of the Big House. The volunteer line stretched down the front steps and into the circular drive, winding around one of the fire trucks. It wasn't even eight o'clock. We still had a missing girl, and now we had a missing BBQ. While completely different emergent situations, one a human tragedy, the other first-world, they both needed attention.

I greeted and hello'd my way through the foyer, stopping in

the kitchen. Carla and her grocery totes crowded the counter where I entered. Orderly rows of cake spinners lined the center island where Chef Carmichael stacked pans and utensils. He had indeed brought reinforcements. Only instead of a pastry team, like Carla predicted, it was Jane Walcott-Hatting.

Carla and Chef wore white chef coats, their respective names embroidered on the front, while Jane resembled a cafeteria lunch lady with a plastic hairnet shower cap and ill-fitting serving gloves. She leaned over a swatch of wax paper holding a piping bag. She squeezed out dots as Chef gently encouraged and complimented her terrible work.

"Did you—" I started to ask, but Carla's single swift headshake stopped me. "Did you find everything okay?"

"Yes, indeed," she said. "Don't you worry. Chef and Jane will have the cakes decorated by afternoon. The pastry team was delayed." She handed me a water bottle with a straw.

"I need something stronger than water."

"Have we met?" Carla said. "You go on now. We all have a job to do."

One long sip of fizzy Pepsi later, I saw Tod crossing the foyer to meet me near the line up to the ballroom.

"Tell me it's a prank," he said, his face pale.

"Definitely not a prank," I said. "At least not a funny one."

Zibby waddled over with her arms wrapped around a dozen clipboards. "What's happened, dear?"

"Someone tore up Oyster Cove Beach," I said. "Right where we're hosting the Beach BBQ."

"Are the baby turtles okay?"

"It's late in the season, and thankfully, we're too close to the sound. No nests near the damage. But they cut it close, that's for sure. Didn't look like they cared."

"Where are we going to have the BBQ?" Tod asked.

"How about the back lawn?" Zibby suggested.

"Hard to have a Beach BBQ without a beach," I said. "And what do we do with all the people here now? Host a party while they are searching for Daphne? It's a delicate—"

"What the bloody hell?" Jane's screech bounced from the kitchen to the foyer and probably down to Parker at the beach. She marched into the hall with her piping bag pointed at me.

Tod and I rushed over before she exploded icing onto the volunteers waiting to check-in.

"There's no beach?" she said. "Literally, no beach? Why didn't you tell me? What are you doing?"

"We're finding an alternative," I said. "You worry about the cakes. I'll find a new place."

"Worry about cakes? Have you lost your mind? This entire party is my responsibility. I should've been notified immediately." Jane ripped off her plastic cap and shoved her piping bag into Tod's hands. "Start piping."

"Have you lost your mind?" he said.

"Fine," Jane said. "Call the Cake & Shake and ask anyone to get over here and start piping. I'm calling the Tidewater."

"I already did and it's no good," I said. "They have two weddings today. It's a longshot, but I have an idea—"

"Edward will be here, in his Big House," Jane paused to check her watch, "in twenty minutes."

"I'm aware, Jane," I said. "We're all aware. Tod, we need refrigerated trucks with freezer capability."

"And exactly where will these trucks be going?" Jane said.

"I don't know yet, but we need to get them here," I said. "Golf carts are out."

"Thank you for your service, Captain Obvious," Jane said.

"I can't call anyone," Tod said. "I need to pick up the Ballantynes. They'll be here in twenty minutes because I'm picking them up in five."

He was right. Their jet was due to land in moments. I

looked around for Tess, figuring she'd help with the cakes. I didn't see her, but I spotted Jona in line. "Call Bay Harbor Yacht Club," I said to Tod. "It's not a beach, but it's water and boats. Call in every favor. I'm sure they'll accommodate us. They've been trying to get the Ballantyne to sponsor more events. Here's their chance. Be adamant, Tod. I'll be right back."

"Where are you going?" Tod and Jane asked simultaneously.

"Three minutes tops, I swear. And I'll text Tess, she's probably here someplace."

"Elliott, I swear, if you walk—" Jane said.

With a quick wave and head tilt, I motioned Jona to go into the library. "Can I talk to you about Daphne?" I texted Tess asking her to call Jane immediately before tucking my phone away. I understood Jane was rightfully stressed over the BBQ, as it was her responsibility, but I was rightfully stressed over the search for Daphne, as it was mine.

"I have to pick up the Ballantynes in five minutes," Tod hollered.

"Call Bay Harbor first," I hollered back.

I waited for Jona by the library's brick fireplace. It was surrounded by floor-to-ceiling mahogany bookshelves lined with nineteenth-century classics, first editions, and decades of bestsellers.

"What's up?" she asked when she joined me.

"What's up with Farrah and Daphne and the next Eligible and a new *Isle* season?" I said. "You didn't mention any of this when we talked three days ago."

"It's all confidential," she said. "I can neither confirm nor deny there'll be a new season of *Down the Isle.*"

"What about the last season?" I said. "You left out the part about Farrah getting kicked off the show because Daphne caught her stealing."

She shrugged. "Water under the bridge. That wasn't even one of the top ten meltdowns. Worse happened."

"Oh? Is another contestant missing?"

She had the good grace to pause. "There's that," she said. "But it would take three months to tell you every sordid story. Besides, that's the point of the show. Drama. Meltdowns. It makes amazing tv."

"You didn't tell anyone about the Farrah situation, though? Wouldn't theft have made amazing tv?"

"It also makes for defamation lawsuits," she said. "We had accusations, not facts. Had we filmed it, you bet your ass we would've shown it. Neither Daphne nor Farrah said a peep about it on camera. No other contestants witnessed it either."

"Were any of those other contestants tarot card readers? Last season, or even the one before? Maybe the one coming up?"

"You mean fortune tellers with a crystal ball?"

"Not exactly," I said. "Tarot cards, like an oversized deck of playing cards. It requires an intuitive connection, not necessarily a psychic one. Any contestants use them or bring them or have large tattoos of cards on their calves?"

"No, but we did have a girl from New Orleans who had a fleur de lis inked on her wrist. Anything else? Wondering if we had a jester or perhaps a pirate on the show?"

"One more question about Farrah," I said. "How'd she take the news that you chose Daphne to be the next Eligible?"

"Truly, I wish I could help you," she said. "But I can't talk about the upcoming season."

"So there is an upcoming season?"

Tod leaned on the French door entrance. "Bay Harbor is out. A founding member's daughter's wedding. No amount of being adamant changes that."

"Seriously?" My stomach flipped and sank. I'd thought for sure the Yacht Club would be available.

"Edward's about to land," Tod said. "Tess is on her way, but Jane's spiraling. Think fast."

He snapped the door shut and my mind went blank.

"Seems like you have your hands full. Is there a problem with your party?"

"Where were we?" I asked. "Oh, right, you were saying there's a season three in the works."

"Nice try. What I can say is that we started renovating Isle House. Take what you will from that statement."

"I was there a couple days ago, and it didn't look renovated. It looked the opposite of renovated."

"It'll be move-in ready next week. From the master suite to the ocean's edge. It'll be as if we never left."

I paused to consider my options. Feasibility and liability. It was also farther than I'd like. Than Jane would like. They'd have to work round the clock, literally, from now until finished without stopping.

"My lips are sealed," Jona said. "I'd help if I could."

"Can it be move-in ready by lunch?"

"Lunch? You mean today? I don't think so. Why?"

"I need a beach," I said. "Right now. Our BBQ this afternoon seems to have met a hiccup."

"I can't authorize that," she said. "Too much liability, and we're filming Juliette and Tucker's wedding tomorrow. My crew's tied up." Her expression faltered slightly. "Wait, are you saying we don't have a location for the wedding? The one I'm filming tomorrow?"

"We do if you let me use Isle House today."

"It can't happen. There's no way I'm going on camera with Isle House less than camera ready."

"It can be camera ready," I said. "It wasn't in terrible shape."

"We'd need to double the maintenance crew," she said.

"Maybe triple to complete it in eight hours. I don't have that kind of budget. We're a cable show."

"I'll pay for the renovation."

"The entire renovation?"

"If that's what it will take."

Jona studied my face, then seemed to believe me. She held up a finger, then stepped over to the broad desk near the window. She rapidly thumb-typed on her phone. Waited a beat. Typed again.

"And we need it in six hours, not eight," I said. "Five to be safe."

She typed, waited. Read, typed, waited. Then smiled. "Done," she said. "It's actually perfect. Everyone will think we renovated the house for the BBQ and not for the upcoming season."

"You really should stop saying that. People will start to think there's an upcoming season."

With a location secured for the party, I needed to move everything from our plantation beach to the Isle House beach. Though calling it a beach was a misnomer. The party would have to take place on the front lawn overlooking the ocean, as the beach below was a rocky edge with a slim strip of sand.

I texted Tod on my way to the kitchen: *All set. Isle House on Thatch Island.*

"Where's Jane?" I asked.

Carla pointed out the window where Jane was furiously waving her arm, pacing, animatedly talking into her cell.

"We're booked at Isle House," I said, tapping on the glass. When Jane glanced at me, I smiled big with an exaggerated thumbs up. She glared and marched toward me, so I smiled bigger.

"What?" she demanded from the doorway. "You seriously found a beachfront to hold three hundred party guests?"

"Isle House on Thatch Island," I said.

"The abandoned bachelor house?" Chef said.

"The same," I said. "It's undergoing renovations. Jona Jerome, the producer, is doubling the crew right now. We'll need to set up and start cooking in the midst of the mess, but we have plenty of time for it to come together."

"Are you insane?" Jane said. "That's seven hours."

"Five, actually," I said. "Keep piping, cooking, baking, whatever you people do in here. Carla and I will get the brisket on."

"You can't be serious," Jane said.

"Did you find a better place?" I asked. "Any available location?"

She took her sweet time thinking that one over. Finally, begrudgingly, she said, "I did not. We'll just make this work. Carla, you get the brisket on. We'll finish the cakes and arrange the trucks."

"A brilliant plan," I said, lifting a grocery tote. I almost dropped it, but played it off even though my arm nearly popped out of the socket.

Carla lifted two other totes. We hustled to the porte-cochere.

"What's in this thing?" I said. "A hundred pounds of brisket?"

"Sweetie, those are only the spices," Carla said.

"Let's grab Rusty," I said. "You okay to ride in the truck with him? He can drive you over."

"I'll take my car," she said. "I'm sure we'll need the flexibility." She hesitated after we loaded the bags into her SUV. "You go on. I know you have plenty to do. Let me load more. I'll get help inside. No sense wasting this trip with just a couple totes."

I jogged to Rusty's Freightliner parked curbside at the base of the drive.

"You know where Isle House is on Thatch Island?" I said.

"Sure," he said. "But for your party? It's, well, rundown, you don't mind me saying. Not exactly Ballantyne standard."

"It will be of the highest standard by the time the guests arrive," I said. "Do your best to keep the layout as close to our original plan as possible. Use the front lawn for the table rounds and buffet, plus the brisket smoker. We'll use the porch for the shake machines."

"You're the boss," he said.

"Please tell that to Jane," I said.

The time-consuming part of moving an entire party wasn't finding a new locale or repositioning tables, tents, and chairs for three hundred people. It was notifying those three hundred people.

As I made calls, repeating the same cheery statement about a slight mishap and the good fortune of a rare opportunity to dine and dance at a local treasure, I made notes.

I still had a case to investigate. I needed to find Farrah and get an alibi for Juliette's accident, and while I was asking, also for the day of Daphne's disappearance. I needed to talk to the Sheriff, and heaven help him if he didn't return my call soon. And mostly, I needed to figure out that burner app.


Notifying party guests was going to take even longer than I had originally anticipated. Which demonstrated how distracted I'd become. As island gossip was more popular than golf, tennis, and mahj jongg combined, my prepared statement was met with questions, comments, and concerns.

My phone buzzed with two texts between my first two calls.

Jona: *Crews confirmed. Done by early afternoon. Sending the invoice shortly.*

Tod: *Side door.*

Happiness washed over me. I wrapped up the current conversation, then hurried down the hall toward the sunroom, avoiding the crowded foyer. Clear blue Carolina skies greeted me once I hit the patio. The sun's brilliant rays sparkled the pool and shimmered against its surface. I followed the pavered path through the vegetable garden, English rose garden, and finally the canopy of hydrangeas covering the porte-cochere.

Tod parked an enormous '85 Rolls Royce Corniche, and I bounced on my toes like a kid waiting to see Santa.

Vivi rode shotgun. Her smile was genuine and kind and just for me. I opened her door, extending my hand to help her out. I hugged her tiny body, she weighed ninety-eight pounds max, and she squeezed back, then kissed both my cheeks. "Elli, my sweet dear, I missed you so."

Mr. Ballantyne emerged from the grand backseat. He was six feet tall and Jimmy Stewart handsome. He held two leashes and out galloped my favorite things on planet Earth: Colonel Mustard and Mrs. White. A pair of pug puppies so vivacious and adorable, I sat on the ground right in the drive so they could greet me proper.

Sufficiently loved by snarfling kisses and curly tail wiggles, I accompanied the whole lot along the same pavered path to the rear entrance. In their seventies, the Ballantynes traveled extensively to promote their life's mission: Caring for humanity and the environment. I knew their work was important and kind and they did so many wonderful things for humankind, but dang, it was always better when they came home.

They entered the kitchen to access the private staircase to their third-floor residence. Chef helped Tod with the luggage, while Jane reassured them the BBQ was hitch-free.

"Let me help you unpack," I said.

"Elli," Zibby said, with a waddle and a shake from the

doorway. "Sheriff Hill is on the telephone. Well, hello, Miss Vivi, let me grab my hat. It's a flamingo!"

"You take the call, dear," Vivi said to me. "We'll come down after a spell." She threaded her hand through Mr. Ballantyne's arm, and they slowly climbed the steps.

I rushed to my office. I did not need the Sheriff to quit me before I could pick up the line. "Sheriff Hill, I'm surprised you remembered my number. I was beginning to think you'd forgotten my name."

"I'm not likely to forget you, Elliott," he said. "Hear you have your hands full this morning."

"I guess it's the one thing you'll confirm. That Alex Sanders did not vandalize Oyster Cove Beach last night."

He laughed. "I can confirm that. I'll go on the record with it, too."

"How about Daphne's tablet? You know where that is? Is Alex working on a deal? Is he talking? Do you need me to ask specific questions, or can you just assume I'd like to know everything that's happening?"

"It's an ongoing investigation."

"Of which I am a part."

"Not as far as the DEA is concerned."

"What about Juliette's car accident?" I asked. "Anything you can tell me?"

"It's an—"

"Ongoing investigation," I said. "Yes, I'm familiar with the term. You're not much into cooperation for a cooperating officer."

"I'm always here if you need me."

"I need you."

Silence stretched from seconds into a minute. "Well, then, good talk. I better get back to it. I have a party to move to your backyard."

"My backyard?"

"Isle House on Thatch Island," I said. "Your backyard, remember? They started renovating it, conveniently working in our favor."

"Convenient, I'd say. Right when the house was never going to see use again."

"So you think," I said.

Tod stuck his head in the doorway. "The Ballantyne's guests will arrive this afternoon."

"Sheriff, you've been of no assistance," I said into the phone. "Let's not do this again sometime."

"Always a pleasure," he said.

I tossed my phone on my desk in frustration. "You know, Tod, a PI-in-training under the mentorship of law enforcement is code for figure everything out on your own."

"If you define 'on your own' to include me, Sid, Milo, every person the three of us has ever met, the Ballantyne name—"

"Fine, I hear you, but it'd be so much easier if the other investigators would simply tell me what they already know."

"Easy is for amateurs," he said. "Can we discuss the Ballantyne's guests now, or do you require more time to complain?"

"I totally forgot about them," I said. "Didn't they want to fly on the Ballantyne jet?"

"They have their own."

"Of course."

He pushed away from the doorframe to leave. "I'll be in my office calling guests. Where'd you leave off?"

"Wait," I said. "How can I get access to Daphne's burner app? Her phone and her tablet are unavailable. Should I call Smithson, that business name I found on her credit card bill? Any chance they'll talk to me? This is new territory."

"No chance they'll talk to you," he said. "And don't even

look for someone who knows someone. Privacy is paramount. That's the point of an app like that. Their customer records will be basic. Name, payment information, phone number. And you'll need nothing less than Supreme Court access to get the kind of warrant that will even get you that much."

"The Supreme Court may be a stretch," I said.

"What other charges did she make on her card?"

I opened my laptop and logged into Daphne's credit card provider. "Clothes, boutiques, beading wholesalers." I scrolled through the last six months, then the six months beyond those. "Here's two I don't recognize: GlamWidget for $12.95 and Nimbostrat for $49.95."

"GlamWidget is a photo filter. The other is likely a cloud."

"A cloud?"

He leaned on the chair across from my desk. "You know, even without access to the actual burner app, you could probably find the calls and texts she made from it. Daphne probably backed it up to her cloud."

"Her cloud?"

"If you know which cloud service, then you might be able to log into her account. The info should all be there. Texts, calls, everything."

"What's this cloud you keep mentioning casually as if I'm supposed to know even though you know I don't know?"

"It's like a backup computer stored off-site."

"Obviously not in the literal clouds."

"Obviously. If Nimbostrat is a cloud service, then Daphne could've used it to store a copy of her data, maybe even the burner app data. She would want to delete those texts and calls from her phone so no one would know about them. That's the point of a burner. But later, if she wanted to read them again, she could access an off-site copy." He walked to the door. "How many guests did you notify about the change in venue for the extravagant annual BBQ that takes place in less than five hours?"

"Not nearly as many as I hoped," I said. "But I emailed Ransom the list of protestors." I opened my email and attached the growing list of protestors we kept handy and zipped it off to Ransom as I spoke.

"Zibby, my dear," Mr. Ballantyne said. His booming voice echoed across the foyer and down the hall to my office. "Vivi is asking about your hat."

"Let's just get the BBQ moved, then work on finding Daphne," Tod said. "It doesn't seem like a party should take priority, but there are hundreds of people working on finding her. And this party isn't frivolous. It recognizes the host families for the homeless, something we all believe is noble and necessary, especially to raise more funds."

"Right," I said. "One crisis at a time."

# SIXTEEN

(Day #8: Saturday Early Afternoon)

After I downed the last of my Pepsis—it was a two Pepsi kind of day—Zibby arrived with lunch. Most of the volunteers were in the field searching for Daphne. A small crew stayed behind in the Big House to continue making posters, bundling flyers, and assigning teams. Tod and I spent the entire morning re-routing attendees, which meant I'd made zero progress locating Daphne.

With thirty minutes before I needed to go to my cottage to get BBQ-ready, I turned on my laptop for a quick search of Nimbostrat.

As Tod predicted, it was a cloud service. In the top right-hand corner of their webpage in teeny type, I clicked the login link. I entered Daphne's email as the username and her universal pearlknot as the password.

Red text informed me I'd entered the wrong username and/or password.

I clicked the reset password link using Daphne's email address, then switched browsers to login into her email service. I refreshed the screen eighteen dozen times in three minutes until, finally, a reset password link arrived. I considered simply using her universal password for the new one, but then decided to create something unique. I wanted to keep unwanted eyes out of her cloud. Ignoring that I was probably also unwanted eyes.

But my unwanted eyes were for good purposes, not nefarious.

The reset worked.

Daphne's Nimbostrat account held only one folder. It was named HushHush. Inside were two additional folders, each with a seven-digit number as its name. The phone numbers from her cell bill.

I opened the first folder to reveal another folder named TEXTS. No folder for voicemails or call lists. I clicked the TEXTS folder and it was exactly as advertised. A list of texts arranged like a spreadsheet with four columns: Two left columns displayed one side of the conversation, one column indicated the phone number and the other for the actual text messages, and then the other two columns for the other side of the conversation. Daphne's number on the left side, and the HushHush number on the right. I quickly scrolled through the content searching for names, but not a single one appeared. I wasn't surprised. Who texts and mentions their own name? Or the name of the other person?

From the brief scan, I determined this particular HushHush phone number must've belonged to Jona. It made sense. They'd need to talk about the whole next Eligible on season three and keep it confidential. I wondered if Jona had given Daphne the idea for HushHush to begin with.

The text exchange was short and intermittent. The columns listed bursts of texts, three or four at a time, over a four-day period the week she disappeared.

Monday afternoon:

JONA: *Don't be dumb. Get what you deserve!*

DAPHNE: *I told you leave it. Seriously.*

JONA: *Meet me at IH. I know you miss it.*

DAPHNE: *?*

JONA: *You go every week. Time for you to be center. Crash heard round the world. Fans miss you!*

Thursday afternoon:

DAPHNE: *Maybe*

JONA: *I knew you'd do it.*

DAPHNE: *I'm not doing it.*

JONA: *Meet me Sat*

DAPHNE: *Can't*

JONA: *You chicken out now you'll regret it. Don't be a wuss. Its win-win. Make a mark. Get your mate. Stop being 2nd.*

DAPHNE: *Maybe. Call me tonight.*

That was the last message, two days before she disappeared. It sounded as if Jona pushed hard to get Daphne to be the next Eligible. I wondered what finally swayed Daphne to accept her offer. Money? Publicity? Love?

Jona alluded to Daphne getting a new mate, but she already had Alex. Was Alex going to be on the show? Well, if he was, he certainly wasn't anymore. It'd be hard to film him from jail.

Or maybe Daphne had told Jona that Alex wasn't long-term potential because she'd thought he was cheating on her. But then that assumed she thought a tv bachelor would be? And after getting dumped on national tv for her best friend, would she really be so open to doing it all over again, even if she was the one in the driver's seat?

What if Jona lied about Daphne accepting the offer to be on the next season? Maybe Jona's actual agenda was to stir up trouble, build excitement right before announcing the new Eligible. The kind of trouble where someone vanished? Bad luck or good that Daphne wasn't here to confirm or dispute Jona's claims?

Their text exchange made things more confusing, not more clear. At least to me. I took notes, then opened the folder with the other HushHush phone number. Again, no names. Just the four columns of numbers and texts. These, too, were terse bursts. With such short exchanges, and the long lines of incoming/outgoing calls to both HushHush numbers on her phone bill, I assumed Daphne was paranoid about someone reading her texts.

And rightly so, as I was reading all of them. I considered whether the cloud deleted older files, because just like the previous text exchange, the only exchange listed occurred the week she went missing. Perhaps the cloud only stored a week's worth of data?

The first burst was the previous Friday.

UNKNOWN: *Take my call*

DAPHNE: *It's over.*

UNKNOWN: *Don't say that*

DAPHNE: *I can't do this anymore. I'm over it.*

UNKNOWN: *We can still do this.*

DAPHNE: *Stop calling! I'm done!*

The second and final burst took place on Saturday, the day she disappeared.

UNKNOWN: *Meet me*

DAPHNE: *I'm not going to do it.*

UNKNOWN: *Please. We'll leave tonight, she'll never know.*

Thirty minutes passed before she replied.

DAPHNE: *I don't think I can go thru with it.*

UNKNOWN: *It'll be worth it. You're worth it.*

DAPHNE: *Ok. Call me tonight.*

This exchange was more telling—and more confusing—than the first one. Daphne was plotting something with someone. But what? And with whom? Alex? He said they fought. Why the burner? And if you're on a burner app, why so cryptic? Though it was probably only cryptic because I had no idea what they were talking about. Was she also caught up in Alex's Charlotte drug scene? Maybe she was the whistleblower? "We'll leave tonight" implied an escape. Were they absconding with something?

"It's time to go," Sid said from my office doorway.

"Why are you here?"

"Hello to you, too," she said.

I glanced at the last line of the text message. Whoever called Daphne "worth it" had called her that night, and she was never seen again. I closed my laptop.

"Sorry," I said. "Hello, Sid, my very best friend in all the land. Why are you here at the Big House?"

"To get you. Carla said you'd probably stay too late. And surprise, here you are."

"She could've gotten me," I said. "Or I don't need getting. I'm a grown woman capable of getting myself."

"Everyone left an hour ago, and you should've left with them. You needed to be at the BBQ thirty minutes ago." Sid held out an outfit on padded hangers. Wide linen pants and a flowy embroidered top. "Change and let's hit the road."

I did as requested, only taking ten minutes to spritz and tame my hair and slap on a fresh coat of lip gloss. "I discovered two interesting tidbits today. I found Daphne's text messages from her HushHush burner phone app. I'm pretty sure one's about Jona. The other? Daphne was planning something nefarious. Said she didn't think she could 'go thru with it.' Possibly with Alex. Or a secret boyfriend. It's a secret somebody."

"Oh? From Atlanta?"

"I don't know. If so, he drove down the day she disappeared. The last message was Daphne asking him to call her, and she sent it about six hours before her cell phone last pinged."

I dialed Sheriff Hill as we walked to the Mini. "Sherriff, it's Elliott Lisbon. Remember me? I'm the one helping with the Daphne Fischer disappearance. I found—discovered, um," I paused, unsure how to continue. "Well, just call me, kay? Or pop over to the BBQ." I disconnected and turned to Sid. "I'm not sure how flexible he is."

"With?"

"Law things. Like me using a pilfered password to access Daphne's personal cloud service to read private text messages from a burner app backup account."

"Could be a gray area."

"But also could involve the last person to see her alive."

"Solid point," Sid said. "Maybe leave out certain details."

We sailed over the bridge to mainland South Carolina, speeding along with the top up. No sense tangling Sid's long mane before a prominent party. It may have been a BBQ near the beach, but everyone who was someone was going to be there. While we were honoring the host families who routinely housed the homeless, the island's wealthiest patrons had ponied up significant dollars to sponsor the tables, contributing to the Housing First Initiative Fund.

Sid's phone buzzed and she pulled it from her handbag. "Oh, it's Brad Jerome from the ATV rental place." She hit the red decline button. "He can leave a voicemail. Probably trying to make sure I don't sue them for my broken boogie board. I may have sold it a little too well the other night."

"Did you say Brad Jerome? That's his name?"

"Yeah, why?"

"Because Jona's last name is Jerome."

"Jona, the *Isle* producer?" Sid asked.

"Yep."

"Maybe it's just a coincidence? Though, I guess Jerome isn't as common as Smith, but it's also not terribly unique like Wigglesworth or Sotomayor."

"Well, coincidentally, Jona Jerome offered Isle House for the BBQ today because our previously pristine and properly permitted beach was wrecked, likely by ATVs."

"And, coincidentally, a Brad Jerome works at an ATV rental hut."

"Too convenient to be a coincidence, right?"

"You want to go back? Stop in Island Rentals?" Sid glanced at her watch. "We can be a little late. Later. We're late."

"And do what? Ask Brad if he provided his sister or wife or some branch of the Jerome family a bunch of ATVs to damage the beach and cause tens of thousands of dollars in damages, not to mention break about ten laws? That public beach belongs to Sea Pine Island, and it's turtle nesting season."

Sid sighed long and deep. "But not tonight after the BBQ, 'kay?"

"For what?"

"To break in and read contracts or trace genealogy or test tread patterns or whatever you have planned."

"Fine, not tonight," I said. "But definitely tomorrow."

"Thank you. Tonight is romantic."

"Where's Milo?"

"He's meeting me at Isle House. I'm arriving with you, but going home with him. Where's Nick?"

"Hopefully meeting me there. But with his big special DEA task force case, it's hard to tell."

"El, your whole relationship is hard to tell," Sid said. "Me? I know where I stand at all times."

"It's straightforward for you two," I said. "You started from scratch only a year and a half ago. First date, first kiss, first everything. So much easier to track and trace where you stand. Ransom and I have history. A lot of history."

"That shouldn't change the present. Or your future. I've never known you to not know what you want. Go get it."

"Slow your roll. It's only been eighteen months or so."

"You two started twenty years ago in college. You're now

forty. What are you waiting for?"

"The other shoe to drop," I said. "You know, the day he texts me to say he had to go. It wasn't our time. Again. Look at his DEA case. It still pulls him in. He's not fully on the island, just like before. He wants to go to Barcelona and Monterey and what if he decides to leave me behind? Again."

She reached over and took my hand. "Sweetie, you were teenagers. He loves you. He came back to you. He wants to take you to Barcelona and Monterey, not the DEA." She kissed my hand and held it in hers. "Don't you dare forget that you are everything. You go get your happily ever after. Fear will only stand in your way."

Tears stung my eyes and tickled my nose and I blinked them back. "You are everything, Sid. Thank you. I love you."

"You know, even with the Post-it, Meredith and Derek got married," Sid said. "He proposed with his mother's ring."

"And then they married on a Post-it."

"And then they married with rings. Because, forever."

"I don't think Ransom believes in forever."

"Do you?"

I squeezed her hand, but didn't answer. We'd arrived at the Ballantyne Beach BBQ and *Down the Isle* set. My plate was definitely much too full to worry about forever.

# SEVENTEEN

(Day #8: Saturday Afternoon)

Isle House dazzled in its antebellum grandeur. The power washed paint practically glowed in the mid-afternoon sun. Every flower bed and planter held mounds of fresh soil bursting with blooms. Valets darted about setting up ingress/egress flow while Rusty's crew loaded the Freightliner with boxes and crates. Catering staff smoothed table linens and stacked plates. Hickory smoke carried by the light breeze promised sweet and tangy brisket slathered in sauce.

Sid and I followed the path to the back where the enormous pool flowed with sparkling cool water. Tables for two and four mixed with luxury loungers and tented cabanas. The tiki bar was stocked and manned with cut fruit and colorful mixers.

Inside the main kitchen, Carla, Chef, and Jane bustled amongst uniformed staffers. They filled a long line of milk glass punch bowls with charred cabbage slaw, peach and plum salad with basil, watermelon pickles, and lemon mayo potato salad. Stock pots held maple bacon baked beans, and split corn on the cob awaited its turn on the grill to be topped with that delicious herbed goat cheese butter.

Tess wiped a variety of cake stands in the dining room. The entire table, a reclaimed-wood stunner, displayed twenty-seven single-tier cakes. Each beautifully decorated masterpiece was an original. Red and blue and pink and green, white and orange and aqua and citrine. Flowers, swirls, and decadent shapes all perfectly placed.

"The *Down the Isle* crew is upstairs," Jane said, straddling the doorway between the kitchen and dining room. "Make sure they stay put. They are not invited."

"They're providing the house we're standing in and the ocean view we're looking at," I said.

"Which we overpaid for, thanks to you," she said. "Guests arrive in ten, so make it happen."

"I've got the cakes, Elliott," Tess said. "They're almost ready for the tables. You talk to Jona. She's in the production suite, third floor. I'm happy to never speak to her again."

I left Sid with Tess to prepare the procession of cakes to the table rounds on the lawn. With a deep breath and a vague idea of how to politely request Jona not join the party, I climbed the two flights of stairs to the top floor.

When I had visited earlier in the week, it was simply a long empty room with a stunning view overlooking the pool. Today, the heavy plantation shutters were closed tight against the windows, and monitor screens were mounted on stands across the wide expanse. Must have been ten total. Six blank and four playing different shows.

Jona huddled with three other people, all with identical *Down the Isle* press credentials clipped to their waists and black over-ear headphones slung around their necks. "I want two angles from the front behind the preacher," Jona said.

"It's a clerk," a girl in side braids said. "County, I think. Or a Justice of the Peace. Maybe."

"Don't care," Jona said. "Make sure both front angles show the aisle. The full aisle. Centered like a runway."

Before I interrupted their camera angle discussion, I noticed Juliette on one of the screens. I stepped over to watch. With my busy week—chased by thugs, almost arrested by the

DEA, Jane Doe in the scrub, ATV-wrecked beach—I hadn't yet streamed a single episode. As I glanced at all four screens, the ones with different shows, I realized they were all *Down the Isle* episodes, or possibly outtakes, featuring Juliette, Daphne, and Tucker in various combinations.

Once I started watching, it wasn't Juliette who held my attention. It was Daphne. She and Tucker sat on the porch swing in the garden. Ocean waves rolled gently in the background while magnolia branches swayed in the foreground. Tucker brushed a lock of Daphne's hair from her face, slipped it behind her ear.

I stepped closer to the screen to listen. The volume was low, but I heard every word.

"This is what the rest of our life looks like," Tucker said.

Daphne laughed. Easy, languid, normal, as if the camera wasn't even there. "We're staying in the house forever? Not sure that was part of the package."

"We'll build a swing on our front lawn," he said. "In San Francisco, we can still visit the beach. Might even see it if we really want to. Expensive, but worth it."

"Yes, but in Nashville, we can visit the mountains. And you can see them for miles and miles. No extra cost."

"California has mountains."

"They're not the Appalachians."

"Wherever you go, I go," he said.

"He really loved her," Jona said from behind me. "Like a forever kind of love. The audience devoured those two love birds. Our ratings shot up as word spread. One blogger called it their love bubble. Hard to stop a love like that. But she tried." Jona pointed to another screen. She tapped two buttons and the volume rose.

Juliette and Daphne sat on a bed with a plastic box between them. It was divided into a dozen compartments, each filled with beads in different shapes, sizes, and colors. Daphne braided threadlike cords while Juliette examined tiny treasures.

"It's fated," Juliette said. "I mean, our grandparents are married, and we'll be married." She sighed and held a bead up to the light. "How romantic."

Daphne twisted the cords tight, sliding beads every so many turns. She remained silent, and it seemed Juliette didn't notice.

"I finally get the family I always wanted," Juliette continued. "Tucker will inherit the family business, you know. And it's on the island. I'll start my business on the island. It's so perfect. We already picked out our house."

"You did?" Daphne finally responded and with surprise. "When?"

"Well, I picked it out," Juliette said. "It's near our grandparents. On the same exact street. It's my dream house, and I know Tucker feels the same. He told me."

"But it's so expensive that close to the beach," Daphne said.

"Where there's a will, we'll make a way," Juliette said.

"I think he loved them both," Jona said to me. "In his own way. It wasn't all for the cameras."

"What wasn't?" I asked.

"The love bubble," she said, pointing to the other screen with Tucker and Daphne lazily swinging on the lawn. "He and Juliette had their moments, too. And he charmed Farrah. Hot and heavy. That kept those two up late, I can tell you that. Plotting and planning."

"You mean Daphne really did get Farrah kicked off the show?"

"Damn right she did," Farrah said. She marched into the room, placed one hand on her hip.

"I've been calling you," I said. "I'd think you'd want to tell me your side of the story."

"I'll tell you now. Daphne knew Tucker and me had a real

connection. Not some ancient fated Juliette Greek tragedy. Not fantasy living in a fairy tale. Real real. Daphne looks all sweet and innocent, but she caused nothing but chaos."

"She's really good at it," Jona said. "And I'm counting on it. Spectacular chaos. You'll see. The entire viewing audience will see."

Took me less than a second to catch her drift and the smug glance she exchanged with Farrah. "You think she's coming back?" I said. "That she's not actually missing? That's she's going to create chaos at the wedding?"

"We'll find out tomorrow," Jona said.

Juliette spoke from behind Farrah. "What are you saying? I don't understand."

Farrah whirled around. A wicked grin lit up her entire face. "Oh, you will, and I want a front row seat for that clown show." She pushed past Juliette with a solid shoulder check. She practically hopped down the staircase.

"Wait!" Juliette shouted, running after her.

Jona frantically motioned the crew. "Go, go, go."

Two crew members grabbed cameras, hoisting them on their shoulders as they jogged out of the room.

"Oh shit," I said and sprinted. I slammed down the steps, my flats slapping the polished wood. I passed the first camera, then the second.

All the while Daphne's texts about 'not going thru with it' with a secret someone flashing in my mind. She wasn't just cheating on Alex, she was cheating on Juliette. No wonder she was stressed out about the wedding. The maid of honor was dating the groom.

Juliette rounded the lower staircase as Farrah whipped open the front door. She raised her hands in victory as if she'd just stuck the landing and was waiting for the judges' score.

Party guests were arriving on the far side of the front lawn.

Farrah waved merrily.

Juliette grabbed the neck of her top, dragging her into the house. "You liar!"

"Don't touch my weave, bitch!" Farrah slapped Juliette's arm down. "Oh look," she said, pointing toward the patio doors visible through the kitchen. "It's Tucker. Let's go ask him if I'm a liar." She bumped the cake table with her hip and Juliette gasped. I gasped. Tess hollered, "Bitch!"

"What the bloody—" Jane said.

Chef put his arm around her, tucking her out of the way as we all sped past.

"I got this," I said.

"Guests are arriving!" Jane said.

We spilled onto the pool deck. There stood Millie Poppy next to Tucker. His face paled as Farrah and Juliette burst forward.

"You and Daphne?" Juliette said. "Still?"

"What do you mean?" Tucker said.

"Daphne's not missing," Juliette said. "That's what I mean. Are we getting married tomorrow?"

Tucker looked visibly shaken. Confusion, fear, anguish. He stepped forward. "She's not missing? You found her?"

"Have you been seeing her behind my back?" Juliette said. Anger lit up her features and Tucker stepped back.

"Of course we saw each other," he said. "We were friends."

"I'm asking about being more than friends. Is she going to crash my wedding?" She laughed, bitterness and pain running deep. "The wedding she was invited to? My maid of honor sleeping with my groom."

"We hadn't slept together, but..."

"But what?" Juliette said. "You wanted to? You were going to?"

"She and I had a connection first," he said. "Way before you and me. It...you pressured me...all that destiny...it just got so confusing."

"Pressured you?" she said. "Confusing? Let me simplify it. Our wedding is tomorrow, Tucker. Tomorrow. You and Daphne had a couple of dates two years ago. Right? Right? The connection is supposed to be ours. What am I missing? You proposed to me, not her."

"We had a connection first, Tucker," Farrah said. "Tell her. We had sex in that very cabana the first week. And it wasn't the only time. And then Daphne ruined it. You knew she lied about those beads, and you did nothing."

"What?" Juliette looked horrified, her eyes wide, her face growing redder still.

"You ruined it," Tucker yelled at Jona, then turned to Juliette. "You both did. All this," he said with an arm wave as Millie Poppy stepped closer to Juliette. "This is you. Not me. Not Daphne. The family connections, the destiny, the whole thing. You poisoned Daphne's mind, and she couldn't do that to you. Even though you did that to her."

"To me?" Juliette said. "Do what to me? Let me marry someone who doesn't love me? Or worse, not marry you because she's going to show up as I walk down the aisle and humiliate me on camera? Her way of getting back at me?"

"It's not always about you, Juliette," Tucker said. "Jesus."

A crowd had gathered. Sid, Jane, Chef, Tess, Zibby, plus catering staff and guests who'd started to stroll the grounds. Jona expertly directed the cameras to film the scene. She worked silently, unobtrusively, so the action would flow naturally.

Farrah turned to Jona. "Since Daphne is in love, and Juliette is old news, I'm the next Eligible, right?"

Jona smiled. "Oh definitely, and this is the trailer."

"I told you I'd get what I wanted," Farrah said. "I always

figure out a way." She blew a kiss toward the camera and left with a sashay.

"How could you?" Millie Poppy said to Tucker. She opened her arms to Juliette whose anger melted into cries which quickly turned to sobs. She was nearly inconsolable.

Tucker looked disgusted and followed Farrah's exit around the garden to the front.

"If you use a millisecond of that footage," I said to Jona. "The closest thing to tv you'll get is from the community room at the prison."

"This is private property, remember? My private property. In your haste to host your fancy BBQ, we didn't sign a contract or a waiver."

"We're only here because you wiped out our beach," I said.

"I did no such thing."

"You facilitated it," I said. "That's conspiracy. An accessory, aiding, abetting."

"Sue me," she said. "Dana, Wayne, why are you standing here? Go! Get Tucker and Farrah leaving. Run!"

"Stop!" I said. "It was a public beach, Jona."

"Then it's a fine," Jona said. "I'll happily pay. It's a drop in the bucket compared to the publicity this will bring. I couldn't have planned it any better." She waved her arm. "Dana, go!"

"Dana, stop!" I said.

"Elli," Zibby said. "The turtles."

"Yes!" I said. "The turtles! You violated the Endangered Species Act when you tore up the beach, which contained Loggerhead Turtle nests."

"So it'll be a large fine," Jona said. "Totally worth it. Dana—"

"Oh no, sister, that's jail time," I said. "Thirty days per egg."

"Let's see," Zibby said. "One hundred fifty-nine nests times three hundred seventy-two eggs each. I know, those little turtles are like a rabbit mixed with a chicken. Those numbers are a superball lottery."

"Yep," I said. "Something like fifty thousand thirty-day sentences."

Jona's face slowly fell, calculations clear in her eyes. She put her hand up to keep her camera crew in place. "You have no proof."

"Other than you just admitted you'd pay the fine," I said. "Why offer to pay for a crime you didn't commit?"

"And your cohort over at Island Rentals," Sid added. "We know Brad very well, and he probably doesn't want to serve the whole fifty thousand thirty-day sentences himself."

"Hand me the footage," I said. "All of it."

"Actually, hand me the footage," Sheriff Hill said. He was out of uniform in khakis and a button down, but he pulled out his shiny badge to identify himself.

"Hand me the footage," Ransom said. He showed his leather foldover directly to the camera crew. It held two badges. The Sea Pine Island shield and the one from the FBI. "Oyster Cove Beach is Sea Pine Island jurisdiction," he said to Sheriff Hill.

Jona held her defiant stance another moment, then acquiesced. She signaled the crew. They ejected identical memory cards from their camera slots and gave them to Ransom. Jona waved for them to follow her, and she dialed her phone as they went back into the house. "Get me a lawyer," she said.

"Don't leave the premises," Ransom said as she retreated.

"What is happening?" Tod said from the patio doors. "The Ballantynes and their VIP entourage arrived. They're greeting party guests by themselves."

Zibby threaded her arm through Jane's. "We should whisk ourselves to the lawn, dear. Those butter beans smell good enough to eat."

"You handled that well," Sheriff Hill said to me.

"She always does," Ransom said. He kissed me softly on the lips. "You look beautiful, too."

"Our Elli always gets her man," Sid said. "I'll catch up with you later, sweetie. Milo's saving me a seat by the band. We'll help Zibby and Jane get the BBQ rolling."

"You left me a message," Sheriff Hill said. "Something about new evidence."

"I think you just heard it," I said.

"I caught the end of the argument," Ransom said. "Were they saying Daphne isn't actually missing?"

"I'm not sure," I said. "Jona intimated that Daphne was going to crash the wedding tomorrow. Some big plan they'd concocted for publicity. I'm not sure I believe her. Something isn't right."

"Agreed," Sheriff Hill said. "I think I'll talk to Jona. How about I bring her round to your station later today?"

Ransom agreed, then Sheriff Hill tipped his imaginary hat and walked away.

"A bit of a fizzle to the end of your investigation," Ransom said. "But at least you got your man."

"Only if you mean you," I said. "Unless you're going to finally tell me that Alex actually was involved."

He held my hand, pulling me under a palm near the pool. "Sanders was not involved in Daphne's disappearance. As far as we can tell, anyway, and we've looked hard. He's been under surveillance for the last month. On Saturday, the day Daphne disappeared, he was completing a drug deal at Island Rentals."

"And you knew this the whole time?" I said.

"Not the whole time, but early on."

"And Sheriff Hill? He knew, too?"

"Pretty much. He didn't want to lie to you, but he couldn't tell you, either. Sanders had stopped cooperating. He didn't want to give up his phone. He was worried we'd see texts arranging a drug buy that day, not anything to do with Daphne. But we didn't need his phone or the text record. His buyer was an undercover DEA agent."

"Ransom, you shit," I said with a firm smack to his chest. "Why not tell me?"

"I couldn't, you know that. I said you were barking up the wrong tree. And Parker also told you to keep looking." He shrugged and half-smiled, trying to charm away my irritation. "I tried to nudge you the best I could."

"I can't always read you, Nick," I said. "I don't want to always read between the lines, deciphering hidden messages."

He kissed me again, then held both my hands. "I'm not hiding. I'm right here." His phone buzzed. He pulled it from inside sport coat. "It's Parker. El, I'm right here in spirit, but I have to go. Sanders just started naming names. Enjoy the BBQ. I'll call you later."

"I'm not staying." I nodded toward to Juliette and Millie Poppy huddled in a cabana.

"I'm sorry," he said. He kissed my forehead and walked away.

I tracked down Tess in the kitchen with the Cake & Shake staff. They looked flustered, lost. "I guess we should serve shakes, right?" Tess asked. "The cakes are on the tables. The presentation was fantastic, by the way. The shake machines are ready. The ice cream is ready. Everything is ready. I think they're just waiting on us."

"Can your staff do it without you?" I said. "Serve the shakes to three hundred guests? Juliette cannot stay here. I think Millie Poppy came with Tucker. I'm sure Juliette would rather leave with you than me. She needs a close friend."

"Yes," a girl said. She wore a tee with the Cake & Shake logo. "There are five of us and two machines. We got this, Tess.

But we need to start right now." She directed her co-workers to the enormous freezer. They hoisted five-gallon ice cream tubs and carried them toward the front door, leaving us alone in the kitchen.

"This is our biggest party," Tess said. "But I guess we've done a hundred events. You sure it's okay if neither of us are here?"

"More than okay," I said.

"Where's Juliette?"

She followed me to the pool. We joined Millie Poppy and Juliette in their cabana, a tented canopy covering a pair of double loungers. Millie Poppy reclined on one with Juliette curled in her lap. Both of their faces were drawn and tear-streaked.

"I know this BBQ is important," Juliette said. "But I just can't even think."

"It's already handled," I said. "Tess put everything in place and it's beautiful." I hadn't seen it, but Juliette didn't know that.

"Can I stay with you, Tess?" Juliette said, wiping her face. "I cannot go home. To that apartment. My God, Daphne could show up any minute. I guess she can't spoil a wedding that isn't happening, right? I guess I ruined her big moment."

"Sara started the shakes, but I'll put Quinn in charge," Tess said. "She's experienced running the team. She'll handle clean up, too. She brought the van. They got this, don't worry." She squeezed her hand. "Be right back."

"Millie Poppy," I said. "How about I drive you home?"

"You going to be okay, honey?" Millie Poppy kissed Juliette's forehead and rubbed her arm.

"Okay enough," she said, sitting up. "You go see Sam. Tess will take care of me. I just need to go collapse somewhere. Anywhere but here. I'll process everything later."

Tess popped out of the house a few minutes later, and they

quietly left the pool area, Tess's arm around Juliette.

Millie Poppy asked me to wait a moment, then went inside Isle House one last time. She emerged carrying a clear garment bag covering a gorgeous beaded wedding gown. "The girls brought it for tomorrow. They'd set up a bride's room on the second floor. Juliette shouldn't have to deal with it. I barely want to."

Millie Poppy slept most of the drive to Sea Pine Island. She started to talk when we first got in the car, but exhaustion took her over. So much had happened in the span of a single afternoon. Really, about a single hour. A best friend's betrayal so deep, it could take years for Juliette to recover. And where was that best friend? Missing or hiding? I wasn't convinced Jona knew more than she let on. At least not about Daphne's whereabouts. While she never seemed worried Daphne was in trouble, she also never seemed confident she wasn't. And I didn't believe for a moment Daphne would cause her parents so much despair, all in the name of publicity for a show she despised.

I parked in the temporary loading zone at Island Memorial Hospital while Millie Poppy stirred herself awake. She stared at the automatic doors leading to the lobby. A couple walked out. The woman carried two vases of flowers, the man carried a cane.

"Sam left me a voicemail," she said. "Right before the accident. I've listened to it a dozen times. That's the hardest part. I can't talk to him. And I never will."

"What do you mean? It's only a dislocated hip."

"He fell into a coma last night," she said. "He'd been in and out of consciousness, and with the pain meds, I'd barely been able to speak to him since he got here. I was going to tell Juliette after she set up the cakes for the BBQ. There wasn't going to be a wedding tomorrow."

"I'm so sorry," I said.

"Sam was talking about our rose garden, that he wanted to tell me something, but in person," she said.

I felt dread. That full wash of heavy that filled my stomach full. Just like when Juliette tried to do the same thing earlier. Telling me she needed to talk, but it had to be later. It's tempting the universe, and the universe does not like to be tempted.

"I always wanted to see the Princess Grace Rose Garden in Monaco," she continued. "I think Sam was going to surprise me. How could it all go so wrong?" She squeezed my hand and opened her door.

"You want me to go inside with you?"

"You go find Daphne," she said. "She's not coming back to stop the wedding. I don't care what they were hollering about. She wouldn't have done that. That girl got herself into trouble. More than she bargained for, and it sounds like she was bargaining for more than she could handle." She reached for the dress in the backseat.

"Let me hold that for you," I said. "I can keep it at my cottage until you're ready. Or I can take it anywhere. You shouldn't have to deal with it either."

"I normally wouldn't consider, but frankly, I can't imagine Emily Post would mind me asking. Could you drop it at my house? Stick it in a closet? Maybe the guest room? Out of sight, if not out of mind?"

"Absolutely," I said. "I'll use your key, then put it under one of the porch planters when I leave. And Millie Poppy, you can always ask me. It's no trouble. Ever."

She thanked me, then slowly walked across the narrow drive and into the hospital. The doors swished open, then swished closed behind her.

No beautiful outdoor beach wedding. No groom to say I do. No forever and ever amen.

Forever didn't always mean forever. But I guess you couldn't plan for that. You couldn't plan for this kind of misfortune. Or plan to avoid it.

I was surrounded by people experiencing unimaginable pain—Juliette, Millie Poppy, Zanna—all stemming from a toxic tv show. It made me count my blessings, and I had many. It seemed almost silly I'd choose to ignore my own happily ever after because of the way it had all played out before. Ransom and I weren't reliving an old episode, we were creating a new season.

As I drove the most beautiful wedding gown never to be worn to a home that may never be happy again, I thought perhaps it was time I figured out my own forever.

Just as soon as I figured out Daphne's.

# EIGHTEEN

(Day #8: Saturday Late Afternoon)

Millie Poppy's street was deserted. It was a beautiful day to spend at the beach or on the golf course or drinking poolside with friends. Once in the driveway, I put the top down in order to wrestle the wedding dress from my backseat. It must've weighed twenty pounds. Heavy silk and tulle and beads. So many beautiful beads.

I slid the key in the lock, and the door handle twisted with ease. The house was quiet. A nearby grandfather clock ticked loudly. The living room and kitchen looked showcase ready, not quite lived in. Like its occupants tidied up and never returned. The rustling of the dress and my soft footsteps lightly echoed as I crossed through the house.

The guest room décor reminded me of a beachside inn. Whitewashed shiplap covered the walls, themselves adorned with sailboat prints and beachy sayings about sand and surf and seashells. The picture window overlooked the patio, fire pit, and rose garden. The ocean barely visible beyond a picket fence.

I hung the wedding dress on the rail along the farthest spot at the back of the closet, pushing the heavy zippered bag behind two storage boxes, and closed the bi-fold door with a soft snap. I glanced out the window. The afternoon breeze rustled the tall seagrass and rose bush leaves.

My mind's inner wheels started to turn. Slowly at first.

Something about the roses. And tv episodes. I continued to stare, hoping the thread of the loose thought would weave into something tangible. After a few minutes, I turned away, letting my subconscious meditate.

The patio slider from the sunroom was open. The distant ocean air drifted in. Almost calling me. I walked outside. Voices from families playing and talking and beaching sounded in the distance, mingling with softly splashing waves and soaring seagulls.

Fragrant flowers scented the air with honeyed notes of rose and jasmine. A short brick path wound around the pretty garden. I followed it.

It was when I reached the last of row bushes that the loose thread of a thought materialized. Sam tending the roses on the morning of the Sea Pine Island Home Showcase. The mulch still looked new. The mounds high and fresh. I knelt closer. Definitely much higher and fresher than the rose bushes toward the front. Why would he tend the roses in the back where no one would see them? Is this what he was trying to tell Millie Poppy in that voicemail?

I dusted my hands and returned to the patio slider, then sat in one of the Adirondack chairs facing the fire pit at the edge of the garden. I called Ransom. He didn't answer, so I texted instead.

Me: *I want to go to Barcelona. I want to go to Monterey. I want forever. Also, I'm having a Columbo moment at Millie Poppy's, can you and Parker and the Sheriff meet me? I think I found Daphne.*

I was contemplating sending a text to Parker to bring dogs when a figure came around the row of yellow roses bordering the side fence. It was Tucker. He had the remnant tears on his cheeks.

"How did you know I was here?" he asked.

"I didn't," I said. "I didn't even see you back there." And it never occurred to me to question the open sunroom slider.

He slid into the chair next to me with a thud. That's when I noticed he held a letter in one hand and a gun in the other.

I jumped at the sight of the gun. I hated guns. They had a singular purpose. To kill. Either people or animals. They were dangerous and deadly and anything could happen.

"So why are you here?" he asked.

"Juliette's dress. Millie Poppy asked me to put it in the closet. She's at the hospital with your grandfather."

"Yeah, I talked to her. She didn't mention the dress. That damn dress. I hate it. I hate all of this." He waved the gun, almost absentmindedly, around the yard and garden.

I sat quietly. Hands in my lap. Unsure of what to say, of what he intended, of why he held a gun.

"We were fine," he continued. Almost casually, barely engaged. "Me and Daphne, me and Juliette. And then Juliette asked Daphne to put beads on her wedding dress. I think she wanted Daphne to feel involved." He laughed. Short and bitter. "She got involved all right. So did I."

"You weren't dating this whole time?" I asked softly. "Since the end of *Down the Isle*?"

"I thought she hated me this whole time," he said. "Turns out, she loved me."

"And you loved her," I said.

"And I loved her," he said.

My phone buzzed with a soft vibration. I hoped it was Ransom saying he was on his way to meet me and not Ransom saying he wasn't. I thought about casually flipping it over to read the screen, but decided against the movement.

"How did you know Daphne was here?" he asked.

"Like I said, I didn't. I came because of the dress."

"I saw you by the roses," he said. "So you know she's here."

"Yes, I know," I said, considering what to say next. "I once saw an episode of *Dateline*. It made me think about the parking ticket. The one you took when you parked Daphne's car at the Sea Pine airport. The night she disappeared."

"But you don't have the ticket. I burned it."

"Yeah, you're right. I don't have the ticket, but I was telling the Sheriff about it on this episode of *Dateline*. The guy had buried his girlfriend in their backyard. Earlier today at the hospital, Millie Poppy mentioned Sam and the rose garden. I remembered him tending it, almost obsessively, the morning Daphne disappeared. Or more accurately, the morning after."

He wiped a tear with the back of his hand, the letter hand. An envelope fluttered to the ground. "Millie Poppy" was written in block letter.

I was so focused on the gun, I'd forgotten he was holding a letter. "Sam left her a note?"

Tucker nodded. His gaze transfixed on the rose bushes.

"You weren't trying to run Juliette off the road. You were trying to hurt Sam."

"He was going to tell her," Tucker said and dropped the note. It landed next to the envelope near our feet. "He did tell her. I came to leave him a note. To say goodbye. I just wanted to get away from this place. But I found this note instead. Now I can't seem to leave it behind. I loved Daphne, but that show, it just messed with my head. It messed with everyone. I was confused. Daphne didn't want to live on the island. Juliette wanted the family. My grandfather wanted me to run the business. Jona wanted ratings."

"And you wanted Daphne."

My phone vibrated again in the silence. Tucker glanced at me as seagulls called in the distance, along with the muted laughter and voices over the fence. And then the faint sound of sirens.

"We argued," Tucker said, seeming to ignore them. Or perhaps didn't even hear them. "Last week. Daph wasn't going to crash the wedding. I mean, at first, that was Jona's idea. She said it was okay because Juliette first cheated on Daphne with me, why not the other way? But Daphne was torn, you know, with the friendship. Juliette just wanted more and more from Daphne, and the wedding was looming."

"What about *Down the Isle*? Did Daphne agree to do another season?"

"Daphne told me she was going to do it with Jona. Take the money and the new show, be the Eligible. Leave us all behind. But then she backed out. She said she'd rather leave the island. Get far away and start over by herself. And I wanted her to leave with me. You know, settle down somewhere, just us. We argued. She couldn't live with the guilt. Wanted a clean slate without me. I thought she loved me."

"She was going to tell Juliette?"

"I don't know. But she didn't care if she found out. It was all too much. Our fight got ugly. I got mad. I pushed her. Just once. She fell in the parking lot. Her head bounced on the asphalt. And that was it. She was gone. One push. One angry shove and my entire life ended. Right there in a random office parking lot."

"You called Sam," I said. "And he helped."

"He helped."

The low whoop of sirens grew steadily louder.

Tucker raised his gun. He pointed it at me and I raised my hands.

The sirens stopped. The gun never wavered. Tucker didn't blink.

The front door slammed, almost like a crash. Footsteps pounded against the floors. The floorboards creaking under the weight.

I sat statue still, not wanting to startle Tucker. I knew he'd heard them, too.

"Tucker," I said gently. "They're here to help with Daphne."

He kept the gun raised. Didn't say a word.

A half-dozen snaps and scuffs. The sounds of guns unholstering.

Voices shouted for him to put the gun down.

I leaned to my right, ready to bolt.

Tucker moved the gun. He didn't aim it at my head. He aimed it at his own. And pulled the trigger.

"No!" I screamed and closed my eyes.

The shot was beyond loud. Like saying a hurricane was breezy or a ghost pepper had a little kick. I covered my ears, but it was milliseconds after the insane explosion.

Someone put their hands on my arms. Held me tight. A strong grip on each side.

"You're okay," Ransom whispered, barely audible. "You're okay. You're okay." His volume rose ever so slightly. I realized he wasn't whispering. He lifted me out of the chair and I finally opened my eyes. He blocked nearly everything around me, holding me close to his chest, gently walking me into the house.

We passed Parker and Sheriff Hill and at least a dozen uniformed officers. I felt tears on my cheeks. My legs wobbled, but Ransom kept us moving, bearing most of my weight.

He eased me onto the front porch swing. He slowly rocked. His arm firmly around me, my head still buried in his chest. "You're okay," he repeated. "You're just fine. I'm right here. You're okay."

I cried. For Daphne, for Juliette, for Millie Poppy, for Sam. Even for me. I'd battled killers this past year. Terrible people who did terrible things. But Tucker battled himself, and somehow this loss ran the deepest.

Once spent, my sobs smoothed into heavy breaths, then deep meditative breathing. I lifted my face to Ransom's. He kissed my forehead. I turned and watched the line of police and rescue vehicles in the drive and down the street. An officer directed residential traffic, another cleared a space. One, I knew, that would be used for Dr. Harry Fleet, the medical examiner.

"Is Millie Poppy at the hospital?" Ransom asked.

"Yes," I said. "I should go tell her. And Juliette and the search teams. Oh my God, Zanna and her family."

"We'll take care of them," Ransom said.

Parker stepped onto the porch, leaned against the railing in front of us. "Can you tell us what happened?"

I nodded, wiped my face, took another deep breath. Eight counts in, eight counts out. I told them what I'd surmised after leaving Millie Poppy at the hospital. Staring out the guest room window. Sam and the flower bed. Tucker appearing in the garden. His confession. The sirens. The gunshot.

"That's enough for now," Ransom said. "We'll talk again later, Parker."

"I should let you two go," I said.

"We need your clothes," she said. She held what looked like a large Ziploc stuffed with pale blue fabric.

My body shook as if she stuck me with a charged electrode. "Is it on my face? In my hair?" My voice trembled with each syllable. Panic bubbled as I stared at Ransom.

"No, honey, no," he said. "He shot away from you. You're clean. You're fine. It's just your clothes. Soil. Residue. It's procedure. You know that."

"You swear?" I asked.

"On all things hand-sanitized."

Parker helped me in the half-bath just inside the foyer. I checked my face and patted my hair. Ran cool water over my wrists and hands and lightly blotted my face with a paper guest towel. My shaking hands made it difficult to remove my pants, even with the elastic waistband. I donned the scrubs and tied the drawstring tight.

Parker hugged me quick. "He's right. You'll be okay. Call if you need me."

I rejoined Ransom on the porch. "If you don't need me here, I'm going home," I said. "It'll be quiet there. Especially with everyone still at the BBQ. I could really use the peace."

Ransom wrapped me in a bear hug. "Text me as soon as you get home. I'll come by tonight with dinner and a bottle of wine."

"I may need two," I said.


Driving down Cabana, I tried to keep my mind focused on the positive things. All the people I love. The Ballantynes. Colonel Mustard and Mrs. White. Ransom. Sid. But my mind wouldn't stay still. It didn't seem right to let someone else, a stranger in a uniform, tell Millie Poppy that her husband buried Daphne Fischer in their garden. That her granddaughter's fiancé killed himself in her backyard. My peace would have to wait another hour.

I parked in Island Memorial Hospital's parking lot and used the automatic swishing doors to the main entrance. The volunteer at the visitor's desk handed me a guest access sticker and directed me to the third floor. I gripped my compact bottle of hand-sani as I waited for the elevator. It wasn't much comfort, but it kept my trembly hands busy.

Sam Turnbull lay partially reclined in a standard hospital bed in the intensive care unit. Tubes ran out of his both arms, his nose, and his mouth. Surgical tape held a ventilator apparatus across his face.

Millie Poppy sat near him. Her chair was against the wall, beneath a window. Not at his bedside. She looked distraught, distant. Mad as hell.

"You know about Sam," I said. "And Tucker."

"He called me," she said. "He explained what happened. He'd already called Juliette. Told her over the phone. Sonofabitch. Tess was with her, thank the good Lord. I called the police."

"That explains how they arrived so quickly," I said. "The island is small, but the entire emergency crew arrived pretty quickly. For which I'll be forever grateful."

"He explained the partial message about the rose garden," she said. "I guess Sam had also written me a letter."

I eased into a chair at the foot of the bed kittycorner to Millie Poppy.

"He'd put it in my desk drawer," she continued. "But Tucker found it this morning. Guess he decided the jig was up. Well, it's definitely up for him. For them both."

The ventilator hissed and thumped. Another machine beeped periodically. The only sounds in the quiet room.

"Tucker killed himself," I said.

She stared at me for a moment. "My husband..." Her voice choked on the word and tears fell down her face. "He knew. Tucker knew. Juliette cried herself to sleep every night. We spent hours and hours, days, searching the marsh land, anguishing. Where could she be? This whole time, they knew. My God, he killed that girl. It's sickening. And Sam. How could he sleep next to me? He buried that girl in our garden. I thought I knew this man."

"I'm sorry, Millie Poppy," I said. "I'm sorry this happened to you and your family. That you had to find out this way. Alone. That I couldn't figure it out sooner. Or figure it out at all. It was always just right out of my reach."

"Oh, sweetie, those two hid it good. That's the scariest part. How well they pulled it together. They killed that poor girl and smiled at me the very next morning. It makes my stomach turn and my blood boil at the same time. It's horrifying me."

"You going to be okay here? Want me to drive you somewhere? I'm sorry, but your house, well, it's inaccessible for a while."

"It's inaccessible forever," she said. "I'll never set foot in there again. The girls are picking me up in a bit. I have some paperwork to sign first, then I'm never looking back." Tears fell down her cheeks in salty streams of anger, devastation, exhaustion.

"But…" I started, though I didn't know what to say.

"My husband buried a girl in my yard. One doesn't get over that."

Two doctors in white coats entered the room and a man wearing a suit walked directly behind them. The older doctor, his hair fully grayed, half-moon glasses perched on his nose, spoke first. "Mrs. Turnbull? You requested DNR papers for your husband?"

"Yes," Millie Poppy said. "I'll sign whenever they're ready. Today if possible."

"Well, we'd like to speak to you about that," he said.

The man in the suit stepped forward. "I'm an attorney with Island Memorial. Your husband's been implicated in the death Daphne Fischer."

"I'm aware of that," she said. "But he's in a coma. One, I've been told, he won't recover from. It's his right to request a DNR designation."

"Do you have documentation of this request?" the lawyer asked.

"We hadn't yet created our living wills," she said. "But I'll declare it under oath. That was his intention."

"You can see how this looks, Mrs. Turnbull," the lawyer said.

"It's Pete," she said. "Millie Poppy Pete. Always has been."

The doctors looked uncomfortable, but remained silent.

"Okay, then, Ms. Pete," the lawyer said. "Your husband's an accessory in the murder of your granddaughter's friend. His own grandson, now deceased, is also accused. The police notified us moments ago."

"What are you saying, exactly?" I asked.

"And you are?" he said.

"Elliott Lisbon with the Ballantyne Foundation," I said. "A close family friend."

"Perhaps we should discuss this in private," he said to Millie Poppy.

"Are you implying I want to pull the plug on my husband because he buried a girl in my roses or because I'm the only person left to inherit and I don't want to wait for him to die on his own?"

"I'm not imply—" the lawyer said.

"How long can he live like this?" Millie Poppy said.

The older doctor cleared his throat. "We can't be sure. He has minimal brain function."

"Can he survive without the ventilator?" she asked.

"No, ma'am," the doctor said. "It's unlikely."

"My inheritance is no matter," Millie Poppy said. "Most of the money is mine, anyway. He's my husband and I have rights. You cannot simply let him languish because he might also be a criminal."

"Excuse us a moment." The three men stepped into the hall to confer.

"Are you doing this for the right reasons?" I whispered to Millie Poppy. "Let the system work. You can't rush his death."

"Oh, yes I can," she said.

The men returned with the older doctor taking lead. "I'm sorry, Mrs. Turnbull, we'll need to refer this to a judge. You should retain legal counsel."

"Again, my inheritance is no matter, gentlemen," she said.

"I'm not removing him from life support for personal gain. He's DNR. You're the ones with financial motive. How much does it cost to leave him here hooked up?"

"That's a discussion for another time," the lawyer said.

"Minimum care, right? Doesn't cost but a small amount of IV bag changing, take his vitals every so often. Yet, I bet you'll charge about fifty thousand dollars a day to keep him alive. Against his wishes. Pretty good racket. You'll make millions. Sounds like you have more motive to keep him alive than I do to sign the DNR."

"Like I said, you'll likely want to get yourself an attorney." The older doctor led the other two out of the room. The door softly swished closed.

"Let him rot," Millie Poppy said. She grabbed her handbag and walked to the door.

True to her word, she didn't look back.

# EPILOGUE

(Day #23: Sunday Morning)

The sun glittered in the brilliant blue sky above me as I rested on a thin quilt. It covered a ten by ten square of freshly cut grass on the Big House's back lawn. I was enjoying a bit of afternoon pug therapy. Colonel Mustard and Mrs. White scurried and hopped, almost like bunnies, as I tossed them their toys. The Colonel preferred a sweet little lamb with a gentle squeaker while Mrs. White pounced and dragged a bright red parrot bigger than she was.

Carla, Chef, and Jane were in the kitchen preparing a Sunday brunch. Fried chicken and waffle bites, citrus French toast, egg white frittatas, roasted potatoes. The Ballantynes would soon join us poolside from their residence.

The entire group had treated me as fragile for the past two weeks. I was using Jane as my gauge. Once her caustic demeaner returned, normalcy would follow.

Ransom walked over to the blanket, then sat close to me. He'd no sooner waved two bully sticks when the puppies abandoned their furry playmates and raced to his side. They quickly settled into their cigars. Paws holding them steady while they gnawed their way to euphoria.

"I heard Sam Turnbull passed away on Friday," he said.

"A relief for all, I'm sure," I said. "Millie Poppy took Juliette to a cousin's in Minnesota. Or maybe Kansas? Idaho?

Somewhere the crisp, cool fall weather could soothe their souls."

"Should make the transition easier for them with Sam departing on his own. No courts, no legal issues."

"Probably too easy for Millie Poppy's liking," I said. "Not that I blame her."

"Sid selling her house?"

"Not personally. Her office is handling both the commercial side for the Cake & Shake and the residential side for the house."

"We'll release it as a crime scene tomorrow," Ransom said. "We were about finished anyway."

I continued to gaze at the sky. Two fluffy clouds slowly crossed my field of vision. An airplane flew through them. "I'll call the Spiritual Center. They volunteered a team to smudge the house and the garden. Sid's office has a team that'll remodel the backyard."

"They really think it'll sell?"

"Rip out the roses, brick the patio, add a big kitchen, some blooming hydrangeas," I said. "It's one of the few homes in that neighborhood with direct gate access to the sand. We'll leave the smudge team's info. May take more than one cleansing."

"Sheriff Hill called me on my way over," he said. "The council is revoking Jona Jerome's permit. No more Isle House."

"Yeah," I said. "Carla said something about a new show in Las Vegas called *Lucky in Love*. Not sure how they'll spin it. I know all press is supposed to be good press, but it's been non-stop bad press. At least it's their bad press and not ours. For once. Tate Keating's doing a full-page next week on the Ballantyne's new homeless shelter."

"I know you don't realize it, but you did good on this," he said.

"I didn't, though," I said. "I didn't solve my case or even help anyone solve it. It solved itself."

"Don't underestimate the power of pressure. Your pursuit

never relented. You kept pushing for answers. You didn't let up for a minute. Tucker Turnbull didn't have the strength to withstand your pressure. You absolutely helped bring Daphne home."

"Thank you for saying that," I said. "I think I'm ready to move on. To wash off the melancholy that's clung to me since I first arrived at Millie Poppy's three weeks ago."

He held my hand, gently tugged me to sit up. "Move on?"

"My next case," I said. "Jane Doe, the girl with the Queen of Swords tattoo. She's yet to be identified. It doesn't feel right to abandon her. Not after we found her."

He stood, then pulled me to my feet. Colonel Mustard and Mrs. White sawed on their bullies without a blink in our direction. "Agreed. But perhaps it can wait until after we return."

"Oh?"

"I've booked us a trip," Ransom said. "I think you'll love it. Fresh air, sea breezes, go at our own pace."

"Barcelona? No wait, Monterey?" I smiled at his smile. "We're driving down the coast?"

"Yes, we are. And the end will be even better than the beginning. It's time you got your happy back."

"Happy? Like the Happiest Place on Earth?"

"A week in the Adventureland Suite," he said. "We leave next Saturday."

"What about your case? You can't possibly be finished with it."

He placed his hands on my face. His thumbs stroking my cheeks. "It'll continue without me while I'm gone and be here when I return." He leaned down and I closed my eyes. He smelled of sandalwood and spice and dreams that come true. He kissed me.

"You two joining us?" Tod hollered from the patio.

I watched him as he set a silver tray of Bellinis on the table, then cranked the large umbrella open.

Carla, Jane, and Chef carried plates and platters and pitchers. Mr. Ballantyne escorted Vivi onto the deck. Her delicate fingers firm in the crook of his elbow.

Ransom held my hand and we crossed the lawn. The laughter of my friends and my family drifting toward us, welcoming us, calling me home. The pug puppies raced ahead, bully cigars in their mouths, not to be left behind.

I felt nothing but joy in that moment. It really was never too late to find my happily ever after.

## Kendel Lynn

Kendel Lynn is a Southern California native who now parks her flip-flops in Dallas, Texas. As an active member of the mystery community, Kendel has penned six novels (the first, *Board Stiff*, was an Agatha Award nominee), plus novellas, screenplays, and countless articles. Kendel has served as president of the board of directors of both Sisters in Crime (national) and Sisters in Crime North Dallas. She leads workshops and attends conferences and conventions where she helps the writerly navigate the publishing landscape. She loves cupcakes, crime tv, and all things pug.

## The Elliott Lisbon Mystery Series
## by Kendel Lynn

## Henery Press Mystery Books

And finally, before you go...
Here are a few other mysteries
you might enjoy:

# PILLOW STALK

Diane Vallere

## A Madison Night Mystery (#1)

Interior Decorator Madison Night might look like a throwback to the sixties, but as business owner and landlord, she proves that independent women can have it all. But when a killer targets women dressed in her signature style—estate sale vintage to play up her resemblance to fave actress Doris Day—what makes her unique might make her dead.

The local detective connects the new crime to a twenty-year old cold case, and Madison's long-trusted contractor emerges as the leading suspect. As the body count piles up, Madison uncovers a Soviet spy, a campaign to destroy all Doris Day movies, and six minutes of film that will change her life forever.

Available at booksellers nationwide and online

Visit www.henerypress.com for details

# PUMPKINS IN PARADISE

Kathi Daley

## A Tj Jensen Mystery (#1)

Between volunteering for the annual pumpkin festival and coaching her girls to the state soccer finals, high school teacher Tj Jensen finds her good friend Zachary Collins dead in his favorite chair.

When the handsome new deputy closes the case without so much as a "why" or "how," Tj turns her attention from chili cook-offs and pumpkin carving to complex puzzles, prophetic riddles, and a decades-old secret she seems destined to unravel.


Available at booksellers nationwide and online

Visit www.henerypress.com for details

CPSIA information can be obtained
at www.ICGtesting.com
Printed in the USA
LVHW040238100320
649437LV00004B/463

9 781635 115871